For Ken

from Dan

on behalf of

Professor P. D. Cawick

2009

LEX MORPHI

more properly

LEX MORPHEIA

vulgariter

MURPHY'S LAW

ൟൟൟൟൟ

a study by the late

Gerald O'Toole

Professor of the History of Science
Univerisity of Munster

ൟൟൟൟൟ

edited by

James Ridell

Reader in Murphistics
Unversity of Man, Douglas,
Isle of Man

**University Press
Munster**
MELROSE BOOKS

Published by

MELROSE BOOKS

An Imprint of Melrose Press Limited
St Thomas Place, Ely
Cambridgeshire
CB7 4GG, UK
www.melrosebooks.com

FIRST EDITION

Front Cover: *Before*, William Hogarth c.1730-31
Back Cover: *After*, William Hogarth c.1730-31
(Reproduction by permission of the Syndics of the Fitzwilliam Museum, Cambridge)

ISBN 1 905226 36 5

Printed and bound in Great Britain by:
Bath Press Limited, Lower Bristol Road,
Bath, BA2 3BL, UK

PUBLISHER'S NOTE

It is regretted that the production of this book falls well below our usual standards. For this there are several reasons, the first being the imposition of certain conditions by the copyright holder. Another, not insignificant, consideration is that at least four people have come to a tragic end during various phases of the preparation of this volume. Despite the risks, Melrose Books is determined to bring this important monograph before the public, a duty hitherto shirked by three presses whose names shall not be mentioned, an obloquy they so richly deserve. This long-awaited study (more than a quarter of a century after it was first prepared for publication) is now presented in the confident hope that its qualities will greatly outweigh the comparatively trifling imperfections in its appearance.

The publishers regret that the captions on page 46, underneath, respectively, the Contessa Ritornella di Tosti and that of her prize cow of the Morfiana breed, have been inadvertently exchanged. The captions and pictures should, of course, be interchanged.

෪෪෪෪෪෪෪෪෪෪෪෪෪෪

Errata

p.xi *for* fragrant example *read* flagrant exapmle
p.1 *for* framer *read* farmer
p.21, footnote, *for* flouted *read* flaunted
p.25 *for* public hairs *read* pubic hares
p.27 *for* patch of quickest descent *read* path of quickish descent
p.29 *for* inflamed by the chill *read* inflamed by the chili
p.29, footnote 25, *for* riotous indignation *read* righteous indication
p.32 *for* swiped with one foul sweep *read* swooped with one fell swipe
p.33 *for* Holy Bedlock *read* Holey Wedlock
p.34 *for* Bulbous Tara *read* Taras Bulba
p.34 *for* errotic *read* eratic
p.35 *for* wholly bedsock *read* holy bedrock
p.35 *for* one fell sweep *read* one foul swipe
p.37, (footnote), *for* Bognor *read* Banger
and *similiter* throughout; but **N B**
p.00 *where for* Bugger Bangor *read* Bugger Bognor
p.65 *for* righteous assembly *read* riotuous assembly
p.65 *for* profolic and ingenious *read* profilic and ingenuous

Errarta (cont.)

p.76 *for* Immaculate Contraption *read* Immaculate Contraception
p.77 *for* one fell swipe *read* one foul swoop
p.77 *for* one fowl swoop *read* one fell sweep
p.79 *for* City of Dreaming Squires *read* City of Screaming Quires
p.81 *for* deflowered *read* befloured
p.81 *for* felt foul *read* fell fowl
p.82 *for* profolic *read* profilic
p.83 *for* one swell feel *read* one full sweep
p.83, footnote 6, *for* one full peep *read* one fell pap
p.83, footnote 6, *for* one foul seep *read* one full pee
p.89, footnote 12, *for* one full swoop *read* one fell swipe
p.93 *for* pogrom *read* pragorm
p.101, footnote 23, *for* cretan *read* Cretin
p.105, *for* one fall swipe *read* one fell swoop

(continued on p. 000)

＆＆＆＆＆＆＆＆＆＆＆＆＆＆＆＆

The editor wishes to thank the reader for the Univerity press, Miss Prince, for overseeing the printing of this volume.

＆＆＆＆＆＆＆＆＆＆＆＆＆＆＆＆

Foreword

THE tragic death[a] of Gerald Richard O'Toole, (always Dick to his friends) Professor of the History of Science in the University of Munster, leaves his great work unfinished. It is published here exactly as he left it, save for a few notes which the present editor has contributed.[b] There has been no attempt to re-order or edit[c] what was a work in progress,[d] undertaken in the face of great difficulties. I have endeavoured to leave what follows, rough hewn and unfinished though it may be, as his memorial.[e]

---

[a] The circumstances of his demise will be recounted in due course.

[b] These being mainly in the form of footnotes, as here.

[c] Nonetheless, one or two fanciful excursions have been suppressed here, such as the reference to the supposed Murphy scion who allegedly travelled to the Far East and was responsible for the exploitation of most, if not all, the tea in China. The story of his marriage to a "Chinee of good family" and the begetting of a son named Tadgh Fu (later corrupted to Typhoo) who is said to have invented the modern tea packet (with its undoubtedly Murphyesque legends 'Open other end' and 'Best before end') is, in the present editor's view, wholly apocryphal.

[d] It is for this reason that certain recent events, although spoken of as occurring in the immediate past, actually took place a decade or more ago*. Thus, the correspondence between Professors O'Toole and Page belong to a period when Oxford had entered its silver age, having relinquished Latin as a compulsory entrance requirement, but not yet having abased itself by admitting female persons to its ancient colleges. Similarly, the chronology of events in Ireland must be interpreted in this light, and it must be remembered that the Univeristy of Man, whose imminent closure has been proposed by the Unversity Grants Committee [Now the Universty Funding Council – Printer] acting upon the orders of the Secretary of State for Education, was still in its prime when the earlier chapters of this book had been prepared for the press by the present editor, and indeed, set up in type.

*IMPORTANT NOTE by the PRINTER TO THE UNIVERSISTY

> Due to circumstances beyond our control, it is considerably more than a decade which has passed between the time when part of this book had been set up in type and when successive editors and printers have striven finally to bring it before the public. It has been found impossible to bring the previously typeset materials up to date. The Prayer Book is no more; nor is Parson's Pleasure, having been invaded by females, who are by now probably parsons themselves. These are but examples of the changes which have taken place since Professor O'Toole's untimely death. At least his own establishment survives: over the water, all British Univerityes have been converted to Polytechnics, by order of the Government, acting on the Murphy report.

[e] The footnotes of the present editor may be distinguished from those of Professor O'Toole by the fact that they (those of the present editor) run alphabetically rather than numerically. The editorial contributions in [square] brackets are those of Professor O'Toole, except when identified as being those of the present editor.

Introduction

THROUGHOUT the world, Murphy's Law is universally renowned, being accorded a respect which frequently borders upon fear. The influence of this Law in every corner of the globe[a] is demonstrated by the fact that it is on the lips of rather more people than can pronounce it. Yet, although his discoveries influence each and every one of us, Murphy's life and works have received hardly any scholarly attention. This conspiracy of silence, for such it is, stems from the fact that so much research is based on his ideas, so many results are achieved using his methods, that if the usual scholarly proprieties were to be observed, his name would have to be acknowledged as a co-author of virtually every contribution to an academic journal: that this is not the case upholds his Law, certainly, but at the same time goes against manifest justice. It has been well said that justice must not only be done, but it must seem to be done.

To take a fragrant example, it is obvious that the so-called 'Catastrophe theory' espoused by Professor René Thom and his followers is nothing other than a usurpation of Murphy's Law [as is the more recent theory circulating under the name of 'Chaos'– J.R.]. The French, too, have brought into being an institution devoted to his principles, if not his name, in *L'École hypernormale des études tostiques renversées*, lavishly endowed, and firmly founded upon the sands of the Mediterranean shores. Surely the land of his birth should honour him properly, and no less lavishly. It cannot truthfully be argued that Irish bureaucracy is not a match for the French.

It is true that at least one institution in Murphy's native land is run entirely on his principles. On the banks of the lovely river Súir, the Queen's head, lately toppled from the pinnacles of the college once named after her, has now disappeared. In strict conformity with Murphy's Law, the whereabouts of the present head of the college are also shrouded in mystery, though rumour has it that it is preserved for posterity in alcohol.[b] As the great man himself said, in an oft misquoted saying, we must do all we can for posterity even though it may have done precious little for us.

Be that as it may, the time has come for one of our universities to put Murphian studies on a proper footing.[c] Only by the establishment of a proper department,

---

[a] Though of course a globe has no corners, thus providing anecdotal evidence of the essentially plane nature of the earth.

[b] Since this was written, the present editor understands that the former head of the College has indeed been finally preserved, and replaced by a Gaelic football. [And information has lately been received that the Queen's head has also been located, though it is still buried – Printer].

[c] Professor O'Toole does not mention the present editor's own Institution (now under threat of closure) where a readership in Murphistics (through the medium of Manks) has been established.

headed by a full Professor, to document and to enquire into the ramifications of the subject, will the shame be extirpated from the national conscience.

The following sketch of Murphy's life and achievements is intended in part to awaken that conscience, for his greatness has not been recognised at home, let alone abroad. Although this monograph cannot lay claim to being entirely original, it adduces some little known facts together with newly discovered material, which clarify various details of Murphy's biography, and his importance in the history of science in its widest sense.

My labours in the field have been greatly aided by the gracious access, granted to me by the Countess Ritornella di Tosti, to papers which can now be identified as autobiographical fragments in Murphy's own hand. Professor Rex [Jack] Page[d] has kindly examined the documents from the palaeographical point of view, and has written to me as follows:

Nuffield Orthopaedic Centre, Oxford

Dear Professor O'Toole,

I have compared the handwriting of the papers in the possession of the Contessa di Tosti with known holographs of Murphy, and can confirm that the hands are identical. As you know, one had some considerable difficulty, partly because the leaves of the volume fell apart in one's hands on the occasion of my British Academy lecture entitled 'How to handle a rare manuscript', and partly because of a slight accident when they became entangled in the spokes of the Contessa's exercise bicycle* which had been placed at one's disposal. In spite of this, there is enough of the work to be, I think, of service to you. The Latin, though of a distinctly Hibernian cast,** is perfectly tolerable, and the contents are not without interest to students of the subject.

I cannot recall whether or not I mentioned to you that one's own family claim some connexion with Murphy. My middle name, Iohannes, I have always been told was given to me on that account.[e]

---

[d] Neville Chamberlain Professor of Fragmental MS Studies and Fellow of St Alfred's College, Oxford: formerly Porson's Professor of Palimpsest Palaeography in the University of Cambridge, to whom we are grateful for supplementing the original title of this book with one that, to use his phrase, "more correctly reflects the Latinity of the time". It has to be remarked that Professor Page steadfastly denies any connection with his former University, even to the extent of saying that his former post was at Birmingham. Some incident of a traumatic nature must have occurred during his Cambridge days.

[e] Professor O'Toole disputed this, remarking that it was "... curious, since it implies knowledge of the Murphy fragments on the part of Page's parents". Professor O'Toole is certainly in error

Please keep me informed, from time to time, as to the progress of your researches. I have time on my hands at present, since I am in hospital, recovering from a slight mishap.

Yours sincerely

Jack Page

* P.S. It occurs to me that the presence of an exercise bicycle may well strike an incongruous note. It was the result of the dear Contessa's difficulty with the English language. She had demanded the return of the papers after my British Academy lecture. I was thus forced to study them in her not inelegant library. One day she interrupted my perusal of the documents, attempting to persuade me to join some form of strenuous activity, the nature of which I was unable fully to comprehend. One replied with a pleasantry, to the effect that one avoided all kinds of exercise, especially jumping to conclusions. This occasioned the bringing of the machine into the library.

** I give one obvious instance. Fragment IV[a], the last (and only) line, has *banjactus erat* – 'it had been rendered inutile' (*vulgariter*, 'banjaxed'). The proper form, however, would be *banjicio, -ere, - ēci, banjectus*.[1]   J.P.

We should like to record our gratitude to Professor Page for giving so freely of his time in connexion with what are now the Murphy fragments, and we should further tender our warm thanks for the encouraging interest he has shown in these studies.

The fragments bear greatly upon certain scholarly matters and show beyond doubt that many of Murphy's ideas were pillaged remorselessly by others, without

---

here, since the names of Jack's elder brother, General R. A. M. Page, were Roger Aloysius Murphy, and his son was named Christopher Robin Aloysius Page: such evidence could hardly be more conclusive that there was a family relationship. See further, p.7.

[1] Professor Page is surely in error here, for how could this supposed form give the reflex 'banjaxed'? The verb is, presumably, *banjacio, -ere, -ēci, -actus*.

Incidentally, the "small mishap" to which he alludes was occasioned by a large articulated lorry which "cut in" (as we believe the phrase to be) upon Professor Page as he was cycling in The High. Professor Page remonstrated with several strident tintinnabulations of his bicycle bell, but to no avail; as a result of these exertions, however, the bell and Professor Page fell to the ground, the latter as a result of his gown becoming enmeshed with certain moving parts of the bicycle. This involuntary dismounting was not in itself gravely injurious, but was unfortunately followed by the distinguished palaeographer being run over by a passing hot-dog vehicle.[f]

[f] What Dean Swift would have termed "running a man down".

acknowledgement. To give one blatant example, Kant's theory of *The principle of contradiction* which he says 'must be recognised as being the universal and completely sufficient *principle of all analytical knowledge*' [his italics][2] is simply an expansion of Murphy's aphorism *inconstantia in constantia* [Fragment V[b], iii].[3] We are reminded of Dean Swift's remark that "there is nothing constant but inconstancy".

As to Dean Swift himself, the question of Murphy's parentage is of course of extreme interest, touching as it does on the possible influence of Swift upon Murphy's philosophy. It has been generally suspected that Murphy may have been the natural son of the Dean, but reputable modern scholars have expressed doubt, adducing evidence for contrary theories. The circumstances of Murphy's earliest years have a direct bearing upon his subsequent career, and will therefore be examined in the light of recent evidence.

---

[2] *cp* Kemp's translation of *The Critique of Pure Reason*, p.190.

[3] The original Latin of the translated passages will be found printed in the appendix at the end of the book.[g]

[g] But see p.16. NB, the [a] and [b] seen in the main body of the previous pages in connexion with the numeration of the Murphy fragments should not be construed as referring to footnotes. On the question of Chaos, or Chassis as Murphy called it, Dr O'Shea of the University of Rockall points out that in considering the equation $f(x) = ax(1-x)$, when x is between 0 and 1 and a lies between 0 and 4, we can iterate the function of f

$ax(1-x)$

$x = 0 \quad 0, 0, 0, \ldots$

$x = 1 \quad 1, 0, 0, \ldots$

$x = \dfrac{1}{2} \quad \dfrac{1}{2}, \dfrac{1}{2}, \dfrac{1}{2}, \ldots$

$x = \dfrac{1}{4} \quad \dfrac{1}{4}, \dfrac{3}{8}, \dfrac{15}{32}, \dfrac{255}{512}, \ldots$

and these are convergent (e.g. the last approaches ½ ever more closely).

The Parish Church, Laracor, Co. Meath, from an old print

(the Parish records in which Murphy's birth were registered were destroyed when the church burnt down in 1859).

AELFRED ᛗEᚳ HEH ᚷEWᚱᚳAN
ÆLFREDUS ME JUSSIT FABRICARI.

*The Alfred Jewel, discovered in 1693,
later appropriated by the Ashmolean Museum, Oxford (see p.2, below).*

Printed in Francis Wise (ed.) Annales Rerum Gestarum Ælfreds Mayni …
(Oxford, 1722) p.171

I. Early Life

Fortunae Filius [a]

ROGER Aloysius Murphy was born at Laracor, Co. Meath, late on March 31, 1690,[1] in which year his mother married John Thomas Murphy, a framer, under curious circumstances. She was the Sally O'Grady concerning whom Dean Swift opined that "she wears her clothes, as if they were thrown on with a pitchfork". She was fastidious neither in her manner of dress nor in her dealings with the opposite sex. It was thus no surprise when she conceived out of wedlock; nor was it of particular remark that there were at least three possible claimants to the fatherhood of the child to be. The three suitors, if that is the correct word, met one night in Laracor churchyard in order to determine the matter by drawing straws. Murphy (senior) having drawn the short straw, the putative son was thus made legitimate and duly baptised.[2]

These things were unknown to the boy until early manhood. Roger Aloysius, now familiarly known as Aloys,[3] had become enamoured of a local girl named Mary Collins, whom he proposed to marry. In seeking parental advice and consent, he became aware of improbity in his father's past, for the latter made it clear that to marry the girl would offend the principles of the church as set out in the Table of Kindred and Affinity at the back of the Prayer Book.[4] This double calamity – for the boy was much taken with Mary, and had looked up to his father as a model of rectitude – was borne with commendable stoicism, to the extent indeed that Aloys' affections were soon transferred to Molly Reardon, whose worth he discussed with his father some months later. His chagrin was unimaginable when he learnt that she, too, was a half sister and an impediment to matrimony. Notwithstanding this new revelation of consanguinity, the boy proved resilient to the extent that he sought the

---

[1] There is some doubt as to Murphy's birth date. The problem hinges on the interpretation of the word *lucescit* in the MS. Does this mean 'he appeared'? If it does, there is no reason to suppose a date other than that given here. If, on the other hand, we take Professor Page's reading of the passage, construing *lucescit* in the sense of 'dawn broke',[b] then Murphy was born early the next day.

[2] On the matter of the phrase 'short straw' see below, footnote 10, and see also p.12.

[3] On account of his clumsiness.

[4] A reference to those days when the Churches of England and Ireland used a Prayer Book.

- -

[a] There is a measure of ambiguity here, for although the natural translation of this inscription would be "son of (good) fortune" the phrase might also be construed as "child of fate".

[b] A reading which, in the present editor's opinion, is greatly to be preferred: one source is perfectly clear on the matter, as it mentions that he was born on the feast of Valerius, Bishop.

favours of the beautiful Lily O'Rourke, whose mother had herself been the toast of the town and indeed still preserved her remarkable good looks. As Aloys soon discovered, however, not only had Lily's mother been toast of the town,[5] but his father (to employ that rake's most regrettable phrase) had "taken a slice" (and more regrettable since he was also heard to say "no one misses one from a cut loaf"). On hearing this, the distraught boy exclaimed, "then how is it that my slice always lands buttered side down?"

Here, then, was a portentous remark, the genesis of a philosophy which would shape the course of history, although at the time its significance passed unnoticed. The junior Murphy renewed his frenetic pursuit of the rest of the nubile village girls, though these were progressively less well favoured and each, when his father was taxed with the matter, appeared to be related. At length, and with considerable reluctance, the youth sought the comfort and advice of his mother. To his surprise she was not shocked by the revelations of his father's concupiscence; the shock, rather, was for him, for his mother revealed that far from being restricted in his choice of a prospective wife, he had no blood ties with any of the village girls whose favours he had sought thus far, having none with the man he had believed to be his father.

---

[5] Professor Page disagrees with this translation, and writes as follows:

> I am prepared to allow a little latitude with *tostum inversum* and even with *frustum tostum*, but *tostus civis* is hardly 'toast of the town', for 'toast' in this sense would be *acclamatio*. I cannot envisage that Swift, from whom the phrase doubtless emanates, would thus abuse the Latin tongue. Incidentally, the word *frustum* occurs in the little ceremony, called The Monstrance, which is celebrated every year in honour of our founder (it originally included a showing of the Alfred Jewel until it was stolen by the Ashmolean Museum – see the illustration on p.xv): each Fellow partakes of the *crustum frustum ambustum* and upon it swears allegiance to the College and its founder, and execrates the use of his name in connexion with spurious claims [a reference to the supposed foundation of Unverity College by Alfred. ed.].

Here, Professor Page is wholly in error. In the Huntingdon MS, p.A, the following passage occurs (one of several of the same *genre* – the 'English' pronunciation of the Latin is necessary in order to ascertain the meaning):

> In mi cum pani praedixit [pray, Dick, sit]
> Claret finis ne ver mixit
> Cantu tellus Dicas tori
> Cingat super Tori rori [sing at supper, 'Tory Rory']
> Aleto claret adit [added] basis
> Tosta laedi, fieri faces

[a satire against Tighe, punctuation modernised: *cp*. George P. Mayhew, *Rage or Raillery*, San Marino, 1967, p.147] We venture to suggest that 'Tosta laedi' is sufficient to rebuff Professor Page's comment.

Thenceforward Murphy did not speak with his father again, which was not entirely just: the guilt of his father and mother, if not equal in extent, were equal in degree; and both had conspired to frustrate his attempts to marry, thereby assisting the operation of what would later be known as Murphy's Law. But as yet the youth knew nothing of his destiny. His sole intent at that time was to discover the identity of his blood father. Although Sally Murphy never divulged any direct information, certain things she let slip caused Aloys to entertain suspicions which gradually strengthened into belief. In order to determine the truth, he journeyed to Dublin to see Dr Swift, only recently installed as Dean of St Patrick's Cathedral.

Crossing the river by the Ormonde bridge [the modern O'Connell bridge] he walked up Fishamble Street, turning left at Smock Alley, after which he again turned left at the Marshalsea. But only when he had turned right at St John's Lane and then left into the Cathedral did he sense that something was amiss. On enquiry, he found that he had arrived at Christ Church, the wrong cathedral. Why this should be, why there should be two cathedrals and that he should be guided to the wrong one, seemed to be in accordance with some law of mischance which seemed to govern more than one aspect of his life; but further contemplation of this problem was curtailed by the realisation that the error had not, after all, been disastrous, since the correct cathedral, St Patrick's, was close at hand.

Having arrived at his true destination, Murphy came through the massive doors into the dark cathedral in heightened trepidation. He asked a verger for directions to the Dean's house, but by way of reply was curtly told to wait. He was greatly surprised when the returning verger said that the Dean would see the boy immediately after Evensong, which was about to commence. Murphy sat down in what seemed to him the vast nave, just as the choir came into the stalls.

One of the clergy, who did not seem to have an active part in the service, seemed to be looking his way. The choir was by now singing the psalms, which had been announced as being those for the twenty-seventh evening of the month. He followed them in the Prayer Book which he found in front of him. They seemed to be about bringing forth good seed, bringing in sheaves, and the fruit of the womb. The priest on the right seemed to be looking at him again.

> Like as the arrows in the hand of the giant:[6]
> Even so are the young children.
> Happy is the man that hath his quiver full of them:

Murphy thought of his seven sisters and six brothers, a quiverful indeed.

---

[6] In the Latin of the MS the psalms are of course quoted in the Vulgate version. I am grateful to Professor Page for providing the contemporaneous English equivalents.

Thy wife shall be as the fruitful vine:[7]
Upon the walls of thine house.
Thy children like the olive branches:
round about thy table.

It was curious, he reflected, that these psalms all appeared to be about procreation, reflecting insistently upon the questions which he had come to ask.

After the psalms, the priest whose part in the service had hitherto been passive now assumed a more obvious role. Moving to the great lectern, he read the lesson, which was then followed by the choir singing a rather dull Magnificat in which the solos were sung by a man with a very curious voice, resembling that of a startled cockerel[8] rather than that of a human being. Once more, Murphy was struck by the emphasis upon the subject which was uppermost in his mind. Abraham and his seed for ever. After the Magnificat,[9] another lesson followed, again read by that forbidding cleric who seemed to have been looking at Murphy: was this the Dean himself?

---

[7] See previous footnote

[8] I had originally translated *quemadmodum gallicantum de improviso* as 'like the random song of a cockerel on a dunghill' until corrected by Professor Page:

> This [he writes] is altogether too free and, if I may say so, mistaken. The phrase 'de improviso' which you have rendered as 'random song' would more properly mean 'read at sight' (of the musical score)[,] implying a lack of adequate preparation on the part of singer and choir; but equally, it might also mean 'startled'. My colleague Dr Thorne, Master of the Quiresters at St Alfred's, assures me that the reference is to a countertenor, which I gather is an effete voice which may well have resembled that of a startled cockerel.
>
> Jack Page

[9] The service in question appears to have been set by Dr Croft. Professor Page demurs, saying (on the authority of Dr Thorne) that Croft wrote no such service. We may legitimately wonder if this statement could be regarded as authoritative, since Dr Root, Fellow and *pulsator organorum* of the College of St Mary-the-Less, tells me that Dr Thorne appears to have published, as the work of Croft, a motet in a much earlier style, by Tallis or some such composer.

Unfortunately, Professor Page showed a draft of these pages to Dr Thorne, which drew forth the following communication:

> Dear O'Toole,
>
> Your comments, shown to me by my colleague, are the most scandalous slander I have seen for some time. Dr Root, who is a communist and a drunkard, is telling blatant lies when he says that I published a piece of Croft, not knowing that it was a bad arrangement of Tallis. Should you publish these untruths I shall sue you and Root root and branch.* Dr Root, by the way, is so proud of being doctored that if anyone asks on the telephone for Mr Root,[c] the old fool hands them over to his ten-year-old son, whom he had presumably sired before he was doctored [this is a typical example of his so-called humour (writes Dr Root)]. That is the kind of petty-minded oaf that you are dealing with.**

Murphy lost himself in reverie, paying little heed to the rest of the service; he was thus surprised when it came to an end. The choir filed out, followed by the verger and finally the priests. Soon, the verger came back, and ushered Murphy along the passage where, at last, he confronted Dean Swift himself, who was indeed the rather fearsome figure which had earlier commanded his attention.

I shall answer no more of your footling questions, and I fail to see what an IRA poof is meddling with these questions for.

Yours sincerely,

Dr Thomas Thorne

*(footnote referring to footnote on previous page)
We are happy to correct the matter, arising from an earlier misunderstanding (on our part) of Dr Root, who has informed us of the true facts of the matter in the following footnote.

** (footnote referring to footnote on previous page)
The man's mad (writes Dr Root). Talk about drunkenness – not for nothing is Thorne known as 'snorter'. It is not merely that his singularly unamusing stories are punctuated by pig-like noises; only partly was he given the name on account of the snort which terminates his mirthless laughter. No, the nickname derives from his habit of guzzling large quantities of alcohol between practice and Evensong; rather more, it has to be said, than a mere 'snorter'. In turn, 'Snorter' was the name was given by the choristers and clerks to the foul concoction of gin, madeira and lighter-fuel that he was wont to imbibe when not under the supervision of his wife, Polly. He refers to her (she of the blue rinse) as 'Mrs Thorne', however, which makes her sound like a charwoman (or char*lady* as she would have it, her mother having been one of that ilk, what in my day was simply called a skivvy, but I stray from the main point in hand). Thorne, too, belongs to the same social milieu, which explains, if not excuses, his manners. In an effort to ape the class to which he aspires, he appears to model his behaviour on Uncle Matthew in one of Miss Mitford's novels.

As to the matter of Croft, I fear that you misunderstood an earlier remark which I made: the work in question was a motet by Byrd, badly arranged by Hayes, and republished by the perverse and foolish Thorne. I enclose a copy of this curious effusion, together with a photostat of the Byrd original, so that you may verify the facts to your own satisfaction. The man can hardly sue in relation to the truth. He is a bladder, a mere bag of wind.

The likelihood that the service was indeed by Croft[d] may be seen from Forster MS 519 (see facsimile printed in the appendix), the beginning of which is transcribed below:

MEMORAND OF THINGS TO BE DONE IN THE CITY

Memds Those only done which are crossed

Full anthems and Dr Crofts book
of anthems

in Fleet-street about
a Clock for St Patr's Cathedrall

"Come to the Deanery, my boy, where we shall have a dish of coffee: later, you shall dine with us and, with good food and drink inside you, you shall unfold your purpose in coming here."

"May I ask, Sir, if you know who I am? For neither you nor your messenger has asked my name or enquired anything of me."

"Of course I know you; you are from Laracor, and are Sally Murphy's eldest son, Aloys."

"Allow me to request that you call me Roger, a name which I have come to prefer. But how …?"

"It appears that you are unaware that I have a house at Laracor. Your family affairs are not unknown to me."

"So – then …"

"Nothing more, I pray you, until we have dined. The man will show you to your chamber, for you will do me the honour of remaining here for a night or two, since

---

Spectacles for 70 years old 4 pair X

Fenocchio and Brocoli original seeds, and
the whole direction about planting them

Melon seeds, and any other garden curiousity

Some presents fluid X

- -

[c] [footnote referring to footnote on previous page but one] It may be recalled that Dean Swift was also somewhat choice of his doctorate. He would have preferred to have been called 'Doctor' rather than 'Dean'.

[d] [footnote referring to footnote on previous page] The present editor opines, with the greatest respect, that it is Professor O'Toole who is in error in regard to this issue. Firstly, the Forster MS list does not include a cross beside the Croft item. Thus, although there is evidence of *intention* there is none of *commission*; secondly, it is Croft's *anthems* which are mentioned in the document. I have again consulted with Dr Mandrake Root upon the matter, who assures me that Croft wrote no services (apart from a setting of the Burial Service). "Quite by coincidence [says Dr Root] Thorne is correct." When shown a transcript of the MS in question, Dr Root was interested in the appearance of 'Fenocchio and Brocoli' [*recte* Finocchio and Broccoli] and took it upon himself to investigate the matter. The College chef at St Alfred's, Mr K. N. Pepper, thinks it most unlikely that these comestibles were at all current at the time in These Islands; but this, of course, is the point: these were novelties to Swift, and, in anticipation of the next chapter, when Murphy's peregrinations in Italy are treated, it is clear that Swift's interest in these things was greatly quickened, if not entirely as a result of Murphy's Italian travels. Interest in 'things fluid' was presumably already established.
[Note by Professor O'Toole concerning his previous footnotes: It may well appear that one or two of the finer points of this argument are somewhat to the side of the main issues, but as every reputable scholar will aver, documentation is the very stuff of literary, historical and scientific research.]

we have much to say to each other." With that Murphy had to be satisfied, until later, after a far from frugal dinner, the Dean hinted that the conversation might now take a more personal course. In response to Murphy's question, the Dean replied:

"Yes, I have known your mother for many years, far more than I would choose to remember. She was never one to pass in a crowd, nor someone who would make a figure in a country church, but she has certain qualities, not least of which is a certain kind of determination.

"When she was with child, bearing you, she was as yet unwed, having been so unwise as to consort with several of the blades of the village, one of whom was the man you know as your father. No one knew who the real father might be, so the three principal actors in the drama met one night in Laracor churchyard (this was before I was the incumbent there, but a churchwarden happened, quite by chance, covertly to witness this comedy with his own ears and eyes). Their purpose was to determine the matter by the drawing of straws. Your father, for such we may call him, drew the short straw. This was the origin of the *sobriquet* by which your father was henceforward known, 'short straw Murphy' ".[10]

"I had no idea that he was called by that name," said the youth.

"This, and rather more, is well enough known in the village of Laracor. Minding

---

[10] Professor Page demurs at my translation of *Iohannes virgula brevis Morphi*. He writes:

I cannot agree with "short straw Murphy". *Virgula* is not a straw, but a twig, though what a short twig might signify in this context, I am at a loss to comprehend. Technically, however, *virgula* is a critical mark in Latin MSS. Thus *virgula brevis* appears to be a marginal gloss by a scribe which has been incorporated into the text by a later redactor. I shall comment at greater length (and on the use of *brevis*) in my notes to the fragments at the end of your monograph. These are coming on apace, since I have enforced leisure occasioned by a slight mishap.

Iohannes (Jack) Page

P.S. It is curious that my parents should have known of Murphy's supposed father's name, even in its Latin form. They died, alas, in a tragic accident, so the source of their information is tantalisingly closed to one. 'Jack' has followed me from schooldays, and has unfortunately been taken up by malicious colleagues for inappropriate and puerile reasons which are irrelevant here.

The last sentence refers to the possibly puerile, but not inappropriate, epithet 'Jack the Ripper', a reference to his dealings with certain MSS. I have to say that I find this objection to my translation contorted and improbable. The "slight mishap" to which Professor Page alludes occurred on the river Isis. A notice saying "when the water rises above this mark, do not attempt to punt or swim" was unfortunately obscured by flood water; thus the accident-prone Professor Page inadvertently did both; that is to say, his inexpert punting was followed involuntarily by comparable attempts at swimming. He was rescued by a Somerville undergraduate, the Hon Emma Royd, who took him to recuperate at Pyles, her family's ["the family being related to the Goodly-Pyles", Professor Page insists on telling us] country seat.

other people's business is the chief occupation of your villager, but he rarely gets to know his own. It does not seem remarkable in the least that you, and doubtless your father, have no knowledge of this. Yet your mother was fully cognizant of the facts and was most exercised to avoid any further *opprobrium* which might be visited upon your father's name. She thus endeavoured to keep to herself a further secret, one which, so far as I am aware, she has succeeded in so keeping from all but her most confidential advisers, such as mine own humble self."

"Then …"

The Dean merely raised a hand to indicate that he would not countenance interruptions.

"There was, as you are perfectly aware, no issue to your parents for several, I think three or four, years. In view of the known fecundity of your mother, does this not strike you as passing curious?"

Murphy, by now thoroughly confused, could not reply. The Dean continued:

"Rakes such as your father, *mittentes semina sua*,[11] hardly trouble that the objects of their lust might well be *portantes manipulos suos*,[12] but in this your father need not have troubled, for the ladies in question were spared the consequences of their actions, and indeed more than one of them may have been aware, like Caelia,[13] that the man whom you call your father was in truth akin to that Greek painter in the epigram, who was unable to get a likeness even in his own children.[14]

---

[11] Ps cxxvi, v.6: "sending forth their seed". The Dean seems to have quoted in Latin at these points, since the phrases are underlined in the source. As will be seen shortly, however, some fragments in English, partially utilised here, have recently been recovered.

[12] *ibid*: "bearing their sheaves".

[13] Professor Page informs me that this somewhat obscure reference is to one of Martial's epigrams. He writes as follows:

Dear Dick,

The reference is to Martial. VI, lxvii:

Cur tantum eunochos habeat tua, Caecilia, quaeris

Pannyche? volt futui Caelia nec parere

The sentiments are somewhat indelicate (as is Swift's poem on Caelia, which may well have been inspired by these lines). The difficulties of translation (by which I mean aesthetic, rather than linguistic difficulties, of which there are none) may perhaps be overcome by employing the *argot* of the stockbroker: she wished to enjoy income rather than growth. By the way, please desist from mentioning any more of my mishaps in the book.

[14] The allusion to the painter, whose name was Marcus, I think, [writes Professor Page] relates, I feel certain, to some lines in the Palatine Anthology, but as yet I have failed to find them again.

"In brief, short-straw Murphy was not, as he supposed, the Onlie Begetter of your supposed siblings, nor yet, as you already know, yourself. For whoever your father might have been, it was not the egregious Murphy, as became clear to your mother after your birth was not followed by the yearly fruit of the womb which is visited upon the fecund. Once she had determined the truth of this, she hid Murphy's shortcomings from him by the simple expedient of finding other tillers of the field and, Ah, sowers of the seed."

The boy was not listening at the end of this disquisition, for a pink dawn of understanding slowly suffused his face.

"So my real father …"

"All I can tell you of your real father are …." [here the codex, or rather fragment, breaks off].[15]

The problem of Murphy's real parentage thus eludes us in the most tantalising manner. The new materials, adverted to below, may well settle the matter. Until this time, to which we may earnestly look forward, allusion must be made to the vast literature concerning Swift's relationships with 'Vanessa' and, more especially, with 'Stella'. Scholarly opinion is no longer willing to contemplate that these relationships were in any way scandalous. If, then, there was no such relationship with his beloved Stella, how could there have been one with Sally Murphy, or O'Grady as she was then? The idea that Swift was Murphy's natural father is nothing short of incredible, although there is some evidence that Murphy himself may have been under that misapprehension, at least for a time. Although the Italian fragments are unhelpful on this point, there is every hope that the new MSS may reveal something of the truth. Yet, whatever revelations they might vouchsafe in regard to Murphy's parentage and to the question of Dean Swift, it is certain that there was a reference to the famous breakfast scene, since this is referred to in the Trinity fragments.

According to this source, the fall to the ground of Murphy's toast, and the realisation that the natural law is and was that the toast should come to rest with its buttered side down was the solemn moment of genesis, when what is now known as Murphy's Law was revealed to the world. As he reflected on the convoluted circumstances of his parentage, and upon the manifold instances of the 'buttered side down' which had governed his life, he realised that he had stumbled upon (indeed, we feel bound to point out, how redolent is this phrase of the workings of The Law) a

---

[15] The lacuna, (or rather lacuna and *anacolouthon*, as Professor Page would prefer it, since the fragment continues inconsequentially with the words *Semper Opus Dei*) is singularly unfortunate. We have high hopes, however, of the recently identified Trinity fragments, in Swift's own hand, which may well shed valuable light on this vexed question. Note the use of the plural verb, clearly indicating that the sentence would have continued "such facts as are known to me …" or some such formula.

momentous discovery.[16]   After breakfast Murphy apparently bade the Dean *adieu*, and journeyed to Dun Laoghaire (then known as Kingstown) in order to get on to a packet boat, supposedly in search of one of the girls he had originally wanted to marry. There is some doubt as to whether he had intended to go to Douai in the Low Countries or to Italy. There is a further story that he mistook the destination of the vessel and landed in Queenstown (the modern Cobh) and thereupon sought out Bishop Berkeley: this latter can be ruled out of court on grounds of chronology alone. With a solitary exception (I. Malone), no scholar has attempted to justify this supposed incident.

---

[16] There is a curious phrase which Swift uses, "I won't quarrel with my bread and butter", which may contain an echo of the toast incident. The medium, as the subsequent fragments show, was certainly toast, even though Swift's reference is to bread; so the statements are not immediately reconcilable. We have, of course, sought the views of Professor Page on this point, our enquiries having elicited the following reply:

> The Churchill Hospital
> Oxford
>
> Dear Dick,
>
> I have your letter in front of me, but I fear I can do no more than agree with what you have written, since I cannot at present move from here and consult the necessary documentation. A trivial incident occurred when I was at a conference near Oxford. I was due to hear one of my American research pupils' brilliant and important paper entitled 'Towards an overview of the use of the verb (excluding the participle) in the works (prose only) of Pseudo-Vegetius the Hun (the younger)'. Unfortunately, on the day on which I was to hear this paper, I came down to the conference breakfast rather early, and, since there was no one to come to my aid, scalded myself on the coffee machine. I will reply more fully, and, one trusts more informatively, when I am able to discharge myself from here.
>
> As ever,
>
> Jack

Another participant at the conference mentioned has described the incident in more detail. It seems that Professor Page mishandled the tap of the urn so that the flow of coffee, once initiated, could not be staunched. With great presence of mind, Professor Page requisitioned another cup, pouring the full cup into the top of the machine and alternately filling the other cup from the malfunctioning tap. Since Professor Page had arrived an hour earlier than anyone else, he succumbed to exhaustion after about three-quarters of an hour of these strenuous labours: unfortunately, as he fell to the ground he failed to detach himself from the appliance, which accompanied him to the floor, anointing him liberally with scalding coffee. Were it not for the seriousness of the injuries (second degree burns [presumably upper second – J.R.]), the incident would be singularly amusing.

Unfortunately, the above note was shown to Professor Page by the research student in question, Miss Virginia Creeper, and called forth his wrathful indignation. For the sake of documentary completeness, I append it here.

Warneford Hospital[*]
Oxford

Dear Professor O'Toole,

I cannot, and will not, tolerate the snide remarks about me which you insist on including in your book, or rather, what I earnestly trust is a rough draft, despite its already having been set up in type. By injudicious remarks you have already alienated yourself from my colleague Dr Thorne of this College[**] (though possibly the fault is not entirely on your side); and, despite repeated requests to desist, you have continued to refer to various little accidents which have befallen me of late. I shall therefore keep to myself the circumstances of my arrival here lest yet again you might remark that I am 'accident prone', a phrase of singular vapidity. How could one be 'accident supine'? Surely an accident is an accident, whether one falls upon one's face or one's back. This, however, is beside the point[***]. I write simply to say this, that I am no longer able to assist you in your work; I feel that I have already contributed too much, and for little thanks, nay, for nothing but covert, nay overt, abuse.

Yours sincerely,

Rex I. Page

_ _

[footnotes to the above footnotes, cont.]

*   The Warneford Hospital is a mental institution much frequented by Oxford dons and undergraduates alike, to the extent that its inmates tend to regard it as a college.

**   The confusion in Professor Page's letter is explained in the previous note.

***   Far from being beside the point, the phrase 'accident prone' clearly embodies a subliminal recognition in the language of the principle of the 'buttered side down', a principle which this monograph has been at pains to document. So also, the use of the word 'befallen' is not without semantic interest.

There is a happy conclusion to this sorry incident. After I had written a conciliatory letter, I received the following communication from Professor Page:

The Ackland,
Banbury Rd.,
Oxford.

My Dear O'Toole,

Quite independently from the kind remarks which you addressed to me, I had already determined to communicate with you. I think I was rather hasty in my last letter. I am somewhat sensitive to what appears to be my unfortunate propensity in regard to accidents of one kind and another, but I would not wish that this should come between us in the furtherance of the great work in hand.

I have also another reason for reconsidering, namely that Snorter (Dr Thorne) was unduly pleased when I informed him that I had written to you in less than warm terms. I would not like him to think of me as an ally, for, to be truthful, he has been acutely exacerbating of late. I went to dinner with him at home the other night and was poisoned in both body and mind. The food was execrable. There was frozen turkey which tasted like cardboard and similarly treated broccoli (*pace* Dean Swift's spelling!) which, in spite of the blue-rinsed Polly's merry chirrup ("It's all home produced!") tasted like a sulphurous purgative. The sweet course was like a poultice, continuing the medicinal theme of the meal which had begun with a soup having all the qualities of an enema, duly acting thus upon Dr Thorne's conversation. All of this was washed down (the metaphor here is of the abbatoir floor) by a singularly noxious potion. I had made the mistake of acquiescing to red wine before I had seen it 'cooking' before the fire, and before I had heard the now legendary phrase "Mrs Thorne and I do not drink red wine, it upsets our stomach". Although the revolting acid concoction began its innocent life as a moderate claret from St Alfred's, after such treatment it is small wonder that they of the Siamese monodenum would be upset; even the stomach of an Afghan would have been turned. My own, at all events, rebelled. I am now in hospital with severe food-poisoning. The Law is again upheld, as you will doubtless observe; but this is of little comfort to me on my bed of sickness. Nevertheless, it gives me time to reflect on matters between us, and I hope that you will take this gesture in the spirit in which it is meant.

Yours sincerely,

Jack Page

PS In a previous note to you I discussed the phrase which you render as 'short-straw Murphy'. I had failed to refer to the *Revised medieval Latin Word-List* (though why the O.U.P. should take it upon themselves to spell <u>mediæval</u> thus, and add an otiose hyphen to Word List, I cannot imagine) which gives a meaning *in sensu obsceno* for *virgula* (*s.v. virga*). This signification, *membrum virile*, may be the one required by the context, in which case the adjective 'short' refers to Murphy, at least in some measure, rather than to a supposed straw. I hope this is helpful.

[Not in the slightest. It seems to us to be wholly inconsequential. G.R.O'T.]

[With this, the present editor emphatically disagrees. J.R.]

Important Note from the Printer of the Univresity Press: It is regretted that a large number of errors has crept into this chapter; please refer to the *errata* on p.iii. Also, events have made it necessary to revise the phrase on p.40, "what is now Yugoslavia" to "what was to be, but is no longer, Yugoslavia". [Even further events necessitate the phrase "the former Former Yugoslavia"].

II. Foreign Strands

O dulcis fortuna, quae passus meos foras egit [1]

FTER many tribulations – in particular, a tempestuous sea journey where he nearly lost his life in the Bay of Biscay – Murphy arrived at length at Genoa in Italy. He was there partly to shake off the dust,[2] as it were, of his former misfortunes, and partly because one of the young women of Laracor, from whom he had been cruelly parted, had journeyed thence. His efforts at tracing her were not wholly successful. His first clue to her whereabouts was that she had gone to Abruzzi. This information turned out to be somewhat misleading, for when he arrived there he discovered that the town had been razed to the ground by an earthquake some seven or eight years earlier.

For various reasons, which are not immediately obvious, he arrived eventually at Bologna, having been told that the love of his life was in that city and, through the good offices of a friend of the family, had secured the promise of accommodation at a Seminary there.

Once in Bologna, those characteristic difficulties which had revealed themselves earlier in Murphy's life became evident once more: as ever, he had severe difficulties in finding his way. He arrived, the noonday sun beating down mercilessly upon his uncovered ginger pate, at the Seminary of St Ignatius, only to find that he had erred by one letter and something like half a league. The seminary for which he was

---

[1] I cannot find [says Professor Page] this quotation anywhere. It does not scan, and thus appears to be from a prose work, probably mediæval. Its sentiments, "sweet fortune (or chance), that led my steps elsewhere" (or abroad) have been echoed by later authors.

[2] For some curious reason,[a] Murphy's Latin at this point is *ut excutabit miculas*, implying crumbs rather than dust *(pulvis)*. It should be pointed out here that the sources for this chapter are firstly the Tosti fragments, in Latin, already used in the preceding chapter, and a new source in English, which is also the basis of chapter three. Although this latter source (to be discussed in due course) is not as informative as we might wish, it does allow the Latin narrative to be fleshed out, as it were.

- -

[a] This is not at all curious: in the opinion of the present editor the undertone is clear, having regard to the toast incident recounted in the previous chapter.

destined was that of St Ignotius, some distance away. He discovered his mistake when making enquiries of one of the Jesuit brothers who spoke French, a language with which Murphy had more familiarity, or so he thought, than Italian. The brother set him laconically on his way, and Murphy trudged off wearily in the direction indicated, though the Frenchman, somnolently enjoying the shade of the tree, speeded his going with a parting insult which Murphy did not at first understand. By the time he had grasped that he had been referred to as an Englishman (an insult quite grievous in itself) going abroad in the heat of the day like a rabid dog,[3] it was too late to turn back and make a suitable riposte.

Murphy, plodding with heavy tread around the airless streets and searing *piazze* of Bologna, turned and turned again in obedience to his instructions: as he did so, he likewise turned over in his mind the events of his life which had led him here, his purpose being both to seek wisdom at the Seminary, and also to seek out the voluptuous Mary Collins, his first and, as now he was inclined to believe, his only love.

His reverie was interrupted by his arrival at the Seminary of St Ignatius [lest it be imagined that this might be a misprint – perish the thought – he had arrived at the same place whence he had lately departed], having failed to reach his correct destination. He expostulated with the selfsame French brother, still contemplating nothing in particular under the shade of a tree, who had given him the false directions.

"I would point out that I am not an Englishman at all, at all,[4] and that you have, probably deliberately, mislead me as to the whereabouts of the Seminary of St Ignotius."

In reply, there were many shrugs, many gestures. The only intelligible words were:

"*Tout droit, tout droit.*"

"Exactly," replied the footsore Murphy, "I turned right, then right again, and kept turning right until, in the end, I came back here to where I started. And anyway, if I were going there I wouldn't be starting from here, to be sure."[5]

---

[3] The phrase, as quoted by Murphy, is "canes rabidi ac Anglici aesto meridiano ambulant". In spite of his initial difficulty (it is not clear whether this apothegm was delivered in French or Latin), it clearly wounded his *amour propre*, for he was to remember the phrase and to use it in his later writings. As some readers may be aware, it has been plagiarised by others, and indeed became something of a catchphrase some years ago, to the extent of being taken up as the basis of a low song. [Professor Page would prefer the spelling *apophthegm* in the above note.]

[4] Professor Page demurs at the translation of this phrase, as will be explained below. He adds that Murphy must indeed have lost his way disastrously in Bologna if he was affected so badly by the sun, since this city had been provided with shaded walkways from mediæval times.

[5] This phrase, likewise, is the subject of interpretative disagreement, to be discussed in the following footnote.

An Italian brother, standing by, saw that Murphy was becoming increasingly agitated, and fearful that the incident might develop into physical abuse, intervened. Coming between the two he pointed and said, shortly,

"*Diretto.*"

"Oh, straight on. Now why wasn't he saying that in the first place, to be sure."[6] As Murphy followed, hot foot, the new route,[7] he returned to his thoughts. The confusion of the Seminaries reminded him of his confusion of Cathedrals in Dublin, and his difficulties in establishing the facts of his parentage. Now, at last, he would perhaps be able to meet once more with Mary Collins, whom he had heard was still unmarried. If he could find her, the wheel of fate[c] could at least be turned back to its former position. No sooner had he come to this welcome conclusion, but his destination was reached. Suddenly, the Seminary of St Ignotius of Tombola, to accord the establishment its full title, was in front of him. Thankfully, for by now he

---

[6] As previously indicated, Professor Page disagrees with our rendering of this phrase, which justly represents *plane*, and of "at all, at all" for *plane, plane*. He objects to differing translations of the same word, writing as follows:

The Athenæum
London

Dear Gerald,

I am off to Italy in a day or two, in order to attempt to procure, or at least photograph, the Tosti fragments which the Countess demanded that I return after the unfortunate British Academy incident. Meanwhile, you have my transcriptions. I fear that my departure has been delayed, however, for once again I am temporarily incapacitated, due to an unfortunate *fracas* at Parson's Pleasure, which you doubtless remember is a bathing place intended exclusively for males. I was with Dr Thorne and others when we were interrupted by females who had seemingly failed to apprise themselves of the regulations governing that stretch of the Cherwell, and certainly had not taken due cognizance of them. All (including oneself) had modestly covered ourselves save for Dr Thorne, who covered his face.

When the embarrassment had passed, there was some ribaldry. "Why cover your face, Thorne" said Harry Stottle [Professor of Aristotelian Logic: widely known as Hintrusive Haitch Arry), "when hall hand sundry must be haware that you are the biggest . . . in town?" "Besides which, Boyoh," said Williams Lloyd Hughes [Giraldus Cambrensis Professor of Latin],

> "Spina quid solium subluto podice perdis?
> Spurcius ut fiat spina merge caput."

Dr Thorne required a translation: one explained that the lines belonged to an epigram of Martial wherein the poet recalled a similar incident, the butt of his satire being advised to submerge his head, opining it to be a more shameful object than those parts more commonly called pudendal. Before I had fully glossed the passage, Snorter (I believe that I have already explained this *sobriquet)* kicked one, somewhat illustratively, in the region of the upper thigh. Since the blame was Martial's, or

- -
[c] The wheel of fortune, surely.

was hot and bothered, he went into its cool portals.

There were several Irishmen there, so he was assured of a warm welcome. There were also Italians, Germans and French, one or two English, Scots and Welsh, and several other nationalities, including a Swiss named Bernoulli, with whom he soon struck up an unlikely friendship. Bernoulli was a relative of the more famous mathematicians of the same name, and it was partly this which drew Murphy towards him. Gérard Bernoulli was a brilliant mathematician in his own right and was already lecturing at the mathematical institute in Bologna (an institute which, in common with Murphy and Bernoulli, had been born in 1690), besides being *lettore* at the Seminary. Only in the previous year, his Uncle Jacques had published the

---

rather Lloyd Hughes', I was particularly discountenanced (though the pain was elsewhere than in my countenance, if you follow me) yet too sick, and too badly winded, to argue. Indeed, one's grip on consciousness was decidedly tenuous. Fortunately, a research student of mine from The House, also a well-known member of Vincent's (he is an able Point-to-Pointer and cricketer of some distinction), Sir Henry Groyne-Straine, rescued me and took me to his country seat, Withers, where I am now recovering, in the delightful village of Horton-cum-Scrotum (actually, he has very kindly taken me to lunch at his Club today, hence the letterhead).

Some of this is possibly slightly less than germane to you. Indeed, since the events are of so little public importance, I would urge that you do not record any of this in the monograph in hand, to the subject of which I now turn.

I have a few minor observations concerning the passages you have sent me; and there are one or two slips which can be corrected at the next proof stage. As to the translation of *plane,* however, given as 'to be sure', and *plane plane* for which you have 'at all, at all', I think you have been altogether too free. 'Quite, quite' would suit the dittographic occurrence but not the haplography (one lapses, perforce, into the *termini technici* of one's avocation). One would have expected *valde* or *certe,* or perhaps *compertum est mihi* on the one hand, and *omnino* or rather *nihil omnino* or possibly *minime* on the other. But I cannot think of any word which would serve both (or rather all four) occurrences. What about 'begorrah'?

As ever,
Jack

We forbear to comment on this preposterous suggestion. Professor Page's arguments are self-evidently untenable, and we stand by our translations (for the originals, see the companion volume, which will replace what was hitherto planned as an appendix[b]) rendering the Tosti fragments to which allusions have already been made. The newly identified source – more fully discussed in the following chapter – is an exciting discovery which promises to reveal much concerning Murphy's biography which has remained hitherto obscure.

[7] By a curious chance, he was following the correct direction in spite of having misheard what was said: what the monk had uttered was *da rettà* ('listen'), though Murphy took it as *diretto.* Two wrongs had, unusually for him, conspired to make a right, since the right way was indeed straight on.

- -

[b] but see p.xiv.

magisterial *De Arte Conjectandi* which, bearing heavily upon the theory of mischance which Murphy was by now formulating, was of considerable interest to him.

They met over Murphy's first dinner at the Seminary. From the culinary point of view the meal was not a success, since artichokes, and other comestibles strange to Murphy, were served that evening.

"What are these?" said Murphy to his neighbour.

"*Carciofi*" was the reply.

"What are they?"

"A gross and rotund thistle" said the Scotsman to his left, with a furious rolling of his eyes and R's.

"Good gracious," said Murphy, "am I expected to eat these things?"

"Zen what do you eat at 'ome zen, Ireesh?" said another voice.

"Cabbage and hairy bacon," said yet another voice, this time coming from the other side of the table. Murphy addressed him.

"Are you Irish?"

"No, Swiss."

"Then how do you know about the Irish national dish?"

"I have *une amie irlandaise*."

"Really? An Irish girl-friend here, in Italy?"

"Yes; permit me to introduce myself. I am Gérard Bernoulli, Assistant in Aleatory Algebra."

"This is most interesting," said Murphy, "this means you have studied the mathematics of the fall of the die."

"And of the coin, and of anything else that has to do with what they call chance."

"You must tell me all about it after dinner."

A monk rose to say grace. Several times Murphy tried to talk to Bernoulli but was stopped by frowns from the rest of the company. Every time the speaker appeared to come to a full stop, it turned out that it had only been a comma, as it were.

"… *et qui manet in caritate manet in ipso.*"[8]

---

[8] Professor Page has kindly communicated the full text of this grace (more usually said *before* the meal), apparently much used in monasteries and seminaries until recently:

"Amen."

Judging by this response, the prayer had at last ended. An instant babble ensued, part of which consisted of taunts directed at Murphy. The word seemed to be '*discrambe*'.

"What are they saying?" Murphy asked Bernoulli.

"Take no notice."

"But what is that word?"

"Two words, not one. It is the Greek equivalent of *crambe repetita*:[9] 'cabbage twice is death', a reference, I fear, to your national diet."

Restraining Murphy, who was set to engage in fisticuffs, Bernoulli took him to a secluded corner of the seminary. When the Irishman had cooled down, they began to talk of the theory of chance.

"My father," said Murphy, "or rather, he wasn't my father, used to speak of compensation in all things. 'If a coin comes down heads the majority of times,' he would say, 'then it will come down tails fewer times'."

"You seem to be confused," said Bernoulli, "but whoever it is, or was, of whom you speak, he is, or was, a dolt."

Murphy went on to explain the problematic history of his parentage and how he was attempting to piece the evidence together. Bernoulli was much taken with the story and said:

"Then the matter of your father, or should we say the *primus inter patres*, certainly has to do with the manner of what some call chance, fate, or fortune, but what my own researches, and those of my relatives, have revealed to be a scientific theorem. The

---

Omnium oculi spectant in te domine: et tu das eis escam in tempore opportuno. Aperis manum tuam; et imples omni animal benedictione. Deus caritas est; et qui manet in caritate manet in ipso. Amen.

The apparent reversal of the first words [continues Professor Page] is due to an earlier recension of the Vulgate, pre-existing the translation by Jerome. You will recall that his version from the Hebrew, though adopted for the most part by the church, did not replace the older Psalter. Thus 'oculi omnium' and 'omnium oculi' coexist in different versions. [Professor Page goes on to explain, *inter alia*, that certain Greek texts of the passage have the nominative for the genitive adjective (i.e. οἱ ὀφθαλμοὶ παντοὶ for οἱ ὀφθαλμοὶ πάντων) and also argues that this grace conclusively rules against vegetarianism amongst the early Christians, but the significance of these observations in this context seems somewhat obscure, as are his comparisons with the form of grace used at St Alfred's College.

[9] δὶς κράμβη θάνατος: I am obliged to Professor Page.

18

tossing of a coin is governed by various forces, some straightforwardly physical, and others which interact according to mathematical constraints.

"In order to understand the way a coin behaves physically, you must understand my uncle's important discovery, dating from six years after we were born. In English it would be called 'the path of quickest descent'. Quite simply,[10] his discoveries of the properties of a cycloid in relation to clock design showed that a particle moving by gravity alone from rest to another point not vertically aligned with the aforesaid point does so by the shortest possible curve. At the same time, a particle sliding down by the influence of gravity (assuming once more that it moves by gravity alone and commences its course from a point of rest), the time taken in the passage between stasis and its terminal point will be the same irrespective of the point at which motion commences. You see the significance of this?"

"No," said the baffled Murphy. "You said you had an Irish girl friend. What is her name?"

"She is an Italian Countess now; but her former name was Lily O'Rourke."

"God in heaven! Would you ever tell me where she lives now? I must go to see her at once."

"By no means. The curfew, for one thing; the Count[11] (a very jealous man) for another. After classes tomorrow I shall show you where to go, and more important, when and by what means you may approach her. The Compline bell is now ringing, so we must cease our conversation. Until tomorrow."

---

[10] *simpliciter valde* in MS: as in English, such a phrase inevitably precedes a convoluted and usually unintelligible statement. Here, as elsewhere, the reader will doubtless be aware that we have rendered *oratio obliqua* into *oratio recta* [against, as Professor Page wishes us to aver, his advice] in the interests of clarity.

[11] The Count was the Conte di Tosti; thus Lily O'Rourke had become the Contessa. We learn that the present Contessa has now disposed of her vital Murphy collection. Professor Page arrived at her villa too late to save them, and also came back to England before the excavations at the Villa Ritornella (alluded to below) had been completed. His travails in the scholarly field have not been without incident. He writes as follows:

> I am resting at present. Perhaps, since you are likely to find out, I should be more accurate and say that once again I have suffered a mishap which is illustrative of those principles which your book will elucidate. The accident itself was a simple one, and took place on Port Meadow (you may recall that this is a large tract of common land in the more westerly part of Oxford through which the Thames runs, though in winter it is proper to say *on* which it runs. Thus, if in a cold spell it should freeze over, as now, much of the area is an agreeable natural skating rink).
>
> On the occasion in question, there was some debate as to whether or not the ice on Port Meadow were strong enough. A vulgar girl, who doubtless dropped her nether garments as readily as her consonants, bet me ("Oill beh' yer twen'y quid tha' ih' won' 'old yer" – her glottal stops were wholly remarkable) that the ice would not

The next day was full of portentous happenings. Another link in the chain of discoveries was forged at breakfast when Murphy's toast fell to the ground, just as it had done in the Dean's house in Dublin. We say 'just' somewhat inaccurately, for the toast fell on the refectory floor, but mocked Murphy as he bent to retrieve it. It lay face upwards. He was aghast. A crowd gathered round at this inexplicable sign from heaven.

---

sustain my weight. "Guineas," one said. "Same ter you," she said, enjoining me, rather improbably, to indulge in self-fertilisation (if I heard and glossed the phrase aright). But even while I was explaining to her that Twenty Guineas, or twenty pounds twenty shillings, was twenty-one pounds in either old or new money, one called to mind an infallible method of winning the wager.

On the journey back from Italy by aeroplane I had chanced to sit next to a young engineer from Sweden, by the name of Jens Bogröll. He told me how he was now an important aircraft designer involved with the problem of strengthening wings, but had originally been a lowly clerk in the drawing office. The company had suffered several disastrous accidents involving fatigued wings: these had tended to become severed in one particular place, but no matter how they strengthened this part of the wing with spars and so on, the fractures continued to occur. Bogröll suggested a series of perforations in the wing on the critical line. The idea seemed eccentric in the extreme, but he pronounced it with such authority that the designers were persuaded to try it on a model tested in a wind tunnel. To their marked astonishment the test was successful, and a subsequent test involving a real flying machine achieved the same result. The redesigned wings gave no further trouble to the company, who were thereby saved billions (I use the word of course in the correct sense, not in the sloppy and exaggerative manner of our transatlantic cousins, who misuse the word in the sense of 'milliards' – but I digress) of pounds. Their saviour was promoted to the post of chief designer, but the moguls were curious to know where he had learned this advanced piece of aeronautical stress science. It transpired that Bogröll's previous employment had been in a paper manufactory, where one of the products was those rolls which people have in the smallest rooms of their houses (what Snorter – Dr Thorne – would coyly term the "minor offices" – a rather pointless liturgical reference). In this occupation he had observed that whatever the design or magnitude of the perforations, the rolls would tear anywhere but along the intended line. It was this brilliant observation of a Murphy principle that my Swedish friend applied so elegantly to the science of aviation.

Further properties of the Law were again proven when I applied the same technique to the ice on Port Meadow. With a spike which I had commandeered from an off-duty litter collector, I determined to win the wager with the girl by fortifying the ice by means of perforations. I had but completed a few penetrations with my tool when the ice gave way. The Law, if not oneself, was upheld. One nearly succumbed to drowning, exposure and other rigours:[d] at least, however, one can claim to have advanced the course of science. I am at present undergoing treatment in the Cryogenics Institute here. As soon as I am fully recovered, I will resume my search for the Murphy fragments.

[d] The unfortunate incident was reported in the *Oxford Mail* and some of the national papers. In his delirium, Professor Page addressed the girl who had provoked him. He was apparently (as *The Times* recorded at some length) entranced by her glottal stops, and congratulated her

After breakfast, he taxed Bernoulli with this unnatural phenomenon. His Swiss friend seemed uninterested, being more exercised with the loss of his double-headed coin, which had rolled down a drain during one of his demonstrations of the laws of chance. Disappointed, Murphy moved to the classroom. It turned out that the subject of discussion was to be the question of contradictory natural phenomena, a most felicitous coincidence. Although Murphy was not a Roman Catholic, he seemed to have been swept along with the tide of learning; and the subject of the class was already close to his heart, even before this latest incident.

There were many tedious discussions, which Murphy either could not understand, or found childishly obvious. Each time he thought he might ask his question, someone was there first, with either an abstruse or inane remark. Thus, the gathering was breaking up for lunch before Murphy had a chance to speak. The Professor, a Jesuit from the nearby St Ignatius (Murphy's sore feet remembered the location of this monastery) was stern, but seemed to be approachable, so Murphy lingered and hesitantly put his problem.

"Father, may I ask a question?"

"Do, but I think the lunch bell will ring shortly; so be succinct."

"Do you agree that one natural phenomenon which is so constant as to constitute a physical law is the ineluctable position of a piece of buttered toast which has fallen from the table? As inevitably as death follows birth, the toast lands buttered side down."

"Of course. The Scriptures tell us exactly this, if only in dark sayings and parables. What is the substance of your question?"

"You have me all confused, Father. What scriptural authority might that be now?"

"Really, Sir, you must attend more closely to your studies. 'The last shall be first and the first shall be last':[12] phrases such as this echo throughout the Scriptures. Take, for

---

on her epiglottis being such a "prodigious organ", whereupon she raped him, as reported in detail by the *News of the World* and the *Sun*. The *Times Literary Supplement* had a substantial piece on Grimm's Law and the Principle of Least Effort which seems to be flaunted in the case of the glottal stop. A long letter from Professor G. Lott *et al.* the following week reflected on the linguistic boundaries of this phonological feature in Oxfordshire. *Marxism Today* carried a piece on the forthcoming *coup de glotte*. As to the question of the assault, the *Guardian* pointed out that this was "a blowr stuck for the Womens' movement", being the first substantiated case of a rape in which (to put it in the words of the *Weekly Law Reports*) the plaintiff was a male and had involuntarily been submitted to successful coition. The unusual feature, according to Professor Lee Gull-Eagle, the distinguished commentator, was Professor Page's weakened state, making him unable to resist. Page, as Gull-Eagle observed in the *Observer*, "was stiff with cold". It will be noted that this incident parallelled, if not exactly, an event which befell Murphy, and which is recounted below (p.85).

[12] Matt. XIX: 30 (the parable of the places at the feast).

example, the forty-sixth verse of the sixth chapter of the Book of Maccabees."

"I am not over-familiar with the Apocrypha."

"Then let me enlighten you. 'He got in underneath the Elephant and thrust at it from below and killed it. It fell to the ground on top of him and there he died.' Is this elephantasmagorical incident not a perfect illustration of what some would call the malevolence of fate, what others would deem to be the mysterious ways in which God moves?"

"But …"

"And, of course, there is the parable of the talents. '*Omni enim habenti dabitur et abundabit: ei autem qui non habet, et quod videtur habere, auferetur ab eo*'.[13] The steward who lost his penny saw it land, so to speak, buttered side down."

"But, Father …"

"No more buts;[14] the bell will sound at any moment. I can smell the *vitello tonnato*,[15] so ask your question without further delay."

"Then it is this. How is it that this morning, when my toast slipped from the plate, it landed *buttered side up*?"

"You cannot have observed the incident correctly. What you describe is simply impossible."

"To be sure; are there not a dozen witnesses? No, Father, there is no doubt, at all at all. So what is the explanation of this contravention of natural law, indeed, as you imply, this apparent suspension of God's own purpose?"

The Jesuit crossed himself and hesitated. Murphy insisted:

"Does this mean you have no answer?"

"**NO ANSWER?!**" thundered the Professor, getting up and nearly knocking down Murphy in the rearrangement of his considerable bulk (he was not a particularly ascetic member of his order).

---

[13] Unto him that hath shall be given: unto him that hath not, even shall be taken away. (Matt. XXV: 29).

[14] The Latin original, *sed mihi non sed ac sed*, is curious. "More than that," says Professor Page, "for the apophthegm 'but me no buts', widely but erroneously attributed to Shakespeare, transparently originates with Murphy, after whose time it became commonplace."

[15] On this matter, Professor Page contributes the following note: Our College chef, Pepper, is irritating, but he does know about these things. He assures me that this particular dish is a kind of cold collation, and would hardly smell in the manner described. Something is wrong here.

"I hear the bell. My nostrils drink in the *vitello tonnato*[16]: I have no more time for you. Come to me this day week and you shall have your answer."

He moved off, visibly perturbed. A Jesuit could hardly admit defeat in disputation, but the impossible seemed to have occurred. Yet, to God, nothing is beyond the bounds of possibility. He ate his lunch enthusiastically at first, but queasiness overtook him as he contemplated the problem which even his prodigious appetite could not put aside. Eventually his food growled dyspeptically within him, so that by the end of lunch he was ill disposed, in a somewhat literal sense, towards Murphy.

The latter, however, rushed off with Bernoulli immediately after grace. On the hills outside Bologna, his friend pointed to a large white villa which, although distant, shone like an iridescent opal in the relentless sun. Having quite forgotten his allegiance to the charms of Mary Collins, Murphy was eager to see the vivacious Lily once more.

"This is the time to go. The Count will be asleep in the taverna. No one, with the exception of deranged dogs and Englishmen,[17] would be abroad in the heat of the sun. Take the path up through the vineyard, and then straight on: when you get to the villa, make the sound of the cuckoo under the large upstairs window facing you. Lily will assume it is me but I am sure she will be pleased to see you in my stead."

And so she was. Murphy had avoided being seen, taking the path of quickest ascent through the vineyard and the secret garden, as instructed by Bernoulli. In some apprehension he gave the cuckoo signal and was rooted to the spot when the casement opened and a diaphanously clothed figure leant out. She was equally surprised, and called out so loudly that the whole valley seemed to echo with his name.[18] He was acutely embarrassed when asked to go up. He found his way, as

---

[16] See above, footnote 15.

[17] The proverbial expression, commented upon earlier, occurs once again in the MS, this time appearing to emanate from the mouth of Bernoulli.

[18] Actually, it was the wrong name, for she called out "Aloys", a name which, as Murphy was at pains to tell her, he had abandoned in favour of Roger. This much is clear from the source, in English, already mentioned, and which will be discussed in more detail in the next chapter. As to the Latin source for this passage, the reader will be aware by now that the style of the document as a whole is often somewhat flowery. The phrase here is *canens 'ave' collibus resonantibus*. As Professor Page (on whose transcriptions we are, as ever, wholly reliant) rightly suggests, this means more literally "singing Hello to the resonant hills"; but we think our translation to be more in the spirit of the original, particularly in view of the gloss provided by the source in English. In addition to this kind of problem of diction which confronts the translator, there is another: in more than one passage it has been deemed necessary that some hints of lubricity should be toned down in order to spare the sensitivities of the reader: [again Professor Page demurs: "prudery is not scholarly" he says – somewhat unaccountably, in view of his own predilection for euphemism] nonetheless, we are sensible of our obligations in this regard.

always, with difficulty, but finally located Lily's room. She was ready for him, but he was not ready for what was to happen.

It will be necessary to pass over the events of the next hour or so, which saw Murphy's shy initiation into mysteries which he was now contemplating barely.

Afterwards, since the wind had changed and the mountain air had suddenly become quite chilly, they put on a few clothes. The conversation turned to those earlier years in Ireland when they had last met in the innocence of youth. He told her of how their plans of marriage had been wrongly thwarted, and how his parentage was now a mystery.

"Ruggiero!" she said.

"Why do you call me that?"

"Because, Roger, your new name is *Ruggiero* in Italian, and with your red hair it suits you down to the ground."[19]

"I see. Now what were you going to say?"

"It was to do with the circumstances of your birth which we were talking about earlier."

"Go on."

"Do you remember the locket you gave me when we had decided to get married?"

"I do."

"I should have given it back when we parted, but somehow I couldn't bring myself to do so."

"It wasn't your fault, it was my wretched father – or to be more accurate, the person I once thought was my father – *ceteris patribus*."

"Well, that is the point: you told me that it was your mother's; but when I looked at it closely, the initials inscribed upon it were not hers."

"I never really took much notice; but presumably they were the initials corresponding with her maiden name."

"Amn't I after telling you that they were not; and you told me that she was given it as a love token just before you were born. So is it not likely that the initials on the keepsake are those of your real father?"

---

[19] The science of onomastics (writes Professor Page) was probably unknown to her, but clearly she had some instinctive grasp of its rudimentary implications. Nevertheless, it seems unlikely to me that his hair was more than shoulder-length.

"Heavens above! You may be right! So what were they?"

"His surname seems to have been O'Donovan or O'Doyle, or something beginning with D, and his Christian name began with an S."

"So the initials were S O'D."

"They were."

"Well, I haven't a notion who that might be. Have you still got the locket?"

"I have; I'll be going to get it. It is in the chest of drawers in the bedroom next door."

Murphy had no time to think further about this exciting development in his quest, for Lily was back almost instantly, bearing a casket. She rummaged in it and found a handsome ruby ring of distinctive design.

"Here is a ring for you: wear it as a little token of our recent reunion. Now where is the locket?"

Murphy put on the ring, which perfectly fitted his little finger. As he did so, she found the locket, chased in silver filigree, enclosing, under glass, two tufts of differing coloured hair, both of which were curled and very short, and which were conjoined in the middle in a kind of plait. Lily showed it to him, saying:

"See, here it is. There are two little cushions of hair. I had always thought that the giving and receiving of the *quei capille*[20] was an Italian custom: I am surprised to discover that the Irish have taken to it."

"What on earth are … whatever it is you said?"

"They are the shortest hairs which show the longest love and the truest colour," she said, prettily.

"Oh, I think I see," said Murphy, glancing downwards at Lily's comate abundance.

"The tufts of hair, red plaited with black, are probably those of your parents," she continued. "The black is your mother's, so the red would belong to your real father …"

"That is a wonderful title for a novel – *The Red and the Black* – I shall write it under the pen-name Sterndale."

"Why Sterndale? Anyway, no matter: look, here are the initials on the back."

---

[20] Public hairs. Apparently this peculiar custom, known to (and kept by) Byron, still persists in Italy.

"They are in curiously formed letters. But mark, there is no apostrophe. The initials are S.O.D."

"Well, that doesn't necessarily mean anything: it might ..."

"On the contrary," he interrupted, "it does. They are the initials of a Latin motto which my mother often used to quote. *Semper Opus Dei.*"

This, then, was another momentous event in history. The alternative title to Murphy's Law seems to have been the acronym of a phrase he was to take up as his own, his talisman against the many buffetings of fate which he was to undergo.[21] Fate was already spinning its wheel. Murphy's new-found lover had tired of the discussion and was close to him, thinking of something quite different. He tried to restrain her, but she merely said,

"Cosa ben fatta é fatta due volte."

"What does that mean?" said Murphy.

"What is well done once is worth doing twice.[22] Now come on," she said, moving towards the bedroom and shedding clothes on the way; but no sooner had they reached the couch than a noise was heard coming from the loose stones on the terrazzo below. Murphy, in a panic, moved towards the window.

"Is it the Count, your husband?" he said, leaning over the chest of drawers, the central one of which was still open, having recently given up the casket and its treasures.

"Surely not; it cannot be," she said, joining him.

Together they peered over the chest of drawers, a handsome Florentine piece, to see who was below. Almost instantly, they discovered that it was only the gardener: but their straining against the open drawer caused it to imitate the action of the guillotine. Since an intropenetrant part of the disrobed Murphy had interposed itself meanwhile, the summary and sudden snickersnee of the drawer caused him to scream with the searing pain which instantly came upon him.

This blood-curdling noise, to add insult to manifest injury, attracted the servants, who pounded up the stairs calling *"Banditti!"*, *"Rapisto!"* and other possible

---

[21] As will shortly be seen, this theory, while attractive, has at least one serious rival, one which Professor Page inclines to believe is more plausible.[e]

[22] Curiously, Chesterton, who was a good Catholic, says more or less the opposite: "What is worth doing is worth doing badly."

- -

[e] Not so: in the present editor's view the evidence is overwhelmingly in favour of the present thesis. See pp.33–34. And, of course it is *Fortune* who spins *her* wheel.

explanations of the disturbance. Murphy, clutching himself in agony, was enjoined to shin down the fig tree growing up to the bedroom window and, having taken the patch of quickest descent, to hide in the well nearby, from which Lily would retrieve him as soon as the clamour had died down.

The defenestration[23] having been accomplished, Murphy found the well, where he shivered, in exquisite pain, during a wait of several hours. It was only at nightfall that he was rescued. Even then, his deliverance was delayed because of the moans, which he could not constrain, of naked agony. In the twilight, the superstitious servants imagined that an evil spirit had been entrapped in the well. Accordingly, they poured libations of hot and, alternately, cold water upon him until, after a last piercing scream, all was eerily silent.

The servants withdrew, thinking the *diabolus loci* to be dead. Not surprisingly, Murphy, although not dead, was unconscious and rapidly moving towards extinction. In the nick of time the Countess raised him to the well head, wrapped him in blankets and conveyed him, on the back of a donkey, into the city, leaving him at the Ospedale.

The Ospedale in question was at the Convent of the Little Sisters of Self Pity. Murphy was delirious and kept asking about the locket: he had still been holding it in the well, but it was in his hands no longer;[24] all he now clutched was a solitary fig-leaf.

---

[23] There is, says Professor Page, a hint of ambiguity in the use of this word (he reminds us that the Latin original displays the ablative absolute construction).

[24] Recent excavations at the Villa Ritornella, under the direction of Professor Rubble[f], have sought to recover this important artefact. In so doing, an incident occurred, of the kind familiar to all archaeologists, and which has a double bearing on the subject of this monograph. The well had been excavated, though there was much altercation between the proponents of the grid method and various other theories of excavation: all, since the site was a hole, seemed equally inappropriate. In the end, a considerable mound of excavated rubble was piled at the side of the well, and it finally became clear that there was nothing remaining at the foot of the well, save water and solid rock.

There is a law among archaeologists called *lex cespitis* (more properly spelled *caespitis*, as Professor Page would prefer). This ordains that the significant finds do not issue forth from the excavation itself, but from the slurry, as it were, (nicely emphasised in the *Anglice* pronunciation of 'cespitis') cast aside. And so it was in this instance, the law being upheld. The locket or brooch was amongst the rubbish brought up by the excavation, but remained unnoticed until a labourer (hired by Dr Rob Graves[g] who was in charge of the casual workers on the site) saw it glittering in the sunlight and promptly pocketed it. The whole incident, coupled with the subsequent flight and disappearance of the labourer turned thief, underlined the operation of *lex cespitis*. As Professor Page explains:

> For those readers whose Classical education may not have been well grounded, *c(a)espis* is the cut turf, which the diligent archaeologist will pile carefully beside his site, but in less careful 'digs' is often mixed up with the rubbish from the excavation.

As he regained consciousness, a further surprise was in store for him.

"Aloys!"

"Where is the locket?"

"There is a ring on your finger: is that what you have been raving about for the last two days?"

He looked at his finger and said, as his eyes travelled towards the Amazonian and pileous Sister tending him:

"No, this is not the locket, it is … Good God! It's …"

"Yes. It's Mary. Once Mary Collins but now Sister Judas (Not Iscariot)."

Gazing up at her luxuriant moustache, he was extremely grateful that she had taken the veil, though unfortunately not literally. How he could have fallen so hopelessly in love with this obese and bewhiskered harridan, he could not now imagine. What a contrast to the vivacious Lily! He thought of her, and immediately tried to get up from the bed, only to discover the severity of his injuries and to realise that he had no clothes. He blushed furiously at the frank, lanate, stares of Sister Judas.

"Your friend is bringing in some clothes for you, so that you will look daycent. He will be here within the hour. But first, Aloys, we must see to your wounds."

Murphy expostulated that he had taken the name Roger, and unwisely told her the story of his parental difficulties.[h] Meanwhile, the ministrations of Sister Judas were both loathsome and excruciating. Prior to coming to the sick ward to see to his injuries, she had been preparing a pasta sauce, characteristic of the district, of rare and vicious power: it was a concoction of chilli, oil and garlic. The oil was not much in evidence, save for a greasy texture to her hands; the garlic, however, was all too obviously present, on her repulsive breath; but it was the chilli which made itself felt, instantly and irremovably. She might better have rubbed salt in his wounds, for the blood blister which figured so prominently on his person, and indeed all that area which, even unruptured, is exquisitely sensitive, was cruelly inflamed by the fiery essence clinging to her hands. Murphy screamed anew in his fresh agony, jumped

---

An alternative and more pithy translation for the 'Law of the excised turf' is the 'Law of the Sod', whence the commoner turn of phrase may safely be said to have derived.

- -

[f] J. C. B. Professor of Conservative Archaeology at the University of Wigan Pier.

[g] Not to be confused with Dr Robert Graves, poet, novelist and latter-day Richard Burton (not to be confused with the actor of the same name).

[h] Unwisely, since the significance of this – that there had been no impediment to their matrimony after all – was not lost on the listener, as will later be seen.

up, heedless of decorum, and fled from the torment. Mercifully, as he came through the door, Bernoulli was there, clothes in hand, so he was able to dress himself, albeit accompanied by the most tortuous pain.

When he had clothed himself well enough to take to the street, Bernoulli and he beat a hasty retreat. Because of his wounds, inflamed by the chill, Murphy paused in distress at the portals of the Ospedale. In doing so, he idly studied the curious notices affixed to the woodwork surrounds, one of which was in broken English: 'The Sisters,' it read, 'is indifferent to language, she harbour all diseases, and has no regard for religion.' Bernoulli urged him on, exclaiming:

"Basta, basta!"

Despite his injuries, Murphy rounded on him and tried to throttle his companion.

"Don't you ever be calling me a bastard …" began Murphy, but Bernoulli restrained and interrupted him, quickly explaining that he merely used the Italian phrase for 'hurry up'.

"Come on!" said Bernoulli.

"Why the hurry? I am in the most appalling pain."

"You saw the notice. This place is a notorious refuge for those suffering from a particular kind of disease."

Murphy understood with remarkable rapidity and allowed himself to be marched, in spite of his agony, to the Seminary. There, he was put to bed, where he slept for several days.

As his condition improved, he became anxious about several things, one being the answer to his question concerning the curious behaviour of the slice of toast. When he had recovered more fully, he therefore persuaded Bernoulli to take him to the weekly lecture given by the Jesuit philosopher. To his desolation, the lectures had been changed: instead, a discussion about Celtic languages was in progress. Someone was asking a question.

"Who is that person with the curious English accent?" said Murphy.

"Floyd,[25] a Welshman," replied Bernoulli.

---

[25] *Unda maris, id est Flood.* So runs the original fragment. It seems that Elway or Edward Llwyd was the 'Floyd' mentioned, for there is a reference to him in a later document [for which see below] and to the fact that a book bearing his name was published in the same year that a mob destroyed a steamboat constructed by a distant relative of Bernouilli's, seemingly called 'Denis Pope'. There was certainly a Denis Papin whose invention was the subject of riotous indignation in 1707, and this was indeed the year in which Edward Lhwyd published *Archæologia Britannica*. But this Lhwyd, Llwyd, Lloyd or Floyd, died in 1709, so the person of

Floyd was enquiring of the Visiting Professor of Philology, an Irishman called Seamus O'Carragheen, as to the Irish equivalent of the phrase *doppio domani* or, as the Spaniards have it, *mañana mañana*.

The venerable Professor was silent for several minutes, then spoke softly and hesitantly:

"I fear," he said, looking round the room, his voice now lowering almost to a whisper, "that there is nothing in the Irish tongue which conveys quite the same sense of oorgency."

There was a respectful silence during which Bernoulli nudged Murphy, whereupon they went out from the seminar, more or less unobserved.

As they left, the silence was broken by Floyd: "Ha, ha!" he explained (in Welsh).[26] Murphy expostulated that he was interested in the debate, but his friend clearly was not, and insisted on going to the *taverna*.

Having some cool white wine on the table, to which Murphy had by now become quite accustomed, they ordered some food. Murphy's Italian, though improved, was not yet perfect, so his first course consisted of toothpicks followed by a fingerbowl. Eventually, some pasta was brought, served with a rich red sauce, after the *Bolognese* fashion,[27] after which they had a particularly delicious melon, which was

---

this name mentioned by Murphy must have been a relative of the author. In 1707, incidentally, there was another riot when Cornelius Meyer and his son drained the Pontine Marshes. Local inhabitants, seemingly fond of malaria, destroyed the drainage works. The Meyers were also indirectly responsible for a particularly unfortunate event in Murphy's career, as will be seen below.

[26] It is possible that he was quoting from the book of Job (39: 25: He saith among the trumpets, Ha, Ha).

[27] Professor Page, as ever, is informative on this point. He writes:

> Our former College chef, Mr K. N. Pepper, was something of an authority on foreign food. He was a good cook, as cooks go, but as good cooks go, he went. He has been succeeded by Mr R. T. Choke, who calls himself an expert on the history of continental cuisine (i.e. foreign food). He confirms that the mixture of oil, garlic and chilli (which you have described to me as the source – no paronomasia intended, I should add – of Murphy's discomfiture) is indeed an authentic receipt; but he tells me that the so-called Bolognese sauce familiar today is comparatively modern. That eaten by Murphy would not have contained tomato. Choke is unable to shed much light on the question of the variety of melon referred to in the second part of the sentence. In College, I might add, we rarely have pasta at High Table, since Pepper used to insist on it being served *al dente* whereas dons such as Dr Thorne demand that it shall be cooked *al* dentures, at which Choke demurs,[j] and which was one of the causes of the peevish Pepper picking up his papers.

[j] Choke chokes, so to speak. On the question of tomato being a modern ingredient of Bolognese sauce, the present editor is informed that the earliest fruits to arrive in Europe

astonishingly sweet, and quite seedless. Murphy determined that Dean Swift should grow these in his garden. Swift had already collected Broccoli and Fennel seeds, both of which outlandish vegetables Murphy had grown to like. Bernoulli promised to procure this new item for his friend's collection.

As they were finishing, the abundant figure of the Jesuit philosopher who had absented himself from the Seminary darkened the doors, quite literally. The *patrone* greeted him fulsomely as *Egregio Reverendo Dottore Padre Professore* and immediately placed before him an antipasto of fish, followed by a pasta dish with a particularly rich looking sauce. He was clearly having the pick of the menu, without having to order anything, least of all the flagon of wine. It was obvious that Murphy would be unwise to raise the matter of his question, since the learned Professor was not to be deflected from the food and drink set before him. As Murphy observed to Bernoulli, he did himself well.

"What is more," said Bernoulli, "he is having chicken *cacciatore*, despite the fact that it is a day of obligation, on which no meat should pass his lips."

With a beatific scowl, the subject of their observation made the sign of the cross over the chicken and intoned, piously:

"*Benedetti le melanzane.*"

"What was that?" said Murphy.

"He's blessing the dish, pretending that it's aubergines."

"What a hypocrite!" said Murphy, throwing up his hands.

"It's called casuistry …" said Bernoulli, who at that moment noticed the ring on his friend's hand, exclaiming:

"That's mine."

"Not at all, at all," replied Murphy, "it is mine. It was a gift." he continued coyly.

"Then whoever gave it to you stole it."

Murphy began to lose his temper, but Bernoulli, who by now was beginning to grasp

---

were yellow, not red, hence the Italian word *pomodoro*, a word that caused an unfortunate incident at a production by the Oxford Operatic Production Society (O.O.P.S) of a work by an early composer called Cesti, whose career seems more than somewhat to have resembled that of Murphy. Professor Page apparently recommended Signora Phryne Gransene, now of the University Chest, but formerly a pupil of his, to translate all the colossal Cesti materials into English. Her knowledge of music appears to have been rudimentary, so the Opera about the Golden Apple was advertised as being entitled *The Tomato,* which understandably caused more than a little discord.

what might have happened, offered to toss a coin to establish the ownership of the ring. This offer was not accepted (Murphy had heard of the double-headed coin), nor was the choosing of a card, nor yet the drawing of straws, a proposal which made Murphy angry again. They were interrupted by a resplendent figure entering the *taverna*. Bernoulli introduced the newcomer to Murphy, who failed properly to catch the name, though it somehow seemed familiar.

"We were discussing, my dear Count, some problems of chance," said Bernoulli. "Murphy refuses to submit the question of the ownership of this ring (by now he had taken it from his friend's finger) on the grounds that he thinks that there is some Law which ensures the worst possible outcome – I gather it has to do with some remarkable details concerning his parentage – but I insist that the scientific laws of chance favour no one; the roulette wheel, the tossing of a coin, the choosing of a card, all are regulated by an aleatory principle which is indifferent to persons, impassive to influence, and disinterested as regards the outcome."

"It is certainly a handsome ring," said the Count, "but I fail to see how its ownership could be in doubt."

"The point is," said Bernoulli, "that the ring is mine, but I mislaid it in the bed of a lady who was so good as to keep me warm against the evening chill of the mountain air: I had removed it lest its sharp edges might thereby leave my inadvertent signature upon her flesh, or otherwise injure her.[28] The same lady subsequently offered similar hospitality to my friend Murphy here, and she gave him the ring. Since he is not entitled to it, and it is mine, it seems more than reasonable on my part that I should offer to wager it."

"That does indeed seem reasonable," said the gentleman, rising, "though in truth the ring should belong to the owner of the bedclothes."

Instantly, Murphy had a horrible premonition of what might take place, but his recent injuries meant that his reactions were too slow, even though the events seemed to take place in frozen time. With a laugh, Bernoulli tossed the ring to Count Tosti, whose name Murphy belatedly recognised. The enraged owner of the sheets swiped with one foul sweep of his swagger stick (not unlike the kind known in Murphy's native land as a Shillelagh) at both of the seated figures, but Bernoulli had ducked, leaving the bemused Murphy to receive the full force of the blow upon his head.

His injuries were so severe that he was taken once more to the Ospedale of the Little Sisters, for there was nowhere else nearby where first aid could be rendered. Once again, Murphy saw the horripilant vision of the adipose Mary Collins as he returned

---

[28] It is probably irrelevant[k] to note that the poet Goethe was wont to prove the scansion of his verses upon the back of his mistress, in not entirely dissimilar circumstances.

[k] It is.

to consciousness. He wondered idly about her Amazonian breast, shuddering at the thought of papillate paps.

"I have had a long talk with Sister Frigida," she said.

"Who is Sister Frigida?" said Murphy, transfixed by the sight of the quivering quiff.

"Mother Superior, known to some of the novices as the Ice Maiden. She is Irish, her name being a rare form of St Brigid.[29] I told her, face to face (Murphy had a horrible vision of hirsute intimacy) that I wanted to leave the order, so that I could marry you."

"Me?" said Murphy, "I can't."

"Can't!" she bristled, "but now we have been reunited by a miracle and you have told me that you have discovered that there is nothing standing in the way of our being joined in Holy Bedlock, we cannot doubt God's purpose."

"I cannot doubt it, certainly," muttered Murphy; "*Semper Opus Dei*, or SOD for short,"[m] he said, as he fled.

Another of the nuns, seeing him flee from the hispid face of wrath said:

"*Contesa vecchia tosto si fa nuova!*"

"How," thought Murphy as he beat an undignified retreat, "can she possibly know about my connexion with the Contessa di Tosti?"[30]

He went up into the hills, running as though pursued by the Devil. He came up through the vineyard, crossed the secret garden, and stood below the casement window of the Villa Ritornella, where he made the sound of the cuckoo.

"Holy Mary, Mother of God: it is a fool that you are," said Lily as she rushed him indoors, "my husband knows of you and is out for your blood."

"So is Mary Collins, now Sister Judas."

---

[29] Professor Page will not countenance what he describes as a popular etymology. "I have consulted (he says) with Dr Violet King, the distinguished Norse mythologist, who confirms that Frigida is a form of Frigga or Freya (from which the English 'Friday' is derived) the goddess of sensual passion, the Norse equivalent of Venus. Vi King assures me that Frigida is a Latin Frigga, rather than a Celtic mutational form, i.e. Frigid/Brigid."

[30] Once more, Murphy had misinterpreted what he had heard. The phrase is proverbial and was a warning, sadly unheeded, as to the perfidy of jealousy: "An old quarrel is soon revived".

- -

[m] The present editor is bound to observe that this and subsequent occurences of the phrase make the theory espoused by Professor O'Toole in a previous footnote less likely.

"She will betray you. She was always a nasty piece of work. I never understood what you saw in her."

"Neither do I. But she is Not Iscariot."

"I hope you are right. Now let us make hay while the pot boils. Ask what you will of me, Roger."[31]

Once more, the delights of venery were revealed to Murphy, though a touch painfully, for he was only recently recovered of his *mentulagra*, as the Italians call it; and once again there was an untimely interruption. A clamour, something like a hue and cry, could be heard coming nearer, ever nearer, towards the villa.

"It's your so-called friend Mary Collins, leading, like some Bulbous Tara, a lynching mob, with my husband as her lieutenant."

"*Semper Opus Dei*, or SOD for short," replied Murphy.

"Quick!" she said, "down the fig tree."

"Not again," said Murphy, who nonetheless escaped by a whisker on account of her cunning.[32]

His escape was temporary, however, for his pursuers, headed by the Count and Sister Judas (seemingly Iscariot, after all), were hot upon his heels. As he staggered on his errotic way, the only means he could see to avoid the mob was to jump into the ornamental lake. His decision, although having much to commend it from a

---

[31] The Latin of this passage is *rogite me, roger!* Professor Page writes:

> The verb *rogito* is the frequentative or intensive form of *rogo*, meaning 'frequently or earnestly to ask, or to stretch after something'. The root ROG is cognate with Greek root ὈΡΓ, from which derive such words as ὀργάω, to swell (esp. with lust, but curiously also to soften); ὄργια, orgies, and many derivatives such as ὀργιασμος; ὀρέγω, to stretch out or lunge, and so on. Since a pun is clearly intended, the phrase might be interpreted as "stretch forth (earnestly) toward me".[n]

[32] Professor Page comments upon this passage thus:

> The phrase here seems, according to a *signe de renvoie* in the original, to belong to a previous paragraph; but in any case, the translation 'by a whisker' seems extremely unlikely in this context. True, the MS contractions in the phrase *apprehend eũ a brev. pil.* might well be read *apprehendit eum a breve pilo,* which could mean literally "she possessed him by a short hair"; but this strains the construction more than somewhat. The plural *a brevibus pilis* seems greatly to be preferred: "she held him by the short hairs". Also, although *causa callidae suae* could mean "on account of her cunning", I am not aware of any usage of *callidus* as a noun. If *callidae* were a misspelling of *calidae*, it would be "because of her heat", but this seems equally inexplicable to me.

- -

[n] Or, to stretch a point, "Hoist the Jolly, Roger!".

theoretical point of view, failed to take into account the circumstances that the Count had engaged the Meyers, father and son,[33] to drain the lake in order to rid the villa of a plague of malaria. All that was left of the lake was an inch of water covering a thin layer of foul-smelling mud, below which was unforgiving rock. Thus, Murphy's dive into the lake, now wholly bedsock, resulted in a fractured skull. As he slipped into unconsciousness he gibbered, in a loud voice:

"Lutum, O lutum; lutum praeclarum."[34]

When he regained consciousness he found himself in a dungeon-like cell, his head covered in bandages clotted with blood. Supposing himself to be, once again, in the Ospedale, he cried out for the sisters. In answer, a series of clanks was followed by the appearance of an uncouth face in what he now saw was a grille. Incomprehensible words came from the toothless grimace, followed by contemptuous spitting. Prison. In one fell sweep it dawned on our hero that this was the latest manifestation of the malevolent principle which was by now ever more clearly formulating in his mind.

He had many months to contemplate these matters. He dared not ask for the Contessa; Bernouilli could not, or would not, visit him. Only the crinite Sister Judas came to dress his wounds and to taunt him: marry her, she said, or suffer the consequences. Although he resisted this tomentous torment of her suit, he was able to prevail upon her to bring paper, pen and ink, and it was thus that he set down his adventures for posterity, though, as he observed, posterity had done precious little for him.

More than a year after his painful incarceration, he was hauled before the equivalent of a magistrate. The charge was read, but in a dialect which he could not understand, and at a speed which made it impossible to construe a single phrase. An interpreter was called for, or so Murphy assumed. Someone had volunteered, but when a question was asked, the supposed interpreter merely repeated it, louder, and with what he fancied to be an English accent. The magistrate, eventually grasping from the uncontrolled mirth of the assembly that something was amiss, sentenced the volunteer interpreter to sixty lashes. The sentence was carried out at once beside the courtroom, so Murphy could not hear anything else for some time; only belatedly did he realise that a real interpreter had now come forward. His name, it transpired, was 'Avocado Pera',[p] but he did not act as a defence lawyer, since Murphy had no money.

---

[33] See footnote 25 on p.29

[34] Yet another phrase which has had some recent currency: "Mud, O mud; O pre-eminent mud".

- -

[p] Hardly. His name is unlikely to have been "avocado pear", though it might well have been Avvocata Pero.

"*Nativo?*" said the magistrate unnecessarily.

Understandably, Murphy was puzzled at the translation. Relentlessly, the interpreter explained, emphasising each syllable.

"Did you come here before you were born, or were you born before you came here?"

"No. Yes. I mean, no, I am not a native of this State, or indeed of anywhere in Italy."

The interpreter translated, and the magistrate noted the answer down with every sign that he considered the matter a crime in itself. By hesitating to answer such a simple question, Murphy was not making a good impression.

The trial wore on, and as it did so, Murphy gradually realised that he was in the dock as an attempted suicide. All the Count's servants gave evidence that he had jumped knowingly to what should have been certain death.

Black as this was, the final witness was sworn in. She gave her name. Murphy could himself have sworn that she said 'Sister Judas', missing out the 'Not' before 'Iscariot'. She looked at him, as though giving him a final chance. He turned away, more certain than ever that this omission was perhaps exquisitely correct, for no sooner had she given her damning evidence (mendaciously stating that he had confessed to her his intention to commit suicide) than the verdict was given.

Guilty.

The court gasped with vicarious anticipation. The sentence was read out. The crowd knew what was to come, but Murphy did not. The interpreter translated the magistrate's words, phrase by phrase, so that the utterance partook of the nature of a gruesome parody of a marriage ceremony.

"… for the crime of attempted suicide … a crime against God … and contrary to the statutes of this City and Papal State … there is but one penalty fixed, … which the law must inexorably exact …" (as he intoned all this, the magistrate fidgeted with his head, apparently draping it with some sort of black handkerchief) " … and I hereby sentence you to death … and God have …"

"This is preposterous!" interrupted Murphy, aghast. "First, I didn't attempt to commit suicide, at all at all; and secondly, if I had tried, unsuccessfully, you would by your sentence be aiding and abetting the commission of a crime." This irrefutable and neatly argued defence fell on deaf ears, however. The interpreter merely explained that the intention to commit a crime, be it larceny or assault, rape, murder or suicide, was in the eyes of the law equal to the crime itself, so whether it might be successfully committed or not would be irrelevant.**

Murphy's rejoinder was never uttered, for he was immediately led away. Judging by the lashes meted out only minutes after the sentence had been passed upon an earlier misfortunate, Murphy feared the worst, and a black mask being pulled down over his head did not allay his fears. Shouts came from all sides. The rabble, it seemed, was lusting for blood. The noise became more and more frightening, and sounded now like a riot. Scuffles were clearly to be heard, and Murphy was unceremoniously bundled into the tumbril. He did not know what to pray, in these his last moments as the cart moved at breakneck speed. [An unfortunate translation, this. J.R.] So he merely said "*Semper Opus Dei!*"

"In short," said a female voice, "SOD."

The mask was ripped from him; so Murphy now saw that he was in a closed carriage and that he had been rescued, with considerable daring, by Lily.

"I could not make a move to free you until the last minute," she said, "but Gérard organised a little diversion, and we whisked you away to safety."

"Bernoulli? I thought he – and you – had forgotten me."

"No, neither of us did, but there were difficulties. Gérard was watched by my

---

** Professor Archie McAndrews, now Vice-Chancellor of the University of Man (in order to secure which post he gamely learnt the Manks language) but formerly Professor of the History of the Sociology of Law, at University College, Bognor (having diligently learnt Welsh), has given the present editor the benefit of his learned opinion on the subject. He says:

> The Law at that point in time was basically, when it came to the crunch, the *lex talionis* which in terms of English is the Law of the Tooth. Quite simply,[q] this was, in lay terms, the conceptualisation of a grass roots socio-moral interaction of cross-cultural religio-ethical standpoints whereby, if you like, the ongoing fundamental rights of the individual insofar as they conflict with the aforesaid rights of another, either on a one-to-one basis, or in terms of the community as a whole, as nowadays expressed by the democratically arrived at decision of their duly elected representatives, were subject to penalties equivalent, in broad terms, but subject to the necessary checks and balances as decided on a regular basis, to the misdemeanour itself. To briefly add one more point, I would say that Murphy's argument that the court should not aid or abet a crime could not, at the end of the day, stand in the sense of a defence in law. In a judicial execution situation the court was *preventing* a crime, in the sense of the crime of suicide, or attempted suicide (in broad brush terms the two are merely variations in degree, not of substance). Execution for attempted suicide (other sentences being in place for actual suicides) was dropped by the late eighteenth century, and in this day and age suicide is no longer considered to be a crime, its new status having come on stream by the end of the nineteenth century. I am not too sure of the exact situation at this moment in time in terms of Italy.

[q] See footnote 10, p.19, for the convoluted significance of this phrase.

husband; but he sends you these seeds which he says you were collecting. For my part," she said handing over the package, "I have …"

Murphy now saw that she had a very small child with her, at the sight of which he let out an involuntary exclamation.

"History more or less repeats itself, you see," said Lily. "The Count, thinking me infertile, went about trying to sire his heir elsewhere. But now he is happy. *Sterilis amator datis.*"

"But is he sterile, or not? And if he is, whose …"

She took the shawl from the child's head, revealing his bright red hair.

"There are not too many redheads in Italy, so the sooner you are out of the country the better for all of us, Ruggiero. I think you mentioned that your father (*putatis putandis*) said that no son of his should fail to give him a grandson. The Count's father said exactly the same thing (though in Italian) on our wedding day. So now both of them should be happy. But the time has come when I must go. Another coach awaits me; but this one will take you on part of your journey, which I have arranged, across the mountains to the coast at Lerici. With luck and clement weather, a boat will take you to Genoa, thus avoiding the almost unusable mountain route. At Genoa, you will join a boat to Ireland. All the necessary transactions have been made, so you will not be at the mercy of those tight-fisted and mean-minded Genoans."

Opening the door swiftly, she jumped down, the child in her arms, pausing only to kiss Murphy lightly on the cheek. He realised that he still had his precious papers on him. He thrust them though the carriage window as she turned to run off. They never saw each other again.

The papers remained hidden in the library of the Villa Ritornella for centuries until they were revealed, only to be mutilated or lost[35] by the ravages of fate, as detailed in

---

[35] Professor Page insists that they are not lost, only missing. He still gallantly pursues the remainder, having had a scent of them in Cambridge, whence his most recent communication is sent:

Addenbroke's Hospital
Cambridge

Dear Gerry,

I have been on the track of the missing Murphy fragments: it appears that they may have become mixed up with some recently purchased Genizah materials (the word is Hebrew for 'lumber-room', so these, you will understand, are collections of Judaistic oddments) which are now in one of the libraries here (though as yet I know not which). I have not yet been able to unearth anything so far, particularly since my visit to the libraries was cut short by a punting accident. As you possibly know, the stance adopted on an Oxford punt is at the opposite end to that in Cambridge, where

these pages. Of the Law they were born; and by the Law they perished.[s]

As to the Tosti family, the present Contessa has already been mentioned in earlier pages. Some of its other scions might well be familiar to the reader, for several found fame of one sort or another. Earlier in this century, the whole of Europe knew the song 'Tosti's Goodbye'; its valedictory nature was reversed, and the sugar-sweet sentiments of the ballad were made more savoury, by Dame Nellie Melba,

---

inexplicably the platform at what should be the front is used as the back (or stern, as I believe the correct term to be) from which the punt is propelled. The reason why the Semites, such as the Hebrews (they of the Genizah fragments), should write from right to left, is perhaps equally mysterious. One divagates only slightly (and indeed I may properly say that I merely divaricate), for I was attempting to demonstrate the relative merits of the Oxford and Cambridge punting positions by βουστροφηδόν progress (that of an ox ploughing, the name being applied to inscriptions which proceed in one direction and then in the other). Arriving at the Oxford end, I was of course able to propel the punt with due vigour, but unfortunately collided with the Bridge of Sighs (not the original Venetian structure, of course, but an *ersatz* copy which spans two parts of St John's College) the propinquity of which I had not noticed.

Although I was badly concussed (if you will allow this blatant back-formation of 'concussion' which I hardly think to be legitimate) I had the presence of mind to retain my grip on the punt-pole, now firmly lodged in the river bed; nevertheless, the punt itself was still moving, independently of me, in the direction of Grantchester, where fetches up much flotsam and jetsam. My grip unfortunately slackened after a quarter of an hour or so, and I dropped into what would have been the water had another punt not interposed itself from under the bridge. As a result, I fell in some confusion into the capacious bosom of that formidable explorer, Fellow of Girton and University Reader in Russian Geography, Dr Wanda Orlova. She was being punted (from the wrong end of course) by her research student, Mr Robert (or perhaps Richard, but I certainly recall the correct initial) Slicker.[r] The two of them proceeded to attack me, supposing me to be a rapist (though I would have thought the twenty stone of Dr Orlova would be proof against a marauder of any kind). Although they eventually recognised me and desisted, it was not before I had sustained severe injuries (less from Slicker's punt-pole than from the hands of the Russian she-bear). Although the two of them attempted to revive me at the nearby Mackerel Inn, an ambulance eventually transported me here, where, since Tuesday, I have been recovering.

The work, however, must proceed. Although I am understandably wary of research students, my own, Miss Virginia Creeper, has greatly helped, both in ministering to my bed of sickness and diligently searching the Genizah fragments for Murphiana. I hope, therefore, to have news for you soon.

J.P.

---

[r] The present editor is informed that Mr R. Slicker is now deceased, having come (so it appears from a communication from Professor Page) to a sticky end.

[s] Blessed be the Name of the Law.

who popularised a new version, thus widely known as 'Melba's Toast'. Yet even she would linger somewhat upon the unctuous melody, so much so that on one occasion in France her frustrated accompanist exclaimed '*dépêche, Melba!*', a phrase which, by a curious misunderstanding, became adopted as the name of some sort of confection.

The Trieste branch of the family migrated to what is now Yugoslavia and became renowned as cooks. One of them made his way to Britain, changing his name to Toste (founding the restaurant chain with the motto *Toste mine Hoste*). He was the author of a host of books on many subjects. The years of his incarceration by the secret police behind the Iron Curtain are the subject of his *Gulash Archipelago*, which won the Cooker prize. His more populist publications included *Too many Cooks, Too many Brothels* and, of course, the *Egon Toste Guide*, together with the posthumous book published by his widow, *Just a Mite*.

Illustration on the next page:

The last part of Murphy's escape route. Since the weather was calm, the difficult route over the mountains was avoided by taking the boat between Lerici and Genoa.
From Barbieri, *Direzione pe' viaggiatoria in Italia,* Bologna, 1771

In connexion with this illustration, it may be observed that Murphy's fear of the sea was justified, not only by his own experiences, but because of an incident that made a deep impression on him as a youth. Most of the English fleet was wrecked off the Scillies in 1707 when returning from a successful expedition against the French. In the foggy weather, the suspect navigation, by outdated charts, allowed the command to believe that it was off the Brittany coast. One of the hands knew otherwise, and said so, and was hanged on the spot by Admiral Sir Cloudisley Shovell for insubordination. The flagship, *The Association,* immediately foundered on the Scillonian rocks, with the loss of all hands, followed by three more ships. Nearly 2,000 officers and men perished, though Cloudisley Shovell miraculously survived, washed up on the beach. He did not land butter-side up, however; he was murdered by a woman beach-comber [a beach-combress, please! (writes Professor Page)] for his ring.

N.20. *Viaggio da Genova a Pisa*
Sono Poste 16. Miglia 121.

III. Return To Ireland[1]

Patriæ pietatis imago [2]

REALLY, my dear Rory," said the Dean, "you confirm for me that, usually speaking, the worst bred person in company, is a young traveller just returned from abroad."

"I would hardly style myself a traveller, Sir, more a fugitive from fate. By the by, why is it that you call me Rory?"

They were toasting their toes by the fire in the Deanery at St Patrick's on Murphy's safe return from Italy. The Dean, rather than heaping on more coals, merely rearranged the fire so that it would burn more economically. He had never lost the frugal habits of earlier poverty-stricken days, when he, too, was at the College of the Holy and Undivided Trinity. Murphy's finances at Trinity were easier, thanks to

---

[1] This chapter is founded entirely on manuscripts which recently came into our custody. The *editio princeps* will be printed in the companion volume to this monograph, together with all the other Murphiana which it is hoped there to assemble. The charge that we are holding this source to ransom is without foundation. The donor, who by his express wish is not to be identified in any way, has insisted that the manuscripts be kept intact and secure (a not unreasonable request in view of the unfortunate history of the Tosti MSS), and in consequence they are now deposited in a special vault in the Library of the University of Dublin (Trinity College), for the sole use of ourselves until such time as they are published in their entirety. The MSS comprising this source, are henceforward identified by the *siglum* **Trin** [*olim* **Getty**]. The slanders uttered, for example by Dr Heinz Zeit, Professor of History in the New University of The Wash at Humberside,[a] originate, we are bound to say, from simple jealousy.

Some use of the MSS comprising this source has already been made in the previous chapter, since Dean Swift was regaled with many of Murphy's Italian adventures on the latter's return to Ireland. Repetition has been largely avoided, for the purposes of this chronicle, by the avoidance of repetition.

[2] As the reader will recognise, the motto is from Virgil; but its significance is ambiguous in that *Patria* may undoubtedly be taken to refer to Murphy's return to his mother country; equally, however, the quotation may refer to his looking for the "image of his filial affection", i.e. his true father.

On the phrase "fugitive from fate", Professor Page reminds us of the lines
> … *fato profulgus Erinamque venit*
> *litora, multum ille et terrus jactatus et alto*
> *vi supernum* …

As always, we are much obliged to him, and send our best wishes for a speedy recovery.

- -

[a] Formerly Goering Professor of the History of Culture at the University of Essen, and protégé of Lord Nacre, who figures at a later point in this narrative.

a supposedly anonymous benefactor. Murphy was in little doubt as to the true name of his patron, but other problems of identity still beset him. There was no time to think of these things, however, for the Dean was speaking.

"It is almost to the very day, when, a few years ago, I was installed Dean here and you visited me soon afterward. It should have been a season for rejoicing, but, in truth, it was an unhappy time. There was much animosity towards me, and I would fain have been at Laracor, and be plaguy busy as I would be if I were there now, cutting down willows, planting others, scouring my canal, and every kind of thing.

"I was happy there, and preferment here was at first far from bringing me an equal happiness. When you mentioned, on that occasion, that you had come to favour the name of Roger, I was minded of my Clerk down at Laracor, where we were often, nay customarily, the only two souls present at Divine Service in the church. On one occasion this circumstance struck me so forcefully that I began the bidding prayer 'Dearly beloved Roger, the Scripture moveth you and me in sundry places, to acknowledge and confess our manifold sins and wickedness to each other …'

"But times are happier for me here now, and the flock of faithful souls at Laracor is growing. Yet I cannot but think of my Clerk Roger when your name is mentioned; furthermore, you have told me that they called you Ruggiero in Italy – you may call me Presto, by the way – so why not Rory in Ireland?"

"But why Presto, and why Rory?"

"You must have learnt at least enough of the Italian language to grasp that *presto* is *swift*, and …"

"O!" groaned Murphy.

"And surely you are not so ignorant of the Irish tongue that you do not know that *Ruadhri* is a cognomen signifying 'red'?"

"Is that so?" said Roger, or Rory. "Speaking of red, there are several matters which I wished to lay before you, one concerning some curious cattle bred by Lily, now the Contessa,[3] of whom I have spoken to you. Unlike most which I had observed in Italy, those on her estate seemed to resemble in colour some of our Irish breeds. Yet, although those with black markings more naturally predominate over those with red, upon Lily's instruction, the husbandmen had succeeded in procuring a

---

[3] Professor Page has brought back from Italy two valuable photographs, reproduced on p.46. The present Contessa di Tosti's features are unfortunately obscured by Professor Page's thumb, which inexplicably came in front of the lens, and the distinctive colouring of the Morfiana cattle, a breed unique to the family estates, is not entirely evident from the black and white photograph taken in rather misty conditions. The pictures, nevertheless, are memorabilia of great interest to students and are therefore printed, untouched, as they were received.

virtually pure red strain, a circumstance in itself quite remarkable, but the more so in consideration of the wondrous ability of this new breed to live in very poor conditions, while nevertheless producing an abundance of milk. I should have examined the matter more closely had not the mob overtaken me …"

"Sir," remonstrated the Dean in sulphurous tones, "no doubt you consider these monstrous abbreviations, or should I say abbreviate monsters, are exquisitely refined, but I should greatly prefer you to use *mobile*, if not *mobile vulgus*, in my company: I know that *physiognomy* is now pared to phizz, and polite ladies say *rep* for *reputation*, and we have officers of the army whose plenipotentiaries become *plenipos*, not to speak of courtiers and templars who *bam* for *bamboozle* and *bamboozle* for *God knows what*. Therefore spare me, I pray you, your pollarded willow-words. Now what, in the proper English tongue, were you trying to say?"

"I fear," said Murphy, "that I have lost the thread of what I was saying. No, it was the m … – the throng headed by the obese and moustachioed[4] Sister Judas, *olim* Mary Collins, of which I was about to speak, reminding me that there were some matters about inherited characteristics which I wished to discuss with you. Are the laws of inheritance which govern the breeding of cows, particularly those of the singular red kind nurtured by Lily, akin to those governing the, Ah, proliferation of the human race, notably those displaying signal characteristics like my red hair?"

At this point Murphy looked at the Dean's wig, wondering what might be the natural colour of the crown occlusively covered by the powdered headpiece constantly worn by his benefactor. He dare not ask, but hoped that knowledge of his hair colour would rule conclusively as to whether or not benefactor and natural father

---

[4] These characteristics, much laboured upon in the materials from which the previous chapter was drawn, are held to be an unlikely combination, according to more than one expert in the field. We have the benefit of the medical opinion of my colleague Dr Candida Thrush, of the Department of Gynaecology at the Medical School of this University. She tells me:

I have consulted with my friends Les and Gay Freemartin, formerly of Middlesex Hospital, and now at the Dublin Institute for Advanced Transsexual Studies. Gay [Dr Gaynor Freemartin, writing on behalf of herself and her husband Leslie] has furnished me with the following expert opinion:

Propensity towards the specific epidermal secondary sexual characteristics mentioned in the documentation is generally found in endomorphic females (I quote from the standard work on transsexual phenomena by A.C. Deasy of this Institute). It is unwise to speak of rigid somatotypes, but there is a distinct tendency for adipose females not to display uncharacteristic papillations, which are more common in the thinner somatotypes.

So you see from this that the details of the case are unlikely to be correct, or, to put it another way, they are a load of undifferentiated gonads. By the way, did you know that oysters change their sex five times during their life-span? Not many people know that.

C.O.U.N.T.

We are grateful for this illuminating comment.

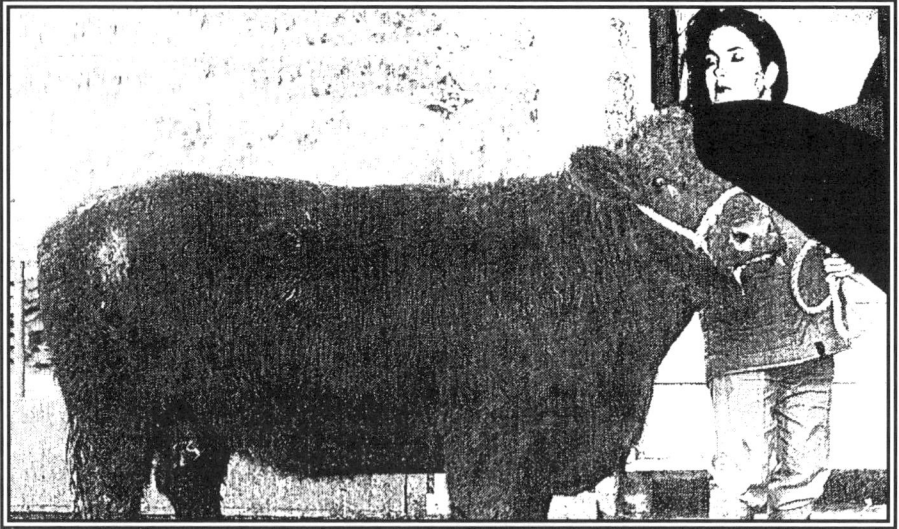

The Contessa Ritornella di Tosti relaxing at her villa, June 31st, 1979

Supreme champion milker of the unique Morfiana diary breed, photographed by gracious permission of the Contessa (same date).

were one and the same. He advanced purposefully toward the Dean and struck out at the wig, as though swatting a fly. Despite a lengthy and undignified scuffle, the wig, however, failed to reveal the colour of the hair underneath, for it stayed rigidly in place, above the now irate countenance of its owner.

"What the D…l?" said the Dean.

"I thought I saw a wasp about to get into your wig, which I feel certain would have caused you a great hurt."

"That being so, I thank you for your prompt action and concern," said the Dean, his frozen features now warming. "Pray continue on your theme, and let us hope for no more insects."

It took some moments before Murphy was able to collect himself, put his disappointment at the failure of his ruse behind him, and to recall the subject of his conversation. Hesitatingly he said,

"If a black bull is crossed with a black cow, the calf will almost always be black. But if the same black cow is now crossed with a red bull, although the calf will generally be black, it might be red."

"Nonsense. The cow will have been spoilt by the first bull. Any farmer will tell you that."

"I am aware of the farmers' lore touching this subject, but I believe it to be false, since Lily's cows have shown the truth to be different."

"This is most fascinating," said the Dean, heavily.

"Furthermore, the red calf, if bred from, will tend to produce a greater preponderance of red, which, in turn with its calves, will increase that preponderance in each generation if bred with more red beasts, subject, of course, to occasional rogue colours."

"Throwbacks."

"Exactly. But although black is clearly pre-eminent over red, the subservient colour can be bred so that eventually it is singled out as a pure strain. I believe this same possibility to be true also of the human race."

"It sounds most unlikely to me,[5] but if you wish to discover experimentally the principles of human breeding, you would do well to follow the career of the Elector of Saxony, Frederick Augustus, subsequently King of Poland. His consort bore him an only child …"

---

[5] Dr Candida Thrush* has kindly introduced me to the duRex Professor of Demography at the University of Malaya, on sabbatical here. Professor Fingerstall is an authority on genetics, and is most interested in these Murphiana. "Johnny," she says, "confirms that Murphy was on the right lines, well in advance of the scientific thought of his time." It is therefore not surprising that Swift was unable to grasp the truth of what Murphy had discovered.

"I fail to see how a singleton might offer any experimental proof as to the laws of inheritance."

"You fail also to allow me to continue. He also sired by-blows in considerable numbers."

"How many?"

"By the time of his death, in your ninth year, and the very year I came to Laracor [i.e. 1699], three hundred and forty-five."

"Good heavens."

"Indeed, you could put it thus. I suggest you study this philoprogenitor's works. Or again, there is something to be said for looking more closely at your own family: or is this indeed your true concern?"

"Well, that is part of it. My friend Bernoulli, who was at Bologna with me, explained to me many instances whereby an apparently random fall of the cards could be predicted if they were shuffled and dealt in a particular way. He had been given the method by his friend Pierre Rénaud de Montmort. Bernoulli showed me an equation whereby, whatever the factors involved, the answer is, as he would say, *Un citron.*[6] Bernoulli's father had also made many important and brilliant discoveries during his lifetime concerning the subject of chance, so called: furthermore, his posthumous discoveries were no less brilliant."

---

* (Footnote referring to footnote on previous page) She has supplied the following additional information:

"By the way, did you know that in common with the Widow Spider, the female Praying Mantis kills and eats her mate as soon as the act of coition is accomplished?" This is a little known fact.

[6] Montmort was hardly an extinct volcano, as a long dead geologist tiresomely observed. On the contrary, he was a very clever Frenchman who contrived to be a friend of both Bernoulli and Isaac Newton at one and the same time. It seems that Montmort, in the game *Treize,* had come across some cardsharper's method of taking a suit and dealing the cards so that one of the cards appears in its correct position. The chance of this happening is

$$1 - \frac{1}{2!} + \frac{1}{3!} + \frac{1}{4!} + ... + \frac{1}{13!}$$

But did Montmort play *Infinité* and reach $1 - e^{-1}$? Alas, although the Tosti fragments have been traced to Cambridge, Professor Page has not yet had sight of them, since they are in the possession of a Professor Ker. [Porson's Professor of Palimpsest Palaeography and Fellow Librarian of St Thomas Didymus College, Cambridge]. The solution to this problem, together with an explanation of Bernoulli's *un citron* (which on the face of it appears to relate to a quadratic equation), therefore eludes us for the present.

Professor Page does not seem to have gained the confidence of Professor Ker, and has furthermore suffered, once again, some personal difficulties. I quote his latest, somewhat lengthy, letter in full:

"Capital!" roared the Dean. "A splendid Irish Bull: much bigger and better than the the red and black specimens you were regaling me with a few moments ago. So your mathematician friend and his father had seen through the ruses of the cardsharpers?"

"Indeed. Further, they had seen, in effect, the workings of the Deity, for 'tis the dealing of the divine pack of cards which controls our destiny."

I had been invited to a College Feast (what we would call a Gaudy) by Dr Bowdler's Reader in Textual Criticism, Dr Quibble. I had more than a little difficulty in getting to the rooms where I was supposed to be staying, since they insisted on calling them a 'set', and the location, said to be in the corner of the second court, was in a quadrangle. Even the name of the College eluded me, for the College, Keystones and Quoins, is written thus but *viva voce* is contracted and ioticised (one digs again, one fears, into the journeyman's baggage of the philological trade) to 'Queens'. Another curiosity is that whereas as they walk to the Common Room, the Fellows of an Oxford College can be distinguished by the fact that they avoid the lawns, peopled by undergraduates and Japanese tourists, Cambridge dons walk to the *Combination Room* on the grass, zealously avoided by the junior members of the College and the hordes of ill-behaved French children which appear to be endemic of that place. I have another curiosity concerning the logomachy of the inhabitants. Cambridge dons wishing to espouse a point of view (or indeed, simply take a view) always "venture to suggest", a curious locution. But I digress.

The "feast" turned out to have the courses in the customary order, the wines of the correct colour, the silver in the accustomed places, and the port circulating in the traditional direction. Incidentally, I had an altercation with an American about this, but I digress again. The central event which I mean to recount concerns that foul-mannered and belligerent librarian of St Thomas Didymus, Professor Ker. He is said to be an authority on Hieroglyphics or something; certainly his own writing requires decipherment. The remove course consisted of roast snipe *à la* something or other, a game bird whose gastronomical qualities are, I venture to suggest (as you see, I have absorbed the *argot* of my host University), not a little over-rated. To be perfectly frank, my gorge rose when I took a mouthful of this bird. To be more accurate, for it had been my desire to get the bird (not only because it is comparatively small, smaller than a woodcock, but also because by such means the disgusting mess could be eaten the more quickly) down in one swallow. Unfortunately, I had assumed that the creature had been boned: I was in error. Thus, the consequence of having swallowed this thing wholesale, which I can hardly retail to you, was that my gorge, as I have said, rose: luckily, with great presence of mind, I managed quickly to manoeuvre my napkin (which incidentally is left in Hall in Cambridge rather than being taken to what they call the Combination Room, but this is what Ker would erroneously call a delapsation) and disgorge the fowl without the process coming to public attention. By the way, have you ever thought that the French *dégustation* is entirely cognate with English *disgusting?* Little wonder that French food is so revolting. But I divagate. The contents of my napkin fell to the floor as I

"No more," said the Dean. "It is not given to man to enquire too deeply into the mysterious ways of the Deity. I have written a few lines which bear upon the matter, which I shall now recite to you."

> Brutes find out where their talents lie;
> A bear will not attempt to fly,
> A foundered horse will oft debate
> Before he tries a five barred gate.

---

attempted to put them in my pocket, so I was confounded by an embarrassing reminder of my exegesis. The loathsome Ker's dog was at hand, however, or rather, to foot, and bolted the obscene carcass in an instant. The creature returned to its master's chair and, thereupon, since the dog's dinner was not, in the last analysis, to its liking (it was an English Setter, after all), repeated the process of disgorgement. Fighting my nausea, my peripheral vision could not but witness that Ker, whose cur's behaviour had gone unnoticed by him, bent down and, in a trice, removed the horrible vestige to his plate and thence to his mouth. At this, I retched once again, but this time did some permanent harm to my vitals, which is why I am, once more, in hospital (have you had cause to confront the dreadful formation 'hospitalised'?). In the interests of science I should say that Ker, such is the state of his palate and alimentary canal, kept the whole thing down, bones and all, and continued, unconcerned, with the rest of the meal. That I had suffered severe internal injury was not immediately apparent to the others at the table, for the gyp (that is what they call a scout) beat me about the back as though I were choking. But eventually, the colour of my face and its contorted features suggested something to Sir Sweeney Barber, the Todd Professor of Chirugery, who ordered that I be carried out and an ambulance be summoned. Even this errand was not without its difficulties, for I had to be unravelled from the lady on my left (I may have omitted to remark that this was a Ladies' Guest Night). Since we rarely wear tails at Oxford, I was not entirely at home with the stiff collar and front, and it seemed to me that the nethermost parts of my shirt recurrently seemed to escape from my trousers. Discreetly, I kept stuffing the recalcitrant garment back, in order not to discountenance the dear lady (who I gather was of good family, being one of the Cambridgeshire Dredgers – the tractor people, you know) whose sensibilities would have doubtless been offended if she caught sight of male clothing which should be decently out of sight. Nevertheless, after three courses of almost constant stuffing, the offending shirt tail seemed still to rear its ugly head (which is a mixed metaphor, I suppose). The ramifications of the problem became apparent as I was carried out. The lady's crinoline (or whatever these female garments are called) was of a similar colour and texture to my shirt, and it was this which I had succeeded, almost comprehensively, in tucking into my waistband. Accordingly, there was something of a scene while the two of us were disentangled. One would have been extremely embarrassed were it not for the fact that one was barely conscious at that moment.

The operation was not entirely successful [for the nature of which see next footnote], and my enforced rest will unfortunately preclude an urgent meeting with Ker.

A dog by instinct turns aside
Who sees the ditch too deep and wide,
But man we find the only creature
Who, led by folly, combats nature;
Who, when she loudly cries – Forbear!
With obstinacy fixes there;
And where the genius least inclines,
Absurdly bends his whole designs.

An earnest silence ensued, after which Murphy said:

"Exactly. This expresses the Law which I have come to regard as predestining our every action. Whatsoever plans a man might make, be they ever so cunning and precipiently devised, are laid waste by a preordained principle of malefaction, to which man can only submit. Some call this fate, but I am coming to see it as a Law, whose operation might seem to the unwise to be perverse, but which is determined mathematically. My friend Bernoulli ..."[7]

"I think that we have had enough of this mathematical nonsense! Did you not say,

---

[7] Here, Murphy tried to explain some of Bernoulli's theories to the Dean, the gist of which will be printed in a later footnote, it is hoped [see footnote 39 on p.76]. Professor Page has been unable to elicit these important details from Professor Ker, though the chances of this are now improved by the fact that he (Page) has now had a second operation, from which a speedy recovery is earnestly to be wished.

The problem, we hear, was initially an hiatus hernia. The operation was unfortunately not conducted by Sir Sweeney Barber, but by another surgeon, Mr Botch-Suture. We understand that the latter is likely to be subject to disciplinary proceedings, not only in respect of Professor Page's treatment, but in connexion also with the unfortunate patient with whom the confusion began. Dr O. M. Script (an Irish friend of Professor Ker, an expert on Runic inscriptions and the like) was mixed up, quite unaccountably, with Professor Page, the latter therefore undergoing a prostate operation in place of Dr Script, who himself underwent a hernia operation simultaneously in another theatre in the expert hands of Sir Forman Saw.

Dr Script's operation was more or less routine (if we exclude the fact that he had to be re-opened in order to retrieve a surgical glove) but Professor Page complained of "gnawing pains" in the region of his bladder. These symptoms were dismissed by Botch-Suture, until Page was quite clearly in agony, from what he now described as 'gnashing spasms' in the groin. Radiography revealed obvious foreign bodies in the region, and a re-opening of the wound revealed a pair of false teeth. How these entered the bladder, or to whose ownership the dentures might be attributed, has not been established so far. The opportunity was taken, however, to repair the hernia at the same time, so Professor Page's scar is now somewhat spectacular in design. Dr Script's collateral operation was successfully completed, we are pleased to note.

[Professor Page later communicated to a pupil that "in nineteenth-century Cambridge the firm of Death and Dyson were well-known undertakers, or so one is informed. Unlike Gush and Dent, the plumbers near Oxford who required no phonetic assistance, the onomastics of their Cambridge counterparts had to be helped along a little by the obliging undergraduates, who pronounced the mortific duo as 'Death and Diesoon.' "]

however, that you and your coadjutor had obtained some choice seeds for me which might add to my collection of rare and exotic varieties and so follow in the footsteps of my learned predecessor Monsieur Nasier?"[8]

"I crave your pardon; I had quite forgot. I will fetch them directly."

Murphy went up to his room and returned almost at once with a packet, embossed with a bright yellow seal which was damaged, however. He handed this to the Dean, who opened it at once. Inside there were several smaller packets, with names written in a florid Italian hand.

"These were the consequence of our meeting a learned lady who had offered Bernoulli an introduction to Signor Fontana of Florence, one of the foremost mathematicians in Europe. She also introduced us to a singer who took us together in his chariot to dine with him. It is a pretty ride. The house is new, not quite finished: 'tis flat all round him, and the Italians have nothing like taste in laying out gardens. However, his house commands a fine prospect of the city of Bologna and of the collines near it, and is plentifully supplied with vegetables from his gardens, which he proudly showed us before dinner. Afterwards he obligingly furnished me with the seeds which you have before you."

"Broccoli and Fennel are familiar to me," said the Dean, rummaging through the smaller packets, "I see we have Artichole and *Melanzane*."

"I fear that I am not able to tell you the English equivalent. The beans are a particularly fine climbing variety which will ascend several feet, hence the *rampicante* of the description."

"I see that they are called *I Fagiolini Antichi*: I assume that they are a similar variety to the French *vieux haricots*."

"Undoubtedly. I was assured that these and others would grow very well in Northern Climes, though I was informed by Bernoulli that those of this last packet are of more doubtful fertility in These Islands. It was he who obtained them, since although Signor Cappone was generous with all of the others, he was reluctant to pass on this rarity."

---

[8] Alcofribas Nasier was of course François Rabelais, under which anagram he published most of his satires on the unthinking conventions of the time, especially of the church, by which he was apostrophised. Swift apparently saw himself as a fellow-traveller not only as satirist and outcast from convention, but as a collector of seeds. The introduction of melons, artichokes and carnations are all ascribed to Rabelais.

Additional note. The Publisher has requested that the footnotes be simplified and shortened. We have thus endeavoured to comply with this request, hoping that no inconvenience is thereby caused to the reader. [Whatever inconvenience might or might not be caused to the reader, it poses problems to the present editor, whose contribution, though in the footnotes alone, is now signalled by square brackets. J.R.].

The Dean's piercing blue eyes peered at the inscription, in a different hand, *Meloni, 'Uovi di Cappone' (senza seme).*

"So these are the seedless melons of which I have heard so much."

He opened the envelope, letting the contents fall on his hand.

"Remarkable," he said. "The packet is quite empty."

"I cannot understand it," said Murphy. "I was promised several seeds of this variety."

"This singer, Cappone: was he by any chance an evirate like the famous Siface, who came to England some years past?"[9]

"Indeed, Sir, he was; it is quite the fashion in Italy, to the extent that they often utter a thanksgiving for the knife, *benedetto il coltello*, or so I was told in the seminary."

"No doubt, but I think the variety of seedless melon called 'capon's eggs'[10] have virtues similar to those possessed by your stoneless singer and, of course, appertaining to your supposed father, neither of whom can be described as seminary."

"Er …You mean…"

"I do mean. You have been gulled by a Capon[11] and trimmed by a Swiss knife."

---

[9] Not to speak of the castrato Tenducci, who some years later visited Ireland and married a girl from Limerick. This union did not please her relatives, who pursued the couple, as already his creditors were pursuing him, so that they were hounded all over Europe. But this undignified story must be left aside. "Undignified or no," says Professor Ker, "it has been made into an opera, whose chief musical qualities are those very things that Tenducci lacked."

[10] Furthermore, the Italian *uovi* has another connotation, we are told, referring to those parts which such a singer has to forgo in order to advance his career, *viz.* 'stones', in the speech of the times.

[11] Connoisseurs of opera will be aware that Signor Cappone sang in the first performance of *Testricles, Ponce of Tyre* and that his life was later celebrated by another opera, *Un ballo in mascara*. "In reply to Professor Ker's uninformed comment about Tenducci," rejoins Professor Page, "he cannot have been a true evirate, as Dr Root of St Mary-the-Less College has rightly pointed out to me: else how can he have entered into marriage, and how can his voice have broken, occasioning, as it did, the end of his career? For it to have been curtailed in this way, there could not have been an earlier curtailment, if you follow my meaning."

Dr Thorne, who does not entirely concur with Dr Root on this matter [putting it mildly], points out that many evirates were married, and their kind was sought after by ladies since they were able to provide entertainment without the eventualities that might have ensued with a man of a different kind. Dr Candida Trush, with characteristic bluntness, speaks of the knife and its consequences.

"Lawks!" said Murphy. To add to his confusion, the clock struck two, the time for Disputation, whereupon he exclaimed, hurriedly donning his gown: "I must hasten to College, otherwise I shall be in bad odour for failing to attend the Disputation."

As he left, tripping over a fishing rod carelessly propped up in the hallway, Swift muttered: " 'The bawdy Hand of the Dyall is now upon the Pricke of Two'. If I do not disremember, that line comes from the same play by the Stratford Bard in which 'Capon's Stones' are mentioned. Wherefore art thou Roger?"

Fortunately, Murphy's late arrival was unnoticed by the Moderator of the Disputation who was, as always, the Professor of Theological Controversies. The subjects were all too familiar. The first debate after lunch was the proposition 'Are women happier than men?',[12] which was followed by 'Can dogs syllogize?' The respondent for the latter topic was Murphy, who attempted to revive elements of the previous subject, ending with a hilarious image of gowned dogs standing up on their hind legs before a lectern and declaiming on the subject of the pathetic fallacy (an obvious reference to Mr Barker who had expatiated on this very topic a week earlier: the point was

---

"Why pussy-foot around the subject in this way? The process of eviration which these singers underwent was not full castration, but a severing of the blood vessels (under a crude form of anaesthetic) that caused the atrophy of the testes (balls to you). In this case what happened was obviously an incomplete severance of what were already retracted testes (orchiopexy – a common enough phenomenon in boys, in any event – and some men I have known); so the strain of Tenducci's ascent to an exceptionally high note pretty obviously occasioned the descent of the scrotal sac and, eventually, his voice. The modern myth that the opposite is possible, that an accident with a bicycle seat can raise the voice by an octave, is detestable nonsense (though fertility may be affected by too much time in the saddle, and in the female also, in whom the much-vaunted sign of virginity is often ruptured by such means). The change of voice at adolescence is irreversible, as is true eviration and its consequences. The other point raised by Dr Root is not very penetrating, for eunuchs are not impotent, merely infertile. Did you know that Sumo wrestlers can retract their testes at will, in order to protect them? Not many do (people know that, I mean)."

[12] "Yes, they are," Dr Candida Thrush is happy to inform us. "It is a little known fact that men dream less (in terms of frequency and in terms of time) than women. Single women, furthermore, dream more than married women. That is why I have stayed single, and a woman."

C.O.U.N.T.

We understand that one of the reasons Dr Thrush maintains this attitude may be due to the unfortunate experience of her mother, whose relationship with the father lasted only one night. This event was commemorated in the middle names which her mother gave to her daughter, Una Notte (the father was Italian). Dr Thrush added a further name, Omphale, doubtless to confirm that she would remain a Spinster (Professor Page protests that the correct form is *Spinstress*). [I doubt that this was the real reason: she could have used the spelling Oona, which would have removed a difficulty referred to by Dr Thorne in a note that Professor O'Toole saw fit to leave unpublished. "The difficulty was that suffered by the Cambridge University New Testament Society, when they unwisely followed too closely in the shadow of their Oxford counterpart, O.U.N.T.S."]

laboured by a reference to one of the psalms recited in Chapel that morning – 'They grin like a dog and go about the city').

"It must be compared," said Murphy, "with an equally unlikely vision which we may conjure up of some strange, uncouth, nation – let us call them the Lillinagians [a reference to the unfortunate Barker's wife Lily, a notorious scold], who may be imagined to have a female priesthood which insists on delivering homilies (or do I mean feminies?) from the pulpit. The idea of dogs syllogizing is no more laughable than the notion of women happily knitting away in the pulpit and discoursing on the œconomy of distributing five loaves and two fishes to a large and indigent family. It is not that we should strain to contemplate that dogs might be able to think well enough in order to be able to syllogize, or that women should take it upon themselves to preach; it is only remarkable that we should be asked to contemplate it at all."[13]

After Evensong and dinner, Murphy broke several College rules concurrently and in succession. 'No resorting to alehouses' and 'No playing at dice or cards' were nicely countered by casting the die at the *Angel* over several sconces of ale, followed by cards and a great deal more ale after he enjoyed the favours of his latest conquest, Marie Louise[14]. As a result of this encounter, it appears, Marie Louise was soon sick in the mornings. Murphy, for his part, was merely sick because of the drink taken.

The Fives court at the end of the Fellows' garden was not an uplifting sight before

---

[13] The reader can hardly fail to be struck by the resemblance of this episode to a Johnsonian quip. As the next chapter will make clear, Murphy became acquainted with the "tedious commoner from Pembroke", and doubtless recounted to him this incident which Johnson later pillaged without acknowledgement. Similar plagiarisms, on the part of Henry Fielding, Tobias Smollett, Charles Burney (the passage concerning the meeting with Signora Fontana quoted above was lifted from Murphy and written up in Burney's unpublished Journals of 1770 [now printed in one or two modern editions]) and many other supposedly original authors, will be evident from this and other chapters. The list is endless, and is not confined merely to his contemporaries, as will be seen.

[14] Curiously, this Marie Louise had the same surname as Murphy: she may or may not have been related to Daniel Murphy, a soldier turned cobbler, who had no less than eight daughters, the youngest being another Marie Louise (1734–1814) who became the mistress of Louis XV of France and tried, unsuccessfully, to supplant Mme de Pompadour by whom she was out-manoeuvred; 'Loiuson' or 'la petite Morphi' ended her days in poverty. Another sister (who had also come to France) met Casanova when she was little more than thirteen: the Chevalier was so attracted by her that he arranged for her picture to be painted by Boucher. The King, seeing this painting, installed her as yet another of his mistresses. She was more fortunate than her sister, however, for her daughter married le Marquis de la Tour de Pin. Boucher painted several pictures of her, but the earliest, reproduced on the next page, shows the marked resemblance to her famous relative, in regard to her facial characteristics, at least. As may be seen, the sobriquet 'la belle O'Morphi' was entirely appropriate, for she could hardly be described as 'petite', as was her more unfortunate sister. [The recently discovered portrait of Murphy will be reproduced in the companion volume].

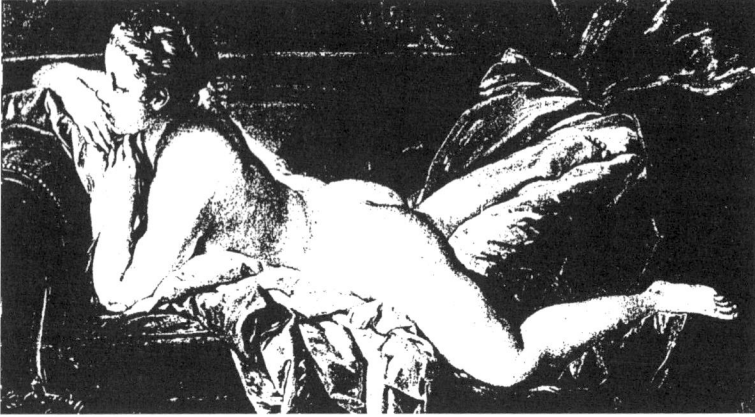

La Belle O'Morphi. *Painting by Boucher in the* Alte Pinakothek, *Munich*

the early service at six o'clock the following morning. There, Murphy was horribly sick in the course of his dyspeptic progress to Matins. After the service, he despoiled the bowling green as he lurched biliously on his way to the seven o'clock lecture. At this, he hardly distinguished himself, sleeping solidly until nine, when he awoke in startled stupidity to find himself being asked to translate a psalm from Hebrew into Latin. Unfortunately, he misheard, and began to translate 'I am wiser than the aged', a sentiment which did not commend itself to the lecturer in question, whose years were his only claim to distinction.

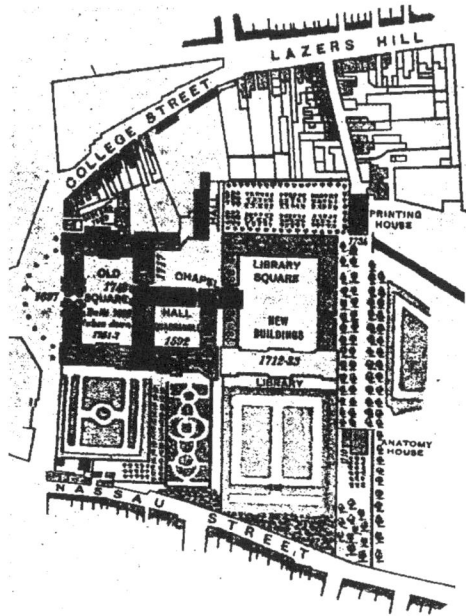

Trinity College in 1750, from Roque's Map of Dublin *of that date.*

Nor was the lecture on the Greek New Testament a greater success. At ten o'clock Matins, Murphy had read the second lesson, during the course of which he made several errors, for which he was reprimanded afterwards by the Provost. To compound his obloquy, he entered into a harangue with the lecturer about the second chapter of St Matthew, saying, quite reasonably, that if the Magi were supposed to have come from the East, and saw the Star in the East and followed it, how was it that they did not arrive in Outer Mongolia and do obeisance

56

to some ancestor of Chinggis Khan? Or had they come from Anatolia? As the lecturer floundered before this onslaught of unassailable logic, Murphy continued to challenge the opinions of the lecturer, who unwisely called the Magi by their apocryphal names. "How is it then," said Murphy, "that they were supposed to be three kings, and yet one was called Melchior, which we might reasonably translate as Mr King? Belshazzar, now, has a fine imperial ring to him, but Mr King sounds to me as dubious as calling a tutor by the name of Mr Wise (catcalls and merriment from the rest, for this was the name of the unfortunate tutor). And then," continued Murphy relentlessly, "why was the supposed purveyor of gold short-changed by being called Mr Silver?"[15]

Mr Wise moved over to the hanging shelves which housed sundry exegetical works, hoping for guidance on this point. His discomfiture was complete, however, when he pulled at a book which was jammed tight into the shelving. Murphy and his cronies had earlier re-enacted the Screw Plot of 1708,[16] in that they

> "Most traitorously stole every screw
> To make that fabric fall"

Thus, by loosening the supporting brackets in the hanging bookcase on the wall of the lecture room and re-packing the books tightly, the outcome was that the dusty weight of learning crashed down upon the head of the unfortunate Wise, knocking him out and summarily ending the class. Murphy decided to beat a tactical retreat

---

[15] It has to be admitted that Murphy's critique was by no means baseless. As Professor Oliver, Regicide Professor of Exegesis at Oxford, and Professor-Elect at the New University of Drogheda has pointed out "there is no doubt that there is a *crux* in this passage, which turns on the Greek word ἀνατολή (hence Murphy's reference to Anatolia), normally translated as 'East'. But it can also mean 'rising' as indeed the Hebrew word מִזְרָח can mean 'rising' and 'East'. The contradiction inherent in the Gospel narrative presumably stems from this. As to the three Magi, Murphy was again right in his assertion that "√MLK has to do with 'king'", and also that Caspar derives from √KSP, meaning 'silver', not 'gold'. It seems that then, as now, the Irish tradition for Hebrew scholarship was, and is, far more vigorous than that of Oxford, where Murphy later found very little on which to exercise his scholarly acumen.

Professor Page (still recovering from his operation) is not entirely in agreement with Professor Oliver. Though acquiescing with the main points, he rejoins "the unwarranted slur on Oxford by a disfigured misfit (this is why we called him Cromwell) cannot go unchallenged. Vigorous the Irish tradition may be and have been, but that is not the equivalent of rigorous. What about the cretinous Bishop Ussher, who computed that the world was created in 4004 BC, a time when, far from being covered in primæval mud, the earth was under water, and God's people (not, presumably, the ancestors of Cromwell) were busying themselves boat-building? Incidentally, when at High Table at The House, Cromwell was unable to fathom the correct use of his cutlery and invariably ended up eating a fruit soup with a fork."

[16] At the celebrations at St Paul's for the victory at the battle of Oudenarde, conspirators had taken some of the bolts from the roof-beams, hoping to extinguish Queen Anne. The intended mischief (celebrated in the poem *Plot upon Plot* from which Murphy quotes in our source) proved to be unsuccessful.

and go early to his lunch appointment at the Deanery, only to find that Swift was about to leave for Ormond Quay.[17] The Dean enjoined Murphy to wait for him, however, saying that he would not be long in returning. He was in something of a hurry, and his wig sat rather loosely upon his head. Seeing this, and the fishing rod still leaning against the wall in the hallway, Murphy was struck with an idea which might settle the question of hair colour. He bounded up the stairs, rod in hand, and positioned himself at an open window, just above the porch.

At length the Dean emerged from the doorway to get into his carriage, and Murphy leant perilously out of the window, angling with his rod to capture his prize. The stratagem was all but successful in that Swift's hat was well and truly hooked, unbeknown to its owner; but having achieved this feat, all Murphy could do was to bear the thing aloft as though it were some kind of trophy. In his haste to retrieve the hat and disentangle the fish-hook from it, he impaled it upon the railings, so that it resembled the spiked head of some executed malefactor from a more barbarous age.

The horse, having followed with increasing alarm the progress of what it saw as a poltergeist, now shied, decanting the driver, amidst voluble language of the coarsest variety, onto the street. Swift, in turn, was alarmed, and unwisely raised his stick to the horse, which thereupon bolted crabwise down the street in such a manner as to overturn the carriage, which began to dismember itself as it was dragged along. Eventually, now pursued by screaming urchins with staves that they had pillaged from the wreckage, it degenerated into a kind of slay, as though drawn by some Lapland reindeer. Thus it receded from sight, as a distant cloud of dust.

Murphy threw down the rod into the street, giving up any hope of retrieving it; but, meanwhile, one of the carriage wheels, wobbling randomly, bore down upon the Dean and bowled him over. Seeing his chance, Murphy ran down the stairs, and under the guise of ministering to the Dean and his servant (who in turn had gone down like a domino under his master)[18], managed to disentangle the hat. Its owner was not discountenanced enough to allow Murphy a further attempt at dislodging the wig, and the hat being clapped back onto Swift's head ended the matter.

When Swift had recovered his composure sufficiently, he went indoors to write a note explaining his inability to keep the appointment at his intended destination and craving forgiveness. This was put into the hands of his servant Patrick, still

---

[17] Presumably to see Stella.

[18] [A further note from Professor Page was suppressed by Professor O'Toole: "Really, O'Toole, this phrase is gratuitously tautologous, convoluted and misconstrued: *domino* does not need to be repeated, and it must surely be an ablative of comparison, though without the complete original one cannot be certain, and would presumably translate simply as 'he fell in a like manner to that appertaining to his master'." It is possible that O'Toole omitted this note on the grounds that in any case the original was not in Latin.]

visibly shaken by the ordeal. Patrick failed to return for a long while, so lunch was postponed and meanwhile Murphy and his host consoled themselves with a pick-me-up. They were joined by Dick Boyle, a particular friend of Murphy's, and a favourite of Swift's.[19]

As was their custom, they amused themselves with various pastimes, one of which was to offer evidence that the Greek and Latin tongues were derived from the English. One of the less dignified of these was the derivation *kiss my a*se* > *m'ars* > *Mars*. This was a sample of Swift's contribution. One of Murphy's was 'Roman', which he derived from 'Rowman', that is, 'Waterman'; to which Boyle added that this was clear enough to convince the most incredulous, for it was evident that the *Gesta Romanorum* were the rough jests typical of these watermen.

When they had tired of capping each others' efforts, they went on to another favourite amusement, the composition of lines that at once embraced Latin and English, of which a specimen of Swift's

> In mi cum pani praedixit …

with its references to 'cingat supper Tori rori' and 'aleto claret adit basis', both already quoted.[20] Boyle, however, took port rather than the claret favoured by Murphy and Swift, the significance of which was apparently political. Referring to the power of his 'Portingale wine', Boyle imparted the line:

> Forte dux fel flat in guttur

for the delectation of the company, to which Murphy, taking up a similar theme, added:

> Itis apis potitis, anda bigone tu.

This latest effusion prompted Boyle to seek what Swift was wont to call the *necessarium*. While he was absent, the Dean said:

"Your friend Dick is a Whig, I gather."

---

[19] Though the Dean often referred to him as the "unmentionable malady", for reasons that we find wholly obscure.

[20] See footnote on p.2. The fruits of the 'derivations' may be seen in Swift's *A Discourse to prove The Antiquity of the English Tongue*. These well-known references would scarcely be worth mentioning were it not for the continued disbelief of Professor Page, now joined by Professor Ker. The publisher has again particularly requested that future footnotes should be kept to an absolute minimum. Accordingly, it has been assumed that anyone with the slightest pretensions to learning will be able to supply references to well-known events, quotations and the like, and that he may easily check on statements which refer to facts which, after all, are virtually common knowledge. [Since some of Professor O'Toole's contributions are henceforward enclosed in square brackets, the present editor has deemed it necessary to distinguish his own notes by [[double]] brackets.

"It is true that he will neither drink claret nor join in the execration of Adrian the Fourth, nor yet would he drink the toast to the horse Sorrel, even in port." [21]

"I think that I am correct in supposing that many of the Fellows of the College of the Holy and Undivided Trinity are of the same persuasion."

"That is so, but the more fashionable of them are Tories."

"So I am informed. And you, not wishing to be numbered amongst the unfashionable Whiggamores, have decided to be a runner."

"What on earth do you mean, a runner?"

"Again, your ignorance of Irish lets you down, a *tóraighe*, a Tory, is a runner, a fugitive, an outlaw."

"Well …"

"And of the many ironies, such as that you, a member of the Established Church, should have been to a Romish Seminary, there is a greater; that before the battle of the Boyne, the Pope blessed King William and his troops, a fact conveniently now disremembered by both opposing factions." [22]

At this point Dick re-entered the room, so the conversation ceased for a moment. When it resumed, the Dean saw fit to chide his guests.

"*Mi dans cinge des aro ver*, but it is incumbent upon you both to apply yourselves more diligently to your studies than I did," said Swift. "For both of you to achieve *mediocriter in omnibus* is nothing to be proud of. Nor am I of my own career at Trinity. I fear that I was admonished (I think it was Easter 1685)[23] for dereliction. I regret to say that in 1687[24] I was also publicly admonished for being absent from the evening Roll, and for failure to attend Chapel and lectures. The following year[25] I wrote a speech for the *Terræ Filius*, commonly known as the *Tripos*, which was not well received by the senior members, and although anonymous, was widely credited

---

[21] As most readers will be aware, port was the drink of the Whigs, whereas the Tories toasted in champagne or claret. [[The present editor doubts that the reader will necessarily have this arcane knowledge, or of Sorrell, the mount of Prince William, who tripped and nearly killed him at the Battle of the Boyne. Adrian IV was of course the English Pope who connived in the annexation of Ireland to Britain.]]

[22] And indeed in the last part of the twentieth century [[except by the Mayors of Belfast and Dublin whose medallions commemorate the same thing]].

[23] This was indeed the date, the record of his achievements being Ph[ilosophy]: *male* G[reek] & L[atin]: *bene* Theol[ogy]: *neglig[enter]*

[24] March 18.

[25] July 11, 1688.

to my pen. So you see that my years at the College were not as profitable as they should have been."

"We also had a little difficulty with the *Tripos* last year," said Murphy. "The stool on which the *Terra Filius* was to sit was uneven in one of its legs, so I sawed off a bit of it. Having done so, however, it became obvious that one of the other of its legs required some attention, so I applied myself to it; but then it became apparent that too much had been sawn off this second leg, so I evened up the other two to suit. Unfortunately, I failed to balance them properly on this attempt, and indeed on several subsequent attempts. Eventually I was successful in attaining a perfect tripod, though its legs were somewhat foreshortened, to the extent that the seat was now only an inch or so from the ground. I relinquished any pretensions to carpentry after this."

"But you have not, I think, given up any pretensions to being a biblical scholar."

"You refer to my altercation with Mr Wise, and my exegesis of the passage of the Gospel of St Matthew concerning the Magi."

"Indeed, Sir. An excellent exposition of the problems."

"There was another incident …"

Here, Murphy's glance strayed to the clock, upon which he exclaimed:

"Good heavens, we must fly, else we shall be gated for failing to attend a surpliced Evensong."

Swift muttered "Tomo rosa nudae" as the two left the Deanery in a flurry of gowns, then returned shortly afterwards for their surplices. They arrived in time for Evensong, though only just, and went into Hall afterwards.

Instead of retiring to his rooms after dinner, Murphy had an assignation with a paramour of some several weeks, so he scaled the walls by the Fives Courts, an adventure which passed without incident, and went to see Bernadette, who was waiting at the *White Hart* tavern. The result of this *liaison* was that a swarthy child had to be left on the Churchwarden's doorstep. It is regrettable[26] to record that this was not the first of Murphy's offspring (nor yet the last) whose fate was to be 'on the parish'.

Another, more momentous, liaison occurred on the way back from Laracor after

---

[26] "Also regrettable," says Dr Candida Thrush, "is Murphy's irresponsible attitude in the matter of contraception. Quite apart from any other methods, the condom had been available for many centuries, fashioned from sheeps' innards, though not many people know that." [Also known as the Irish letter, despite claims by Monsieur Jean-Jaques Condom [[No, it was a Colonel Condom]] to have been its inventor.]

one of Murphy's forays to his birthplace. There, he had hoped to elicit information from his mother, but whatever he was able to glean was not particularly useful; so his return journey was leaden-footed. He fetched up at a rather disreputable inn, and easily responded to the charms of a freckle-faced girl whose features seemed somewhat familiar to him. After their dinner, and a great deal of drink, he became the more familiar with her.

In the morning, she lit the candle to look closely at him, and, causing him a rude awakening, asked him to repeat his name: her memory of it, she said, was vague, though she remembered that it sounded like Harry or Airey.

"Though Hairy might be most appropriate. Anyway, it sounds most unusual. What is it, so?"

"Well, it's a nickname which some have given me. It's the Latin for ram, aries, which coincidentally is my star sign."

"Aries. Latin for ram. Up the airey mountain ..." ("Down the rushy glen," interpolated Murphy). "Then 'tis small wonder that you pleasured me so nicely," she said, dimpling.

"Well, it's not so much that," said Murphy, now wondering where he had seen those dimples before, "but RAM is what it is; I mean," he said, now becoming thoroughly confused as, for some reason, a picture of his mother came before him, "I mean, the initials of my names spell RAM."

"So what are they? What is your real name?"

"Rory. Rory Murphy, though I used to be called Roger."

"That's a very ..." The girl seemed to be taken aback, but then rallied, speaking quickly.

"Just for a moment, I began to wonder ..." She stopped, and then said more slowly:

"Did you always answer to the name of Roger?"

"No." The girl paled. Ashen faced, she asked:

"What does the A stand for?"

"Aloys."

"O, my ..." but with these half uttered words, she fainted. She had, of course told him her name, but it meant very little to him. Was she the younger sister of Molly Reardon, or any of the others from his Laracor past? And why had she become so agitated? Though something about her was familiar, and in particular those dimples. A chill possibility overcame his thoughts as his mother's face was drawn before his memory's eye in sharp detail: he too, paled, his face taking on a greenish hue in deference to the quantity of the drink with which he had fortified himself the previous night.

"Wake up! Rouse yourself!" implored Murphy. "You told me your Christian name, but what is your surname? Tell me your name!" he pleaded, his voice rising.

"Henrietta. Henrietta Murphy, your sister."

"Jaysus! You were little more than a biteen of a baby when I last saw you."

"You didn't see much of any of us: you were always after the village girls."

"And much good it did me. Perhaps you don't know the true story."

"No, you went away suddenly, and very little was heard from you from that day forward."

Murphy guided her through the labyrinthine events that surrounded his father's (or supposed father's) waywardness. She followed him through the reproductive maze in increasingly better spirits. But before he had come to his peroration, the colour had come back to her face, the life into her eyes.

"So we're not related after all!" she said, blowing the candle out and jumping upon him, almost in one movement. It was with great difficulty that Murphy finished the story and relit the candle. Henrietta rejoined:

"Oh, well, at least I'm only your half-sister. There's not many that have an adventure like this."

They discussed the matter at length, and talked over the history of the family. It seemed clear now that the many brothers and sisters shared by the two of them were probably not even of the same father. Henrietta told him that since his being given the name by which the family knew him, Aloys, his mother had followed this by naming all her subsequent children in alphabetical order, Bernadette ("O, No!" groaned Murphy – but then realised that the ages could not possibly have matched), Catherine Richienda, Daniel, Eustacia, Frederic, Geraldine …[27]

"But why are some of the names unusual, not to say outlandish?" They pondered on this matter for some time; Henrietta, showing considerable intellectual acumen, eventually reasoned:

"Because, I think, Mother wished to use the names secretly to record not only the year of birth of each child but also its father's identity, by a second name if necessary, like hallmarks. Would you ever give me a piece of paper?" She wrote rapidly on the

---

[27] The system of date letters was, of course, taken up by the British Vehicle Licensing Authority some centuries later, without due acknowledgement.

proferred leaf, and showed him the result, in the form of a list. "It is the girls' names which are often outlandish, as you put it: the respective fathers were surely Bernard, Richard, Daniel, Eustace, and so on. ("Brilliant!", interrupted Murphy, "and yours was Henry"). Anticipating the troubles that you experienced (she went on), it is evident that she did not wish to visit similar problems upon the rest of us. So despite having mostly different fathers, she could still tell whether or not we would be related to a prospective spouse, so that the question of consanguinity would be settled, and the sanity of the offspring protected."

"Now I come to think of it," she continued, "one or two of our siblings had a second name which corresponded to an earlier one in the list. So Patricia Danielle must have had the same father as Daniel."

"Or else Mother could not work out whether it was Patrick or Daniel who was the father. But then …"

"Wait now! Our Aunt, Mama's sister, also married a Murphy. I do know that he was unrelated to Father ("Everybody is," interjected her half-brother), but his name was Daniel." Murphy now became solemn, and asked in a low voice:

"Was anyone's middle name Aloys, Alice or something of that sort, or even Roger, Rogetta, or anything resembling my names?"

"Well, there was your distant relation, Nicolette Alicia …"

"My God! How distant?"

"She was the fourteenth."

"I must return to Laracor and find out more. I shall go to the graveyards there and in Trim where many of our relatives lie ("Indeed they do," said Henrietta, "but most of them habitually lie above rather than below the ground, especially on a Saturday night."). But that will have to be several weeks hence, for Term starts in two days. Let us travel back to Dublin together, and tell me where you are staying. We shall discuss the matter further in the light of your astounding deductions. But let us hope, and that fervently, that the problem of consanguinity of issue does not arise in our connexion."

This momentous phrase was another step on the road to the full realisation of an understanding of the workings of the Law that was to bear his name. For the issue did indeed arise, as will be chronicled in due course. Here it should be said, however, that the foregoing incident is one of the few that can be given at least a *terminus a quo*, thanks to the foresight of Murphy's mother. Another may be presumed to date from nine months afterwards, thanks to Murphy's lack of foresight. In general, the events recorded in this chapter apparently begin no earlier than 1716 or so, when Murphy was in his mid-twenties. In common with Boyle, he appears not to have hurried to take his degree, and was still *in statu pupillari* at Trinity several years later, when the following events took place. There is no way of dating them accurately on the evidence to hand, but it may be surmised that the period was 1719–1725. The next incident recorded is not earlier than 1719, and not later than 1722. This much can be ascertained from College records.

Dr Fitzpatrick was a singularly pompous and foolish gentleman. His ignorance, widely supposed to be without parallel in the college, was as profound as his inability to admit of it. His pupils' regard for him could hardly have been lower. Lampoons were posted to the effect that 'Gerald Fitzpatrick and Patrick Fitzgerald' (this coupling being a reference to the supposed gross practices of these two individuals) or 'Fitzpatrick got my goat' (which bestial allusion is perhaps self-explanatory). The college was on tenterhooks, bearing in mind some of the rioting that had overtaken it in past years,[28] especially in 1699, when on Trinity Sunday, Provost Taylor died from a brickbat thrown from the righteous assembly.

In this instance, the brickbats were verbal rather than real, and the animosity towards Fitzpatrick simmered, but did not boil over. His goose was cooked, however, in a stew assembled by several of his pupils, including Murphy, the chief cook. The latter alluded to Isaac Bickerstaff in one of his tutorials with 'Fitz' (as he was generally known). Fitz, of course, had no knowledge of this author or his works, but nevertheless agreed with Murphy that in common with Martinus Scriblerus, Bickerstaff was "a profolic and ingenious author" with whose writings he was intimately conversant. Murphy left the matter thus, but planned a particular vengeance for the following week.

A note arrived from Murphy asking if Fitz would be so kind as to excuse his pupil from attending the tutorial in the usual place, the physician having confined him to his rooms. Murphy assured his tutor that no contagion was possible, and forwarded what nowadays would be called a Doctor's Note. He implored Fitz (to use his own sycophantic words) to conduct the tutorial in Murphy's own rooms "so that the pearls of your wisdom shall be unconfin'd". The gullible Fitz needed little persuading, and by this means events were set in train.

Murphy's cronies, Boyle and Canning, had arranged an arras in his rooms and had persuaded two of the college dignitaries to hide behind it. One of these was a stickler for academic standards, and the other had a hatred of what he termed 'abominable practices'. Both were already ill-disposed towards Fitzpatrick on account of his habit of blowing a post-horn and holding soirées devoted to horn blowing (or rather, mostly to informing the audience of the difficulties pertaining to the instrument and thereby hoping to excuse the incompetence of his uncontrolled eructations). On a previous occasion, they had aided and abetted Boyle and Canning to sabotage these activities: having obtained a wasps' nest, the two dons (Mr Duffy

---

[28] And in later years, too, for there was a serious riot in 1749 when Oliver Goldsmith was an undergraduate.

and Mr Sterne) persuaded the three undergraduates (Boyle, Canning and Murphy) to introduce the nest into the offending instrument. This cornucopia of wasps, more musical to the ears of the long-suffering audience than was the recital, proceeded to sting Fitzpatrick into silence (apart, that is, from some satisfactorily mortal sounding groans). Thus it was that a *quid pro quo* was easily exacted, and witnesses to the next act were installed behind the curtain as Fitz sat down, prepared to act as a latter-day Socrates.

"I suppose," said Murphy, "that you are familiar with the horn concertos by Virelli?"

"My dear boy," replied Fitzpatrick, "I have played them often; indeed, the last time I did so was in the presence of his Serene Highness the Archduke of Austria."

"The latest ones to be published, it is said, are filched from works by his teacher Vermicelli."

"That has been known for some time," said the pit-digger. "They are manifestly inferior works."

It need not be said that all within the room save for Fitzpatrick were alive to the joke being played. The victim, wholly unawares, slipped further into the pit he had digged unto himself when Murphy showed him his essay.

"I have taken the liberty of quoting from Isaac Bickerstaff's latest publication, which is entitled *Paris and Sporus*."

"An admirable work," said the gull.

"You approve, then of the epithets 'a cherub's face' and 'beauty that shocks you'."

"Quite so; they are phrases that I have often used."

"Have I not heard Mr Fitzgerald use a similar turn of language?"

"Quite probably, though he will have got such phrases from me."

"So you are the *Paris* to his *Sporus*?"

"O, undoubtedly, for he absolutely treads in my footsteps."

"Indeed," said Murphy, forsaking the push gentle for the shove direct, "so you would describe him in phrases such as the 'white gourd of Ass's milk'?"

"O, emphatically, for his complexion is of singular beauty, quite creamy, like a milkmaid's," said Fitz, quite unknowing of the chasm.

"Then …"

The two dons broke through the arras, Sterne crying:

"Enough of this, you 'Reptile all the rest. For as the Prompter breathes, the Puppet squeaks'.[29] Rightly did Nero put the effeminate dancer Paris to death, as would I, if I had sway over matters such as these. As to the eunuch Sporus …"

Sterne spluttered to an enraged silence and left, telling Duffy to command the porter to throw Fitzpatrick and Fitzgerald out of the college, thus ending the careers of two universally unpopular tutors.

"By the way," said Boyle, "why do milkmaids have such wonderful complexions?"

"By dabbling in the dew, or so they say," replied Murphy, "though I have other ideas on the subject."[30]

This was the last major event of the term, so he and Boyle went their separate ways. Boyle[31] was engaged by Lady Lucan to manage the estates of her husband, who had

---

[29] In common with Murphy, Sterne was of course quoting from Pope's *Epistle to Dr Arbuthnot*, doubtless communicated to them by Swift. In this satire against Lord Hervey, the libertine (who apart from sharing a mistress with the Prince of Wales, also had less natural appetites), Pope was originally intending to pillory Hervey as Paris, the homosexual mimer executed by Nero. Later, however, the base Sporus came to mind. He, the eunuch 'slave wife' of Nero, seemed a sufficiently revolting parallel.

[30] Although it is more than possible that Murphy had anticipated the discovery that cowpox, which milkmaids met every day of their lives, made them immune from smallpox and its disfigurements, it is more likely that Murphy was referring to the fact that milkmaids retired early to their nocturnal activities, in which he had often participated. "Anticipated is the wrong word," says Dr Candida Thrush. "Lady Mary Wortley Montagu had introduced inoculation against smallpox into England in 1717, though she may not have made the correct connexion between the aetiology of the milkmaids' regimen and their resistance to smallpox." [What connexion? we ask ourselves. Brushing this matter aside, the chronology seems, for once, to show that Murphy's part in events was not wrongly credited to someone else.] "By the way," continues Dr Thrush, "do you know that women suffer more injuries from ski-ing accidents than men?" [Doubtless because they have to remove more clothing when they are caught short, and probably get tangled up with their ill-designed garments subsequently.] This having been said, the young Professor (or rather, pre-Professor) Page when ski-ing in Switzerland had his head turned, in an almost literal manner, by a female in such a state of post-micturational undress, whose renewed descent of the slopes was clearly involuntary. The sight of this pulchritude, which was the more revelatory as she progressed and her apparel regressed, resulted in Page turning violently [[*plus ça change…*]] and himself involuntarily joining the procession, meantime sustaining several fractured limbs. They ended up in adjacent beds in the hospital, since the staff thought they were related (he, not yet having insisted on being called Jack, was known as Rex, so it was a natural assumption that Régine (as she was then known, being at a Finishing School) was his consort. This accidental coupling was hallowed by matrimony when the couple returned to England.

[31] Who, as Professor Page (still recovering from his operations) reminds us, was related to the fourth Earl of Orrery*, "he of the spurious epistles which engaged Swift's attention in *The Battle of the Books*. More to the point, he was also related to the Hon. Robert Boyle of Lisemore, a founder member of the Royal Society." [[What point?]]

unaccountably absented himself. The work principally involved a certain amount of coppicing, but also attention to the Great Avenue, some of whose trees required felling and replacing. These Boyle duly indicated in the time-honoured fashion immortalised by Cowper:

> Like crowded trees we stand
> And some are marked to fall

Unfortunately, the estate workers, having little knowledge of poetry, felled the unmarked trees, an error that was unkindly and unjustly blamed on Boyle.

Murphy, meanwhile, had again set out for Laracor in order to make a further attempt to elucidate the mystery of his lineage. He decided to follow the route which would have been taken by Swift many years before, and to make enquiries along the way. His first stop was a tavern often mentioned by Swift: by good chance, there had since been no change of landlord, whom he questioned as soon as the opportunity arose.

"Well, Sir," said the landlord, "I recall perfectly well the last time Dr Swift came here. Like you, he was journeying to Laracor on foot, and stopped here for the night, just as you are. He was taken with the fact that I came from the same parts, as he, too, was born in England, in Leicestershire; and my name was of no little amusement to him."

"What is your name, then, landlord?"

"Belcher, Sir. Jonathan Belcher, at your service."

"Then, Belcher, did the Dean say anything else? Did he, for example, make any reference to the inhabitants of Laracor?"

"O No, Sir. He asked me how long I had been out of my native country, and I told him thirty years. He asked if I expected to visit it again. 'Never', I said. 'And can you say that without a sigh?' 'I can Sir,' I replied, 'for my family is my country.' And he commended me for being a philosopher and asked if I were reconciled to my fate. When I replied that I was happy here, liked the people and though not born in Ireland would die in it, and that's the same thing, he was silent for a long time. Then he said '*Ipsis Hibernis Hiberniores!*'. It was only after Dr Swift had departed that I found out what that meant. So I am content to be more Irish than the Irish. He came back this way again on his return, but said very little, that I recall, and nothing of the village of Laracor."

"Thank you, Belcher. I will take my supper now, if you please."

---

* (footnote to footnote on previous page): not to be confused with the Earl of Ossory, a title assumed by the disgraced Fitzpatrick as he wandered in exile through the Balkans

Murphy supped, and drank deeply the while, in order perhaps to lighten the cloud that had descended upon him, since he seemed to have achieved little. As he drank, he became aware of a an older woman at the other side of the room, whose charms were undeniable and whose features, such was his inebriate imagination (though he was not so drunk as to imagine himself sober), seemed familiar.

It is not inappropriate, for reasons which will become clear later, to quote *verbatim* from the Trinity MSS.

> To say the Truth, the Behaviour of *Murphy* was a little inexcusable. To the Dose of Perry which was by no Means pure, he had received the Addition of above a Pint of Wine, or indeed rather of Malt Spirits. Now that Part of his Head which Nature designed for the Reservoir of Drink, being very shallow, a small Quantity of Liquor overflowed it, and opened the Sluices of his Heart, so that the two lovely blue Eyes, whose bright Orbs flashed Lightening at their Discharge, flew forth two pointed Ogles. But happily for our Heroe, they hit only a vast Piece of Beef which he was conveying to his Plate, and harmless spent their Force. The fair Warrior perceived their Miscarriage, and straightway came to his Table and from her fair Bosom drew forth a deadly Sigh ….

[desunt non pauci]

> No sooner was the Cloth removed, than she again began her Operations. Gently lifting up those two bright Orbs, she discharged a Volley of small Charms at once from her whole Countenance in a Smile. This Smile our Heroe received full in his Eyes, and was immediately staggered with its Force. To confess the Truth, I am afraid Mr *Murphy* treacherously delivered up the Garrison, and the Lady, having his Heart entirely taken, enjoyed, as Conqueror, the usual Fruits of Victory.

> Here the Lovers entwined themselves in the Manner of their Kind; meanwhile, the Graces think it proper to end their Description.

[desunt non nulli]

The lady journeyed to Dublin, and Murphy continued in the opposite direction to Laracor. He had not the slightest hint of her identity, save that she was a widow woman, but no longer living in the country (her husband had been a strong farmer [i.e. of some substance] in the village of Trim). She was returning from thereabouts where she had attended the funeral of her sister Sally's husband, John. As Murphy cogitated upon these names, however, their coincidental nature began to alarm him more. Eventually, in considerable agitation, he turned round, and made to follow the lady. He must ask the name of her late husband.

Had he involved himself unnaturally with his Aunt? If so, neither had recognised each other. And the funeral. Was his unfamiliar father dead, and beyond being able to reveal anything of the past? Murphy hastened to Dublin, but failed to catch up with the lady. In considerable distress, he went to the Deanery, where Swift broke the news to him.

"I fear that your poor father, or at least he whom the world regards as your father, perished last week."

"This is indeed a sudden and double sadness," said Murphy, "for, as you well know, I have been estranged from him these past few years. With the callowness, not to say callousness, of youth, I judged him too severely when I found that he was not my natural father. Of late, however, I have come to realise that he, like me, was merely a card played in the great game of mischance of which we have spoken so often together. Now having recognised my folly, it is too late to make amends. So the blow, as I have said, is a double one."

"You must not distress yourself, though Heaven knows, his death was distressing enough."

"How did he die?"

"He had been behaving a little strangely for some time. One evening, walking by the Knightsbrook, that river by my garden's end (in former times), he amused himself by making the noise of a rutting deer, an imitation which he had recently perfected. Its very perfectness was demonstrated by the response of the nearby female deer who rushed, with considerable enthusiasm, upon your *quemadmodum* father ..."

"O God! What a horrible end."

"Pray, do not invoke the Deity in vain. The matter was not as you suppose. The harts were not deceived, nor yet was a stag that arrived almost at once upon the scene, thinking there to be a rival with whom he must do battle; but the two sexes, upon eyeing each other, rushed headlong to conjoin after the manner and inclination of their kind; and in the ensuing mellay, Murphy, now face down in the Knightsbrook, was unable to regain his feet. He therefore drowned, held under the comparatively shallow waters of the brook by what otherwise would have been the harmless passion of the deer. Although it is true that the hart desireth the waterbrooks, there is no desire like unto the greater one which indirectly caused your father's (*sicut dixit*) demise. In this, there seems to be some poetic justice. They that live by the [*desunt pauci verbi*]. So, the sad and final enactment of Murphy's lore[32] is to be seen as a fulfilment of God's justice."

---

[32] We cannot fail to observe a homophonic pre-echo which must have reverberated in the ears of Murphy junior, to be recalled after the due effluxion of time. A comment by Dr Candida Thrush upon the mating habits of deer was the last thing that she wrote prior to her untimely

"Indeed, you have put my mind at rest and so have greatly comforted me: I can see that the die was cast in heaven which ruled my father's *(pater inter pares, passus)* destiny."

"God does not play at dice.[33] It was a divine card, a card stacked, so to speak, after the precise and scientific manner which we have discussed earlier."

"So you think, after all, there was something of substance in the theories of my friend Bernoulli, which I attempted to explain to you?"

"Of course, of course; but you must not think that because some fiddle-faddled figures are offered as mathematical proof of a law, that law was not well understood. There are countless pertinent references in the Scriptures;[34] and the Greeks were

---

death from psittacosis. Unfortunately, it lay unfinished, and came into our hands only through the good offices of her executrix, Dr Robin Cox-Sparrow. The gist of the fragment was "Did you know …." The knowledge that it might have imparted is immeasurable, but it has been well said that we must be thankful for small mercies. As we are indeed. [[Indeed, indeed. That impossible bird-brain nearly succeeded in having my univeristy renamed almost as soon as she arrived here (having already caused immense trouble at O'Toole's own university – he was highly relieved when she moved). Imagine the Unversity of Man being renamed The Unvirity of Person. And she wanted to change our motto and crest. Our well-known emblem of a triad of three Manks cats' tails with the legend *quocunque ieceris evanescit* was to be changed to an entirely different badge with a motto reading *viri viritim evirescunt vireone* (the *vireo* apparently being some kind of finch or thrush, that would emasculate us all one by one). Furthermore, my department was to be closed in favour of an Institute of Wimmin Studies *(sic)*, of which the 'chair' (God help us all) was to have been a Doctoress Gelda Juturna Unman. Luckily, this was scotched (or manksed as we prefer to call it, which is an entirely different thing to welshed) by the fact that she failed the linguistic requirements of this Unverity. Although it is preferred that members of staff be fluent in Manks, this is a formality really. But the Unmanner protested in an unmannerly fashion at the title 'member of staff' and became purple in what passed for her face when she was questioned as to the unique peculiarity of the plural form of *ben* ('woman', which as everyone knows has the curious plural *mraane*). When the topic of conversation (if this word can realistically be applied to a shouting match) turned to the matter of gender mutation, she became apoplectic and had to taken to an Asylum where she remained Confined At the Pleasure of the Tynwald until she died, in a screaming fit. So my department is safe for the present.]]

[33] A remark erroneously attributed to Einstein, as is well known. The original of this passage, *Deus aleatoribus non ludet*, must somehow have passed, through unknown intermediaries, into the cognizance of the twentieth-century scientist, who, as will later be seen also plagiarised what he called his theory of 'relativity', an idea anticipated by Murphy, and fully exploited by him, two centuries previously.

[[It is not so well known that Einstein was invited to give a one-man show at the *London Palladium*. Nor are his sexual exploits usually documented.]]

[34] *vide supra*, pp.23-4.

hardly without knowledge of these *phænomena* as they would call them. Witness the Athenians to the Melians, as recorded by Thucydides:[35]

> For of the Gods we believe, and of men we know, that by a law of their nature wherever they can rule they will. This law was not made by us, and we are not the first who have acted upon it; we did but inherit it, and shall bequeath it to all time, and we know that you and all mankind if you were as strong as we are, would do as we do.

Reflecting sadly upon what the Dean had said, and upon the events of the past week, Murphy excused himself and retired to bed. The problem of his parentage, whose true nature seemed to elude him at every turn, was uppermost in his mind as he tossed and turned in his sleep. In his dreams, however, fragments of a plan began to piece themselves together, and, when he awoke, they came to him fully formed.

At the unaccustomed hour of seven, Murphy rose excitedly and went downstairs to the kitchen, suggesting to Patrick that he (Murphy) should take up the breakfast tray this morning, in order to play a little surprise on the Dean.

"Himthelf won't like it, Thor. Himthelf thortainly don't like thorprises. And, though he'm a just man, he'll likely blame me for not doin' mi duties."

"I shall tell him that you have a sore throat, and that I suggested this exchange of duty so that you wouldn't cough over him."

"A thore troath, you thay. Well …"

Although the servant was still puzzled that Murphy should want to usurp his task, the shilling he was offered silenced any doubts. Accordingly, Murphy took the breakfast up, congratulating himself that, at last, he had settled on a foolproof method of ascertaining the colour of Swift's hair. For although the wig was never off his head in the daytime, he would hardly sleep in the thing.

A respectful knock at the door elicited a grunt. Murphy entered and put the tray on a table near the bed, while he went to draw back the curtains. As the grey morning light reluctantly illumined the room, Murphy turned from the window. At once, Swift became aware of the substitution, exclaiming:

"Boy, what is this? Have the staff left home, or succumbed to the ague?"

"Not exactly," said Murphy, "but the servant has a sore throat, and we deemed it unkind that he should cough over you; so I took his place."

---

[35] Swift quoted, of course, in Greek; we have here rendered the passage (from *The History of the Pelagian War*) in Jowett's translation, in the sincere hope that it will not (*pace* Professor Ker, whose comments are left unrecorded) be thought anachronistic.

"Most considerate. Kindly convey my breakfast tray to me, and my wishes for his recovery to Patrick."

During this conversation Murphy stood stiff and open-mouthed, as though paralysed. The whole drama had been enacted to no purpose. Dully, he proffered the tray to Swift, who now was sitting bolt upright in bed. The wig, it was true, was on its stand on the dressing table, not on the head of its owner; but in its place Swift wore a resplendent black silk-tasselled nightcap[36] which quite covered any trace of hair that might have answered the crucial question of parentage. Disconsolately, Murphy left the room.

In the autumn, some time after these happenings, Murphy became the father of another child, a redhaired boy. Its mother, his half-sister Henrietta, refused to leave it 'on the parish' as Bernadette had been willing to do (alas, she now repined in the Bridewell, opposite the College); so they took it to the Poor Clares' in North King Street. At the Poor Clares', moreover, word was passed to Murphy that Professor Genno, Professor of Casuistics at the Jesuit University of Leuven, had presented his compliments, and had high hopes of an early solution to his problem.

At first, Murphy had no notion as to who the learned man might be, or of the nature of the problem, but then he realised that this was the gluttonous Professor of Philosophy at his former seminary at Bologna, and the problem was none other than that of the toast which had unaccountably fallen buttered side up. On enquiry, it appeared that Genno had been in Ireland for some months, but had hurriedly left for the Low Countries.

Events now caught up with Murphy. Bernadette,[37] released from the Bridewell, demanded earnest conversations with him. Before she could tell him her news, however, he insisted on recounting to her (though not in all details) his meetings with his sister Henrietta, and that for a moment he had thought that she, Bernadette, might have been another of his half-sisters.

---

[36] In conformity with the *Constitutions and Canons Ecclestistical* of the Church (Canon 74: 'Decency in Apparel'), though the tassel would hardly be in keeping with the injunction 'plain'.

[37] As Professor Ker is kind enough to point out, she was the model for Swift's 'Corinna' who

> in the morning dizened
> Who sees, will spew; who smells, be poisoned

The last word was of course pronounced *pizened* as in "a cup of cold pizen". I have long meant to tell you that, unlike the accident-torn Page, I am genuinely related to Murphy, but to no ill effects: although my first name (which I no longer use [[this is because he was called 'the Bilker' as an undergraduate]]) is William, a family name, and my last Christian name is Nicholas, on account of being born on December 6. Aloys is my middle name, given to me as a recognition of my famous forbear. Cordially,

Nick Ker

"That I may be, for your father was very friendly with my mother", she said, not knowing that this particular blood relationship was precluded. "I know that he stopped you from marrying my sister on the grounds that you two were related. Which reminds me …"

"Your sister?"

"Yes, Lily. Lily O'Rourke is my sister."

"Heavens above. Now I see that you resemble her more than somewhat."

"If that is a compliment, I accept it. But I must tell you …" She did not continue, but blushed prettily closing the top of her cloak, where Murphy seemed to take considerable interest. In every way, she certainly seemed a great deal larger than the wench with whom he had romped before she had been confined to the Bridewell, more than eight months ago. She was speaking again: "By the way, do you know that Mary is back in town?" But Murphy was staring not at her, but beyond, and had failed to hear the last remark.

"Oh Hell!" he said, "here's my Tutor." After a haughty glance at the girl, the Tutor, Mr Dawson, said to Murphy,

"Who is this person?" to which Murphy replied, with great presence of mind:

"My sister Deirdre, Sir."

"Nonsense! She is a known woman of the streets."

"Yes, Sir; and Mama's terribly cut up about it."

"Tcha!" said the Tutor contemptuously. "See me in the morning." He turned on his heel and walked towards the College.

"That won't improve my standing. I'd better get back to College myself, before worse befalls."

It befell. They had walked only a few yards towards the College gates in the September gloom when the august figure of the Vice-Provost loomed ahead.

"Good evening, Vice-Provost," said Murphy in a sycophantic tone.

"What do you think you are doing?" Murphy could not repeat the witticism he had used to the Tutor, and would not have dared. "You know very well the rules of the College, and should be within its gates unless in pursuance of an approved purpose, and this …" – he peered short-sightedly through his rheumy eyes at Bernadette – "is not an approved purpose."

"She is just a friend."

"In that case, you must choose your friends with more care, for she is a notorious prostitute, as all the Fellows of this College know."

"And," said Bernadette, "by none better than you, Tommy. Meeoww!" At this, the Vice-Provost flinched and made off hurriedly, glancing malevolently back at Murphy, who said:

"I think that ends my career at Trinity. What was all that rot about Tommy? That isn't his name, surely."

"A pet name, merely. I used to call him Tomcat for various reasons, one of them being that he used to call himself by a monkish name, Prior Puss."

"I think you mean … No matter." In the aposiopesis she had begun to look very unwell. It now became clear that the news she wished to impart was now of an urgent nature. When she had recovered, she said:

"The seeds of love, my dear, are about to fruit again." Speechless, Murphy said:

"Are you sure it's mine? There have been others in your bed."

"Not just then. You were my only man."

"Oh well, I suppose it's the Poor Clares' again."

"I'm afraid that gate is closed. The nuns have been taken away again by the priest-hunters."

"So that is why Professor Genno beat a hasty retreat, leaving me without a solution to the problem of the toast."

"Maybe. I haven't a notion what you're talking about, but we must go to St Jude's."

"I didn't know there was one. St Jude is obscure to me; I think he must be the Patron Saint of lost causes."

"He is, to be sure. The nuns that have founded it are come over from Italy this year past."

And still Murphy failed to read the signs. The results were catastrophic, and dogged him for the rest of his life. As Murphy had anticipated, he was instantly sent down from Trinity, a sentence immediately communicated to Swift, much to his distress. This divine eventually, and reluctantly, agreed to send Murphy to Oxford instead. But the visit to St Jude's[38] was disastrous. Who should take in the child but Sister

---

[38] Which Swift later thought of buying to re-found St Patrick's Hospital for which

He gave the little wealth he had
To build a house for fools and mad

Jude herself, *olim* Mary Collins, her pilosity only slightly disguised by her having shaved her moustache. The petrified Murphy turned and ran as fast as he could, pursued by three women, the bristling Sister Jude, Sister Mary of the Immaculate Contraption, Bernadette, and a fourth, a mysteriously veiled figure carrying a bundle, but who seemed at first to be behind the rest but eventually seeming to come from nowhere.

"Quick!", she said, catching him by the sleeve. "In here." She bundled him into a coach, uncannily re-enacting events which had taken place years before in Italy, but now horribly refreshed in his mind. And, to complete the parody, she showed him a redhaired child. "Your daughter," she said, taking off its swaddling-clothes and then unveiling herself. His Aunt.

"Jaysus!"

"Now that St Jude's and the Poor Clares' are ruled out, I shall have to keep the girl, but I don't know how I am going to explain this, having been a widow for a month or so too long. But I shall call her more or less after my late husband, and that should stop the tongues wagging."

"What were your husband's names?" He knew the answer before she replied,

"Daniel Aloys Murphy."

"DAM!"

"Yes, I am the Dam, you are the Sire, and the little foal is Danielle Alicia Murphy."

"But do you know who I am?"

"I realised who you were after that night at the inn. These things happen. It's the sort of thing that happens in books and plays, so why not in the sodality of real life?"

"SODality," he said, stupefied.

"We must get away from here. Where can you go?"

"St Patrick's Deanery. My guardian will think of some stratagem."

And so they parted. The Dean made immediate plans to take Murphy to Kingstown and to put him on a boat to Chester. But even now, fate[39] was to play another hand, to boot. As Swift was waving a fond *adieu* to his protégé, the wind got up and his wig became dislodged. Thereupon, a sea-eagle seized it, and carried it away, in one

---

[[the intellectually accident prone and differently sane, as the late Thrush would have said, before she fell off her perch.]]

[39] The figures given by Bernoulli to Murphy, proving that what is commonly known as 'fate' is expressible mathematically, are appended below. They have been rendered into modern

fell swipe, as its prey. This was not the only indignity to be suffered by the late owner of the wig, for as Murphy gazed astonished at what had been revealed as an almost hairless head, another eagle[40] came down in one fowl swoop and settled on the pate as though it were an enormous egg to be hatched. In the confusion, for the boat had now cast its moorings and was making unsteadily out to sea, Murphy had to strain his eyes to catch a glimpse of the colour of the Dean's hair, such as remained, now resembling the form of a novice's tonsure.

It was the colour of the leaden sky into which Murphy was sailing, which perfectly reflected Murphy's heavy heart and the depths plumbed by his falling spirits. Grey.

---

mathematical notation due to the kindness of Dr Rick O'Shea, Reader in Ballistics at the University of Rockall.

$$\lim_{n \to \infty} P\left(\left| \frac{\mu}{n} - p \right| < \varepsilon \right) = 1$$

[40] A bald eagle, it is said.

The River Knightsbrook at Laracor, the scene of the demise of Murphy senior, described by Swift's as "a river at my garden's end". From an old print.

IV. OXFORD DAYS

City of Dreaming Squires [1]

THE circumstances of Murphy's removal to Oxford were painful enough, particularly since Swift was unwilling for his ward to leave Trinity and attend instead what he saw to be a manifestly inferior universitry,[2] writing, as he did on April 28, 1726 to the Earl of Peterborough: "There is a Univarsity in Ireland founded by Queen Elizabeth where Youth are instructed with much greater Discipline than either Oxford or Cambridge."

The parting from Ireland was the more painful since, closely following upon his father's death, his mother also passed away peacefully.[3] As the Dean observed to Murphy on the boy's embarking for Chester,

"To lose one parent ...." The subsequent words were, however, lost to posterity when the eagle bore his wig aloft.

Murphy did not find his way immediately to Oxford (and here it has to be admitted that we are very uncertain in the matter of chronology[4]); but the general run of events probably follows much the order as set down in this chapter. The treatment has had to be abbreviated more than somewhat, at the request of the publisher, and

---

[1] Matthew Arnold, who is said to have coined this phrase in *Thyrsis,* lifted it directly from Murphy, as will shortly be seen.

[2] "This really will not do," says Professor Page. "For all its inadequacies, This Place produced some of the finest brains of the time." "And," rejoins Professor Ker, "the worst addlepates. Has Page never heard of Gibbon? Probably not." "One will deny oneself the obvious retort about the simian Ker," retorts Professor Page, "anyway, Swift condemns the Other Place equally. I suppose you know that Nick Ker's Cambridge undergraduates call him ...." [curtailed].

[3] [[Footnote suppressed]]

[4] "And are likely to remain so, while that [suppressed: a reference to Ker] hangs on to those Genizah fragments and fails to release them to the scholarly world," comments Professor Page. "Scholarly world be [omitted]" avers Professor Ker. "Jack the Ripper is no more a scholar than my laundress. About the only influence that Oxford has had on the world is the spread of Ragwort in Britain: once confined merely to the Ripper's Port Meadow, it infected the West Country and Wales by means of the GWR. It's a pity that the railways exported this particular Oxford Weed (poisonous to horses, but not unfortunately to that nag Malfolio) for it has been found difficult to exfoliate this toxic [footnote curtailed]." We might introduce a lighter note to this unfortunate exchange by mentioning that in Ireland too, the railways were responsible for the dissemination of a characteristic plant, in this case the rather more benign Ox-eye Daisy, which graces the railway tracks of this country. Professor Ker's comment (suppressed here) about the Cinnabar moth being imported from Cambridge to Port Meadow to eradicate Ragpaperwort from Oxford is based, we feel, on somewhat confused evidence.

the footnotes have had to follow suit, having regard to the publisher's particular and repeated wishes; but full documentation will be presented in the volume of source materials, which we hope will satisfy the most rigorous of scholars, and also Dr Quibble, whose protested 'scholarly open-mindedness' is more succinctly described as vacuity.

We know for certain of only one adventure before Murphy's undergraduate career at Oxford: this was in the company of Swift himself, who seems to have visited Murphy in England a year or so after the latter's departure from Ireland. (After the death of Stella in 1728, a year after their supposed 'precipitant marriage', Swift never again ventured out of Ireland, so this event must date from 1726–7, at the conclusion of one of his last visits to England). On the way to meet the boat at Chester by which Swift was to return to Ireland, the pair stopped at Lichfield, where they appear to have met Samuel Johnson, who himself was soon to become an undergraduate at Oxford. Shortly after setting off on foot again towards Chester, however, a summer thunderstorm broke out which necessitated their sheltering underneath a tree. They were joined by a couple, the woman being obviously pregnant, who were in great haste to be married at Lichfield. Seeing that no time could be lost, Swift kindly offered to perform the ceremony himself. They gratefully accepted, were married, and went on their way as soon as the skies cleared. Suddenly, however, the tyro husband turned back, on recollecting that he had no document that would prove the couple's new status to a disbelieving world. Accordingly, Swift obliged with the following 'marriage lines' which evidently satisfied the illiterate couple:

> Under an Oak, in stormy Weather,
> I joined this Rogue and Whore together;
> And none but He who rules the Thunder
> Can put this Rogue and Whore asunder.

Murphy's eventual arrival in Oxford, probably in 1727, must have been about a year after his hasty departure from Ireland. Although our knowledge of this period is scant, it seems that his journey to the Univercity was shared by none other than Henry Fielding, who recounted to Murphy his conversation with the Earl of Denbigh, a kinsman. When asked why his branch of the family spelt its name in a different way from that of the Denbigh branch (Feilding), the novelist replied:

"I cannot tell, my Lord, except it be that my branch of the family were the first that knew how to spell."

This story greatly amused Murphy, who was prompted to recount to Fielding some of his own adventures bearing on his own family background. Unfortunately, more than one of these was remembered *verbatim* by his interlocutor and found their way into various novels of his, the most celebrated of which, *Tom Jones*, contains large passages that are known quotations from Murphy.

Upon this vexed question there will be more later, but the source that recounts the coach journey with Fielding clearly places one of the conversations at the Tollgate in St Clement's [now vanished – all that remains is a deflowered traffic island on the approach to Magdalen Bridge. The illustration below shows it in Victorian times]. This must mean that Murphy came to Oxford from the South, in which case it is not unlikely that he was returning with Fielding from Wycombe,[5] where we know that Murphy had dealings with the notorious Monks of Medmenham, more familiarly known as the Hell Fire Club. Sir Francis Dashwood and Harry Fielding were both at Eton together, so it can be surmised that the connexion between Murphy and Fielding was at an early meeting of what was to become the Hell Fire Club: indeed, perhaps it was through the latter's offices that Murphy became a member of that brotherhood.

It appears that Murphy felt foul of the university authorities quite soon in his career. The first occasion was when, after a drunken spree, he was crawling back to his college with his countryman O'Nions, popularly known as Pickle, with whom he had made friends almost at once. They were accosted by the Proctors and asked for their name and college. Although the first reply was prompt and half-way truthful ("Pickle, St Alfred's") the second was contumelious and prevaricatory.

The Toll-gate at The Plain, much as Murphy would have seen it
(Victorian photograph in the collection of Professor Page)

---

[5] To anticipate Dr Quibble, although the fully fledged 'Society of St Francis at Wycombe' (to give it yet another of its names) was not to take shape until Sir Francis had returned from his Grand Tours, there is no doubt that some form of Hell Fire Club, if not under that name, was in existence many years earlier, in succession to the Duke of Wharton's Hell Fire Club, which had to be disbanded in 1721. It was not until 1726 that Dashwood set off to France, Italy and Germany, so the chronology fits.

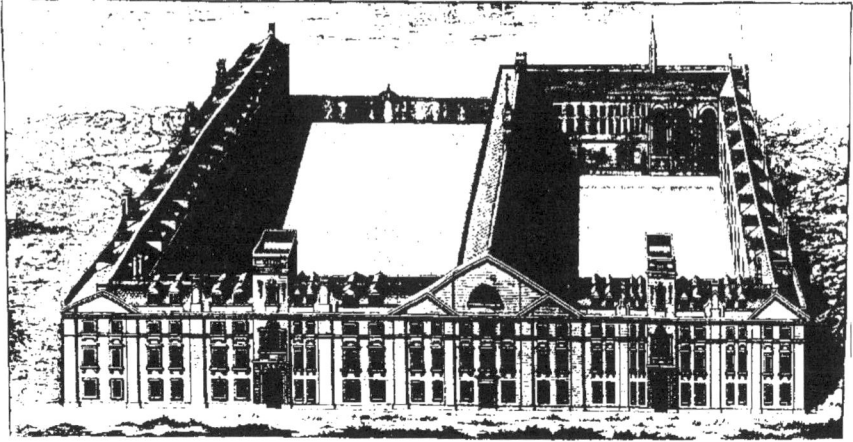

St Alfred's College, as rebuilt in Murphy's time
(Print by Boggan, 1742, in the collection of Professor Page)

"My college is the one with the tower", slurred Murphy, unconvincingly; then, at a venture, "MMMagdalen. Whence I was ppperegrinating with my friend, pepperegrinating, pperegrine… PPPickle. And my name is Rory…". He swayed dangerously, and with what was left of his conscious processes tried to focus on some surname that might suffice for the moment; but his thoughts were entirely… "RANDOM!", he proclaimed triumphantly.

This event had repercussions far beyond its apparent insignificance. As will be seen, this adventure was relayed in due course, together with other stories, to Tobias Smollett, with the consequences known to all who have read the novels of this author. Not only were the doings of the pair mercilessly traded upon and incorporated into these works as though original, but the very titles of the volumes (the names of the pair that Cadwallader – this being the name of the Proctor – had temporarily accepted) bear witness to this act of calumny. The other consequence was a hearty dislike on the part of Cadwallader for Murphy, an aversion which hardened into hate.

An added reason for this antipathy was that Murphy became enamoured of a Junoesque lady named Melissa, unaware that she was Cadwallader's niece. Whether or not she was the model for Richardson's Clarissa is dubious (and we do not require the opinion of Dr Quibble in this matter, nor in regard to the fact that Smollett's *Peregrine Pickle* was published only a year prior to Murphy's death), but she was certainly a profolic letter writer.

Although her letters furnish some details of her *liaison* with Murphy, the evidence of Cadwallader's animosity is to be found in legal records of the period. We shall deal with these sources somewhat out of chronological sequence (the events to which they refer occurred later, and indeed subsequent to the arrival of Johnson in Oxford, and of several incidents recorded below). The reasons for taking these matters out of order is solely to show that Dr Quibble, who is now disputing the authenticity of these sources, is wholly in error. Having said this, the first extract from the court records relates to an earlier year in Murphy's career in Oxford, soon after meeting up with Fielding.

> M. fuit indict in le spiritual court eq p̃ [*deeest*] car ceo est malum in se donque le marrying dun frere & soer, au testimony de quel certaine persons, notablement H.F. Il la plead que la marriage non fuit ni lege ni cubiculo (car M fuit que, in ipsissimis verbis suis, *having the drink taken prodeegeeously*). Sur mesme reason M non as reconnaitre que la femme fuit son soer. Sparrow Justice dubitavit, mes Haddock Justice semble que l'indictment fuit contre justice. Judgement pur plaintiff.

[Mich. 1 Geo. II Le Roy *versus* Murphy]

The H.F. can be none other than Fielding, who as a magistrate would doubtless be believed; this entry absolutely proves that he was no friend to Murphy, and emphasises that incidents recorded in the previous chapter were but grist to the novelist's mill. The court records of some years later reveal two other incidents, however, in which 'C.F.C.' laid information that 'Miss M.G.P.' was espied by Murphy when she was airing 'son nude corps in un Balcony at Iffley' for which he was arraigned in the matter of what is nowadays described as a 'Peeping Tom' and severely punished for 'tiels profane actions' and 'derelinquy'. At virtually the same time, the records of the Ecclesiastical Court at Oxford (popularly known as the 'Bawdy Court') show that Murphy appeared before it on the grounds that while making water he had exposed 'his privities to the sight of the said Melissa Plenitude, on the testimony of Dr Caradog Floyd Cadwallader of Jesus Colledge'. Murphy was sentenced to be paraded in a white sheet for four Sundays at the Parish Church [St Mary the Virgin]. Thus, in one swell feel, he was arraigned twice on information laid by Melissa's uncle, whose identity was now clear to him.

As is pointed out by that distinguished authority on the subject, Professor Flashman, Murphy's virtually simultaneous appearance in two courts for what appear to be contradictory offences may seem illogical but was, and indeed is, according to the law (which is clearly an ass, as Dr Tom Leer rejoins[6]).

---

[6] His wife (or *partner* as she prefers to be called) is the distinguished writer on Women's Issues Dr Jenny Tay-Leer, who comments as follows. "Not so. It is quite obvious that the poor woman was being ogled by this lecherous beast. Of course, she would hardly have been sunbathing, a silly habit which became fashionable only in our own century; the court records make it plain that she was merely relieving herself into a chamber-pot, and could not do so in peace because of the odious Murphy. The Law was quite right to come down on him in one full peep for this offence. Whether simultaneously, or on another occasion, is not obvious from the records, but the fact that he also exposed himself in this detestable manner meant, quite rightly, that at one

By the time Johnson arrived at Oxford, relationships between Cadwallader and Murphy were strained, though the Melissa affair had yet to take place. 'C.F.', as he was unpopularly known, had a malformed upper lip which he sought to hide underneath a moth-eaten moustache and beard, which made his baryphonous diction even more curious than was due to his flawed physiognomy alone. (His accent, which when he became heated betrayed him as having a North Welsh origin, he normally disguised to some effect). His mumbling yet pompous mode of speech underlined the impression that he was born at the age of sixty-five (as Murphy put it, "the Gods bestowed on him the gift of perpetual old age"). Until Murphy's later clash with him in the courts, the undergraduates knew his initials but not the names for which they stood, so not unnaturally they invested the ciphers with meanings of their own, apparently in reference to the facial defect of 'C.F.'

It seems that Cadwallader was aware of whatever interpretation the undergraduates had put upon these letters (though they are not known to us, nor were they, apparently, to Murphy at that time), but he chose to ignore it. Murphy, in company with Johnson, had for some reason sought the opinion of Cadwallader on the question of the sippet of toast that had famously fallen buttered-side up. The answer, murmured portentously into the latter's beard, did not satisfy the enquirer, who harangued his senior with relentless chapter and verse. This caused the Jesus Fellow to draw himself up to his full height[7] and to exude all the *gravitas* he could muster. The argument became increasingly heated as Cadwaldr (as he now presented himself) repeatedly, more sibilantly and adenoidally, denied that toast could possibly land buttered-side up. Murphy's shrill reply, in which he, too, retreated momentarily into his native brogue, to the effect that the Tutor was blind to the truth, began:

"You can't face …", but was interrupted by a shriek as the insensate Cadwallader, frothing at what would otherwise answer for the mouth, advanced towards Murphy with the intention of strangling him. Johnson, interposing his considerable bulk between them, averted a more disastrous scene, and led Murphy away.

It was after this incident, when the two of them gathered with their cronies in the Turl Tavern, that Murphy and Pickle told Johnson of their earlier encounter with Cadwallader (later to be recounted to Smollett). Murphy, of course, was Johnson's senior by some twenty years, so it was not unnatural that the junior should have stood considerably in awe of the older man, and to have hung upon his every word. They drank gin, a new-fangled habit that had overtaken the British a few years since, and the members of the company were regaling each other with their various adventures, of which Murphy's were by far the most colourful.

---

foul seep he was also punished for this offence. So the gander's goose, as the source makes plain, was cooked."

[7] Murphy's duodecimal system of numeration has not yet been deciphered, so we do not as yet have first hand [[or feet]] information, but a secondary source gives the figure five foot five and five eighths.

Johnson was most taken by Murphy's description of his times at Trinity, especially the occasion when he had argued with Mr Wise about the Magi, and had painted the verbal picture of a dog preaching on its hind legs. When the proctorial visitation of Cadwallader was recounted by Pickle, Murphy's presence of mind, when he had all but lost it, was lauded by Johnson:

"That, Sir, was great fortitude of mind."

"No Sir." replied Murphy, "Stark insensibility."

Boswell, as we know, garbled these events very badly, and blotted out the name and contribution of Murphy in order to further the cause of his hero. A cogent example concerns the habit of The Athenians (as they styled themselves) of skating on thin ice in Port Meadow, an event unsuccessfully reconstructed by Professor Page, as documented in an earlier chapter. On one occasion, the soles of Johnson's shabby shoes were so outworn that he could scarcely take part in these frolics, so that on the way back from the meadow, Murphy having recently won a considerable sum on a particularly disreputable wager, bought Johnson a brand new pair of shoes from Crispin Bros, the cobblers in Carfax. They repaired to the rooms of Pennymoney at Christ Church, and toasted each other in brandy, which as Murphy observed, was the religion of the damned. Johnson was disinclined to try on his new shoes, since his feet were too wet. Murphy accused him of being a hypochondriac, which he stoutly denied, saying that in any event "A hypochondriack suffers from no disease save that of no disease". Murphy's rejoinder, to the effect that he had invented a medicament for no known disease, which would therefore cure Johnson's complaint, is too well known to repeat here.

Eventually Johnson, still dangling his shoes upon his arm, left The House to go across to Pembroke. He retired to his room in order to sleep off the effects of his exertions and the brandy, both of which he heartily disliked, but was soon rudely awoken by what he conceived to be the noise of corncrakes at the foot of his staircase. Peering out of his door down the stairs, he expostulated with the noisemongers who, it turned out, supposed themselves to be poets, reciting their ill-scanning lines in the manner of a raucous twittering at the tops of their drunken voices.

"What corbilious drivel is this?", demanded the irate Johnson, using a word unaccountably excluded from his famous *Dictionary*.[8]

"Sir, we are a nest of singing birds," came the reply.

"Then it is time the fledglings were ejected from the nest," said Johnson, throwing down the missile nearest to hand, which turned out to be, to boot, the shoes.

---

[8] "Unaccountably no," says Professor Page, "for no such word existed or exists. Perhaps this was a misprnt for *atrabilious*, applying not to the poettasters, but to Johnson's choler?"

It is manifest, *pace* Dr Quibble, that Boswell's account of this incident, including his mistaking Port Meadow for that of Christ Church (the idea of skating on Christ Church Meadow is laughable), not being able to spell the name of that House correctly, and transposing, misconstruing and misrepresenting these and other happenings, is wholly unreliable.

Meanwhile, Murphy had gone with Babbage, one of his fellow Athenians, to the tower of St Mary's. They proposed to re-enact the experiments that Bernoulli and Murphy had undertaken many years earlier at the leaning tower of Pisa, in which they had attempted to verify the Law described some years earlier by Newton. In this new experiment, as in the old, Murphy had some parcels of feathers of a known weight, which were to be dispatched from the tower at the same time as parcels of lead of exactly the same weight. At Pisa, the parcels of feathers had drifted somewhat, so the law of gravity could not be proved before the two were led away on some trumped up charge or other. At Oxford, conditions were better – though, for some reason, the lead parcels arrived at the foot of the tower before those containing feathers. If this were not bad enough, one of the leaden missiles hit a bystander who sustained not inconsiderable injuries. In accordance with that malevolent Law, the nature and formulation of which this book seeks to document, the bystander (or rather belowstander) was Cadwallader, whose view of the gravity of the situation owed nothing to Newton's (and whose centre of *gravitas* was peculiarly low). And he had seen and indentified his assailants, though when later questioned they hotly denied any part in the matter.

It was thus singularly unfortunate that the cronies should have to attend one of Caldwallader's lectures soon afterwards. Apparently the lecture was comparatively short, because of the nature of 'C.F.'s' injuries. The next week, however, he was fully fit, as the following account of the subsequent lecture shows.

"You will recall," said Cadwallader, "that last week's disquisition concerned the nature of Truth. I trust that all of you diligently took to heart the importance of this Cardinal Virtue?"

"Good," he continued, on receiving earnest nods of assent. "You will also recall that I desired you to study the seventeenth chapter of the Gospel according to St Mark. I take it that you have all complied with my request?"

More silent, but hearty, assent.

"If any of you has been unable, for any reason, be it ever so venal, to study the text in question, let him be good enough to indicate this deficiency before we proceed further."

Once more, a silence, though this time no one stirred.

"I require and charge you …."

Murphy thought that the Lecturer had slipped unknowingly into the Marriage Ceremony (this sent a shudder down Murphy's spine, for it brought back the horrors of his Italian adventures), but what followed were reasons, severally enumerated, why certain of the assembly might not have completed, or even started upon, the task. In preternatural silence he was running though the Seven Deadly Sins, and pointing to likely exponents of each of them as he surveyed the class in an arc.

"Accidie, I suppose, would be your excuse, Mr Johnson; and Gluttony yours, Mr Pp … O'Nions? In that you were doubtless dealing in trinkets to secure yourself an even greater income, we must suppose that Avarice would be your mark, Mr Pennymoney."

And in due course, inexorably, Cadwallader came to the end of the arc.

"Lust, Mr Murphy? The blonde and buxom harpy from The Golden Cross? ('The Golden Crotch' said a wag, *sotto voce*) Or the more sinuous, darker, charms of the daughter of the house at the Mitre? ('he did'n daughter, but he Mitre', whispered another).

"These, however, are but jocular speculations about your characters," he continued, without betraying a scintilla of jocularity, "which you will instantly belie, having by silent assent confirmed that each of you has diligently perused the seventeenth chapter of St Mark, as I requested, especially in regard to its relevance to the question of Truth. Am I correct in this assumption? If anyone must needs disabuse me of this notion on his own behalf, pray let him not feel intimidated in any way."

He paused, purely for the purposes of intimidation.

In the silence, a cock crew.

"Ha!, the bird reminds us of The First Apostle. But St Peter's was a thrice uttered denial, which was at least positive in nature. You, on the other hand…" (Here the cock obligingly crew once more, but it failed to elicit any merriment). "On the other hand, you have complaisantly agreed with me thrice. For this, your punishment shall be to learn the whole of St Mark's Gospel in Greek, by this time next week, word perfect. This is a fitting task for you, severe enough, though not in truth as onerous as you may have imagined. For, as you will now discover, St Mark's narrative comes to an end at the fourteenth verse of the sixteenth chapter. There is no seventeenth chapter."

Professor Page had hoped to contribute a note bearing upon this incident, but was prevented from so doing by an immense personal tragedy, the death of his wife Regina (more familiarly known as Queenie). She and Rex (or Jack, as he is more generally called) were a devoted couple, and he was wholly reliant on her. When in Cambridge, she would ensure that Page turned up at the right place by giving him the exact bus fare. When they moved to Oxford this stratagem did not seem to work, since Professor Page regularly arrived at a less than salubrious estate called

Blackbird Leys rather than Boar's Hill, his intended destination, and where he lived in some comfort.

Jack Page was unable to drive, since he had lost his licence a few years earlier. Colleagues have made unkind fun at this mishap, but undergraduates were full of admiration, thinking him to have lost his licence as a result of having been driving under the influence of drugs. Although this was literally true, the reality was that he had come from having a tooth extraction undertaken by Mr Pullen-Payne, an old-fashioned dentist who insisted on administering laughing-gas as an anaesthetic. The wisdom[9] tooth was removed smoothly, but the subsequent passage of Professor Page through Oxford (or rather, up Beaumont Street and into the foyer of the Playhouse) was less smooth, since his somewhat ancient vehicle, rather jauntily named *Lily Christine III*,[10] failed to respond to the somewhat haphazard ministrations of its driver. When Page ripped through the glass doors, accompanying himself with hysterical peals of laughter, he was assumed by the astonished staff to be drunk. Since he was a governor of the Playhouse, the matter was glossed over, and no charges were laid. Nevertheless, his driving licence, which had been on his person at the time, disappeared at some point during the incident, together with the medal of St Christopher Page was luckily carrying at the time; but he was too embarrassed to report these losses to Queenie, excusing himself from driving by saying that after the accident the College doctor had advised him not to do so (which was perfectly true, though the reasons for this advice were not medical).

So it was that when it became necessary to remove some furniture from Great Tew, it fell[11] to Mrs Page to do the driving. Her husband had attended a country auction intending to buy the Falklands Desk – of which later – but had been distracted by the use of split infinitives and other grammatical solecisms by the auctioneer. He thus failed to secure the Desk, but his subsequent gesticulations of protest were interpreted as increasingly enthusiastic bids for an entirely different article. It was therefore his wife who had to drive the van hired for the purpose of carrying this unexpected purchase. Although Queenie was a careful driver, her friend Mrs Mundy, who had been enlisted to help in the removal, was not. Unfortunately, it turned out that the latter was prone to violent travel sickness, especially as a passenger in a van; so to prevent Gloria Mundy being sick in the Transit, Queenie gamely allowed her to drive. Travelling from Enstone to Oxford, they narrowly avoided a head-on collision with another van belonging to Gush and Dent, the Witney plumbers (despite his acute loss, Professor Page has indicated that he will provide a note on the subject of onomastics which he hopes will grace these pages). It was this near accident that

---

[9] Note by Professor Ker suppressed.

[10] Bought, so we are told, from a colleague of his at St Christopher's College who retired some years previously to Devon. [[Professor Fen, no less, who in turn had bought it from an undergraduate who had been sent down. Unhappily, Gervase Fen is no longer with us.]]

[11] See footnote 9 *infra*.

caused an even more woeful lack of attention on the part of Mrs Mundy, for she failed to notice and avoid a tree falling[12] across the road. The driver survived to see another day, but the passenger was crushed, to be pronounced dead on arrival at the Radcliffe Infirmary.

Professor Page's grievous loss was not even mitigated by possession of the furniture (a rare Manx Dresser), for being riddled with woodworm, it turned to dust with the impact of the accident. Nor was he able to take comfort from the legal remedies he sought from Oxfordshire County Council (the owners of the errant tree and the works site on which it stood), despite Page's having turned over the case to Dr Richard Trickie, Fellow in Jurisprudence at St Alfred's and a successful barrister. The County Council's defence, upheld by the court, was that the driver had been forewarned of the likely behaviour of the tree, since there was a prominent notice displayed on the roadside saying CAUTION. HEAVY PLANT CROSSING ROAD. Appeals to higher courts were of no avail, and the Minister of Transport, Sir Laurie Driver, would have no truck with the matter.

The Oxford career of Murphy was significantly hampered by his being hounded by Cadwallader, especially when the latter's niece became entangled with our hero, whom Cadwallader regarded as an incestuous lecher. As soon as the don had wind of the relationship, he did everything he could to stop it, both by having recourse to the courts, as we have seen, and by other means. Despite this, Melissa[13] and Murphy managed to meet up often enough, not least at the festivities of the so-called Hell Fire Club at Sir Francis Dashwood's Wycombe Park.

It was the practice of the participants at such gatherings to be masked, or disguised in other ways. Thus it came about that although Melissa and Murphy were able to recognise each other easily, they did not at first realise that the ill-favoured runt in a goat's costume was none other than her Uncle. Only when he started to fumble with her pleasing plenitude, and mumble pompous platitudes, did she realise that here was a potential crisis that must be averted.

---

[12] It fell in one full swoop.

[13] Dr Quibble has pointed to what he ill conceives to be an inconsistency in the narrative, that the 'M.G.P' does not necessarily refer to the same person. Since Murphy frequently referred to her as 'God's Plenitude', and her middle name was Godiva, we can lay bare this abortive criticism. She appears to have been given the name on account of her mother riding a white horse into Banbury, an event made famous in a children's rhyme whose transmission into modern times has suffered mainly by phonetic corruption, since 'cross' manifestly should rhyme with 'horse'. As Professor Page, who is slowly recovering from his bereavement adds, however: "This is not the only *crux* in the poem, for the dittographic appearance of 'horse' [he says] is suspicious, and may be a euphemism for something else, rather coarse." Incidentally, Dr Quibble is grossly in error in his proposition that Melissa may have been the model for Defoe's *Moll Flanders*, which he stupidly takes to be a corruption of 'Mel Phlinders', a play on 'philanders'. The chronology is all wrong, and so is Quibble.

As luck would have it, Cadwallader eventually fumbled to greater effect, so that Murphy, seeing what was happening, strode over to have business with his rival, unknowing of his identity. Before Murphy revealed himself, however, the masks (and much else) of uncle and niece were discarded in the struggle, so Cadwallader at once knew that the tables were turned and that the spectre of the unnatural crime of incest was ineluctably raised above him, and that his identity could hardly be in doubt. He took the only course of action open to a man of his honour and standing. He fainted.

A brief but intense discussion between Murphy and Melissa followed, so that by the time her uncle had regained consciousness they were ready. Murphy retained his mask, and affected a guttural and near incomprehensible accent.

"Great luck," said Melissa. "I met him passing by the door."

"*Metto dowsei pulsum,*" grated Murphy, taking to himself the role of a doctor of some indeterminate foreign race. Luckily, Cadwallader was drunk enough not to see through the rather makeshift nature of the manufactured tongue which they hoped (this is why they later called it *Esperanto*, though the term *Macaroni* was later favoured by the Hell Fire habitués) might be a palaver that would serve to deceive the listener into imagining it to be a real language.

"He desires to feel your pulse."

"Can't he speak English?", said Cadwallader.

"Not a word."

"*Palio vivem mortem soonem.*"

"He says that you have not six hours to live," said Melissa.

"O mercy, what did they put in that drink?"

"*Pizenatus.*"

"He says you've been …"

"Yes, Yes, I can understand that I've been pizened. What will be the effect?"

"*Quid effectum?*", enquired Melissa.

"*Diable tutellum*", said Murphy, drawing slightly on a remembrance of misspent hours in Swift's Drawing-room.

"He says you'll die presently."

"O, horrible! What, no antidote?"

Some of the rest of this dialogue, pillaged almost word for word, may be seen at the end of Sheridan's *St Patrick's Day*, where Murphy is thinly disguised as Lieutenant O'Connor. The upshot of the true encounter at Wycombe was that the victim was informed that three thousand pounds would procure an antidote, a vast sum for those days, and which Cadwallader could not possibly raise. After some prolonged whispering between the two conspirators, Melissa proposed the alternative: that the curious doctor had expressed warm feelings towards her and was prepared to effect a cure instantly, without fee or reward, other than the hand of herself, Cadwallader's niece. This prize the abysmal creature offered without demur. Melissa, however, insisted that the troth be plighted in front of witnesses. The company assembled around them, thinking that something more racy was about to happen, and the ceremony was duly performed by the Revd Laurence Sterne, who was fortunately, but not fortuitously, present at the time.

Cadwallader became impatient, since he was increasingly fearful of his condition and terrified that he might die before the remedy was ministered to him. Murphy wrote on a piece of paper and gave it to Melissa, who handed it to her uncle.

"I don't need a prescription," he wailed. "I need the nostrum itself."

"That is it," said Murphy, not troubling to dissemble further.

"What the Devil …? Plain English?" Cadwallader was reading out what he thought to be the receipt. "*In reading this you are cured by your dutiful nephew-in-law.*"

As Murphy revealed himself there was an apoplectic explosion, Cadwallader's erstwhile pale features turning towards a dangerously purplish hue tinged with brown, something like puce – though its pre-volcanic precursor should more properly be described as a pre-puce colour. His many dire and imaginative threats were silenced by Melissa, who pointed out that the arrangement was a preferable alternative to the courts, which would take a dim view of her uncle's advances toward her, there being so many distinguished witnesses. Had he but known, no one would have borne witness to such things, which were commonplace at the Club, but not of their nature noised abroad by its members. Indeed, there were, supposedly, the naked figures of the Egyptian god of silence Harpocrates, finger characteristically to his lips, and the equivalent Roman goddess Angerona, in a similar pose, the pair acting as sentinels at the Club.[14]

---

[14] And, inscribed above the door the Horatian motto

Ne fidos inter amicos
Sit qui dicta foras eliminet

which may roughly be rendered 'what is said between friends should not go further than these four walls'. "*Very* roughly," says Professor Page.

Some days later Murphy and Johnson were sitting in The Old Tom, a favoured place on which Murphy waxed eloquent:

"There is nothing which has yet been contrived by man, by which so much happiness is produced, as by a good tavern or inn. I would place it above even the endearing elegance of female friendship."

On the latter subject, Johnson enquired of Murphy's other female friends at the Mitre and the Golden Cross, to which he answered,

"Oh, they were but un-idea'd girls", and proceeded to recount the Wycombe adventure (from which it is clear that the scrofulous Pembroke man was the intermediary through whom this scene was culled by Sheridan). When Murphy had finished, Johnson was full of admiration. As on an earlier occasion, he commented on Murphy's presence of mind in the face of disaster.

"Depend upon it, Sir, when a man knows he might be sent down in a fortnight, it concentrates his mind wonderfully," replied Murphy.

"And this lady to whom you are espoused. Is she, at bottom, a good woman?"

"Indeed she is, Sir, remarkably callipygian, and she has also … Well, anyway. Yes."

"I gather that we have seen the last of her uncle, the infamous Cadwallader."

"Really? How do you mean? The last I heard of him was when Melissa dealt with him after the Tetsworth incident. [recounted on page 112]"

"Whatever she did to him, it finally tipped him over the edge of reality. It resulted in his going over to the Romish faction. He was last heard of trying to peddle sickly religious daubs, fervently ill-executed by his own hands but signed *AMDG*, around Brittany."

"So …"

"So Jesus College rightly terminated his Fellowship for blasphemy."

It was at about this time that Johnson told Murphy that he would have to leave Oxford, for he had finally run out of funds. Murphy was sympathetic, and on hearing that his young friend had hopes of a literary career, gave him some well-chosen advice:

"Read over your compositions, and where ever you meet with a passage which you think is particularly fine, strike it out. And you will find it a very good practice always to verify your references, Sir."

They were to meet again, in London, but by that time Murphy had realised that Johnson, even if unwitting, had passed on accounts of his adventures to Smollett, Boswell, Sheridan and many others, so he felt that his erstwhile companion had betrayed him. Johnson sought to repair the damage by belittling these authors, as for example by calling Sheridan "naturally dull" and opining that "there is more knowledge of the heart in one letter of Richardson's, than in all of Tom Jones". But the damage was done. Indeed, a few years later, in 1738, when Johnson tried to inveigle Swift into giving him a Dublin MA, Murphy, when asked his opinion, said:

"That fellow seems to possess but one idea, and that is the wrong one."

This made sure that no degree was forthcoming.[15]

At this juncture we find ourselves having to contend with two detractors, whose mission as naysayers seems to be to deny the authenticity of the Murphy documents from which this narrative is assembled. Of the arguments (if they may be dignified by such an epithet) of Professor Gerry Bilt, Rupert Murdoch Professor of Deconstruction at the New University of Darlaston, there is little to be said. Insofar as there is anything that can be grasped from amongst the plethora of gibberish about structuralism, semiotics and the rag-bag of other pseudo-critical postures which he affects, the sum of it is trivial and puerile. What he understands to be his trump card, a supposed analysis of the 'subtext' (what ever that might mean) of Murphy's writings by Doctorin ter Techst, Reader in Derridory Studies at the Institute of Dutch Letters, Amsterdam, is but a Joker.

As to Dr Quibble, our patience is exhausted. The latest folly of this charlatan has been to put the Murphy materials that he has obtained from our work (Professor Ker having communicated them without our authority) on his computer, and to declare that his Text-Critical program proves that it is impossible that all of the passages were written by the same person, least of all Murphy. I have news for him. A friend at the Cambridge computing laboratories, Dr R. O. M. Emery, has kindly obtained a copy of this pogrom, entitled StyleCruncher, for our own use. My diligent pupil, Ann O'Rach, engorged the machine ('keyed in' is the appalling jargon, she tells me) with the whole of Dr Quibble's writings, and the thing pronounced that he alone could not have possibly written them. (Miss O'Rach tells me that something very similar happened many years ago when doubt was expressed about the true authorship of St Paul's Epistles: the manner in which he employed the Greek particle γάρ, thought to be stylistically inconsistent, was subjected to statistical analysis by some precursor of Quibble. This was no less than the authority on Greek Particles, Professor Martin East, Fellow (and Worshipful Chief Swan-Turner) of Porterhouse College, Cambridge, who purportedly 'proved' that St Paul could not have written the Epistles in a triumphant paper appearing in a learned journal. This latter, however, was also analysed by the same method, which duly confirmed that it could not have been written by the proto-Quibble, so East's

---

[15] Johnson's fortunes were not furthered, it has to be said, by Addison, who had written to Stella to the effect that it would be a bad idea "to encourage a very absurd man in his absurdity rather than strive to pull him out of it".

theories went West. She is now putting the works of Professor Bilt and Doctorin ter Techst into the jaws of the StyleCruncher, so we shall probably learn that they were written by a child of three.

Through the good offices of Professor Page (happily restored to better spirits), the Clarendon Laboratories at Oxford have performed some tests on those Murphy documents presently in our possession. A distinguished visitor, the Russian Academician Professor Chestikoff of Chernobl has analysed the ink by a method known as Proton Induced X-ray Emission. He tells me that this is a non-destructive process capable of detecting any element from Sodium onwards in the periodic table (elements with atomic numbers below 11 cannot be so detected) at trace levels (i.e. a few parts per million). This was effected by bombarding the sample with a narrow beam of high-energy protons from the isochronous cyclotron at Culham and examining the characteristic spectrum of X-rays emitted by computer analysis (see Professor Chestikoff's charts on the following page).

The full documentation of the results will be given in the second volume, but in sum, it can be said that the papers are all identical chemically, and the paper+ink spectra (since the proton beam passes through both) show that 90% or better of the ink samples are identical. The characteristic spectra, seen in the following figures, are the same for all the paper samples, and identical in all but 10% of paper+ink spectra, of which 5% are near identical and 5% so similar as to be the same ink in all probability. The signature identified as Murphy's holograph by Professor Page therefore matches chemically as well as calligraphically all, or virtually all, of the other writing in the MSS. The papers have also been tested at the Ashmolean Museum's C14 laboratory, and have been dated to 1714, the very year that Murphy escaped from Italy; so the theory that large portions of the MSS were inserted at a later date falls to the ground.

As indeed did Professor Page. One of the dons at Freddie's (the popular name by which St Alfred's is known) had suggested a Bore's Head dinner. Not in imitation of The Queen's College nearby, which holds its Boar's Head celebrations on Christmas Day, but a dinner at which each Fellow would bring a guest, the most tedious of whom would be adjudged the winner and the prize, a bottle of College port, would go to the host. Needless to say, there was to be utter secrecy, lest the word get out that the guests were being audited in this manner. All went according to plan initially, and Page had high hopes of success, having invited A. J. P. Taylor from Magdalen. He was thwarted somewhat by Dr Thorne having invited Lord Nacre of the House, who found Taylor a natural irritant, to the extent that their long-standing feud was instantly rekindled and continued to smoulder at table. Indeed, it was just after Lord Nacre's discomfiture (having declard certain documents as "incontrovertibly authentic") at these papers being proved to be forgeries. Taylor was quick to remind the company that the method by which they had been shown not to emanate from Himmler was very similar to that of Prefessor Chestikoff's, described here.

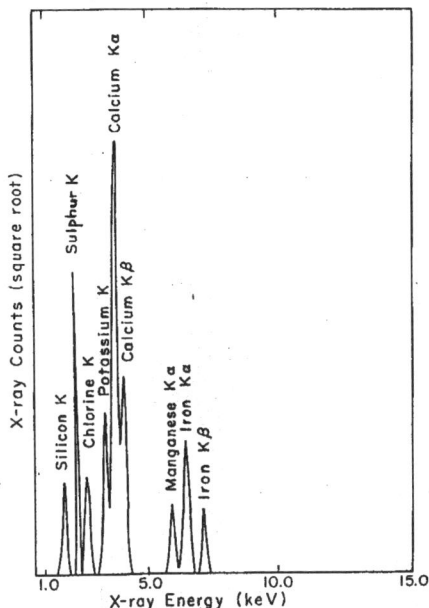

A. Characteristic X-ray spectrum of paper from the Murphy documents

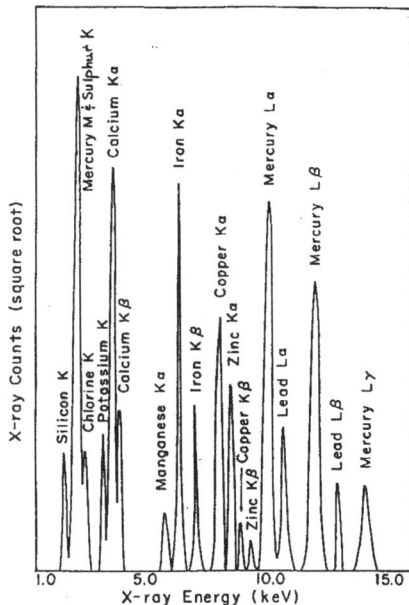

B. Characteristic X-ray spectrum of paper plus manuscript ink from the Murphy documents

K, L, α, β and γ show the atomic electron transmission responsible for the X-ray emission in question

© 1979 & 1984, Ivan Nastieichi Chestikoff

By dessert, things had gone from bad to worse, and when Lord Nacre made some witticism about how ghastly the food and drink was, supposing that Brown Windsor Soup, Liebfraumilch and the like was the sort of thing relished by the class from which Taylor came, fisticuffs ensued. Someone[16] said that this was boorish behaviour, another (Professor Bo Zart, a Swedish Visiting Professor of Painting at Freddie's, who rather liked to show off his understanding of the English language)

---

[16] The first speaker is widely assumed to have been the Boring Bosnian, from St Mary's. His name fluctuated between *Crucis* and *Cross*, by which he later attempted to be more English than the English (he invariably wore a brown tweed jacket, even at this dinner) and to disguise his original surname, which sounded like an obscure disease that might exclude him from the polite society with which he sought so earnestly to ingratiate himself. The assumption that the Lord High Canard, Professor South, of Our Souls' College, was present in a drunken state, is founded upon a misunderstanding. South (though it would be difficult to tell whether drunk or sober, and although not attired in brown, he habitually wore shorts with his dinner-jacket) was certainly present at a later Bore's Head dinner (as was the aforementioned Crućić) but at the time of the earlier dinner in question he was still Professor of Linear C Epigraphy in the Unversety of the North Bank.

that this was the wrong kind of bore, and yet another, probably Dr Fuzzel, that the dishes and wines had been carefully chosen to match the occasion as being the most acutely boring. Now whether he added "like the guests", or whether the phrase came from some other drunken voice is a matter of dispute, but it meant that Page, at that point having had some small success in separating the two combatants, was now rounded upon, not only by the original belligerents, but by all the guests to a man (one of whom was Mrs Thatcher, the future Prime Minister), for all of them, even the most befuddled (i.e. Dr Paxman, who was delivering the Kalashnikoff Lectures in Peace Studies) had now realised why they had been invited.

As we have said, Professor Page fell to the ground. Although he was rescued with considerable promptitude by one of the scouts who had seen active service in the SAS (and whose opinion was that this skirmish was one of the most violent in his experience), it was not before substantial injury had accumulated. At the Radcliffe Infirmary, where his wounds were dressed and his bones set, Dr Tibi (a Lebanese specialist in injuries of this nature) told his colleagues that although the damage caused by trampling and kicking was characteristic, the worst insult (a rather curious medical term) was caused by some metallic object, which left a deep and ugly imprint on the Page countenance, and which was judged to be something akin to a type of knuckle-duster used by thugs.

The identity of this object remained a mystery until, by chance, one of the doctors (Tibi or not Tibi, that is the question that the popular press has frequently posed: whether the honour for this discovery was due to him or some colleague, has not been settled with any certainty) saw a picture of Mrs Thatcher in a newspaper, in which she was seen clutching a handbag with a murderous looking clasp. [[Margaret Thatcher was refused an honorary degree by Oxford, many years later. Though the reasons for this refusal were widely assumed to have been in revenge for her educational policies, or more correctly, for giving less money to the universities, it was an unspoken sympathy for Jack Page and the memory of this abominable incident, enduring long after his death, that caused Congregation to close ranks on this issue.]]

By a curious coincidence, a similar dinner had been held at St Alfred's a couple of centuries earlier, though this was a more elegant and civilised affair. It was a meeting of the Narcissus Club, of which Oscar Wilde was later a member. There was a tradition that Irishmen should be elected President, and on this occasion Murphy was duly installed in that office. There was also a tradition that the newly-elected President (the incumbency of which office alternated between Magdalen and St Alfred's) should become quite drunk, and Murphy duly obliged (his own words being that he "was stocious altogether"). It was therefore particularly burdensome to him when he awoke the next morning, realising that his Schools *viva* was to take place that day.

When his scout brought an unwelcome breakfast, he also handed him a note which alarmed Murphy considerably, for the time of the viva had been brought forward to 10.a.m., only a matter of minutes away; the venue had also been changed, but at least this was to New College, next door. So he gathered up his gown and beat a hasty and dyspeptic path to an upstairs room in the front quad of New College.

The gowned adversaries looked like so many black beetles. All of the examiners had luxuriant beards, entirely engulfing any facial features which the supposed subject of their study (assuming that He has any connexion with theology) might have provided. As a result, each member of the board looked identical and particularly menacing. Murphy was told to sit down.

"Name and College?"

"Murphy. St Alfred's."

"*Quære*. What are the armorial bearings of that College?"

"Three cakes, burnt, proper, upon a platter argent, impaling King Alfred, couchant unregardant."

"*Satis*. And the motto?"

"*Quicunque placentæ torruit, biscocitum autulerit.*"

"Which is construed?"

"He who burns the cakes takes the biscuit."

"*Vix satis. Quæstio*. What, Mr Murphy, is the Ninth Beatitude?"

"So far as I recall there are only eight."

"That is not so. I suppose you will claim ignorance of the Eleventh Commandment?"

"I know there is some variance between the versions of the commandments as vouchsafed in Exodus as against Deuteronomy."

"This is mere quibble. Iterate the commandment."

"I fear that I am ignorant of it."

"Indeed. Then be so kind as to inform us as to the identity of the present head of the Church of England."

"The head of the Established Church is the King, His Majesty King George."

"Incorrect. *Quære*. What is the likely outcome of your examination here?"

"I fear that I cannot anticipate the consequences."

"Here, I can enlighten you. The probability of failure is so strong as to verge upon the inevitable. Good day."

A lump came to Murphy's throat; his stomach heaved and his legs seemed to liquefy. With great effort he moved from his chair and out of the room. His perturbation was intense, his misery complete. Seeing a friendly face at last, he hailed his companion Babbage, whom he espied on the other side of the quadrangle.

"I have had the most minatory examination, the like of which I hope I shall never again experience. The questions seemed simplicity itself, but the learned professors of theology brushed aside my answers as though they were wrong."

"What questions did they ask *you?*"

"The ninth beatitude, the eleventh commandment, and the present head of the Church of England, which they said was not the King."

"The answer to the last, I think you will find, is the Duke of Lancaster, for you were with Jacobites who refuse to acknowledge whom they call the Duke as King."

"Then how can these dons be loyal members of the Church? And what of their curious questions?"

"The ninth beatitude, you will find, is 'Blessed are they who expect nothing, for they shall not be disappointed'[17] and the eleventh commandment is 'Thou shalt not be found out'."

"But …"

"As you say: but. It is clear that your adversaries were not *Sacrae Theologiae Professores* (in any case this is a curious phrase – for what is Theology if it is not sacred?) but were the perpetrators of what is clearly a prank. What did they look like?"

"They were heavily bearded and moustachioed."

"Then they were undoubted undergraduates, for moustaches are against Canon Law.[18] What time is your real *viva voce* examination?"

---

[17] It is surprising that Murphy should not have known this, for it was a favourite phrase (though in a slightly variant form) of Pope, a great friend of Swift and whose work was well known to Murphy, as seen in the previous chapter. Murphy also visited Pope on several occasions, as detailed below.

[18] Here, Babbage was in error, for it is moustaches when worn *without a beard* that are forbidden by Canon Law. In the nineteenth century, when the priesthood seems to have taken no notice of it, beards were worn by the High Church faction, moustaches by the Low. [[Nowadays no one takes any notice of the priesthood, and bitch-collars are all the rage, quite often worn with

"I thought that was it: a card told me that my viva in the Divinity School at Eleven of the clock was transferred to Dr Foster's room here, an hour earlier."

"Dr Foster died last week in Gloucester.[19] I suggest that you cut along to the Schools with due haste and face your real inquisitors."

This he did, and the genuine examination to which he had to submit was by no means as rigorous, the questions being "What is the Hebrew for 'the place of a skull'?", and the like. The proceedings lasted little more than a few minutes, and Babbage was waiting in the Schools quadrangle for him.

"There seems no great purpose in my studying Hebrew, Greek and all the rest of it, if this is all they require of me. It appears that the sum of my learning in the School of Hebrew and Greek is scrawled upon its walls."[20]

"Be thankful for small mercies," said Babbage. "Let us go down to *The Bear* for something of a celebratory nature."

As they crossed from the Schools[21] through Catte Street to St Mary's, they talked

---

the moustaches sported by the priestesses. The foregoing footnote by O'Toole is in any case misinformed: he cannot have checked his references, as Routh seems to have advised Murphy. Canon Law 74, correctly cited by O'Toole in a footnote in the previous chapter, contains references neither to beards nor moustaches, unless "newfangleness of apparel" was what he had in mind. Mistakenly.]]

[19] Apparently in an untimely inundation (writes Professor Page); but he never reached Gloucester. The facts of the matter are these: Foster was fording the river at Nether Piddle when a flash flood overtook him, suddenly engulfing him up to his midriff. Unbalanced, he was swept away. He was rescued by a kindly householder, who also saw to his needs when it became evident that he had contracted a severe cold; despite solicitous nursing, however, this malady turned to pneumonia from which he subsequently died, still some way from his intended destination, where he was to meet his tailor. A children's ditty, surviving unto the present day, records his demise, though its last three lines are manifest corruptions of the original, which may be reconstructed thus:

> When caught in the Piddle
> It rose up to his middle
> And soon after he died in great pain.

[[Piddle and Puddle are but differing spellings of the same word, originally pronounced the same. 'Puddle' is often a mere euphemism, which has its counterpart in 'Ruddle', a form that has been resisted by most branches of my own family, correctly spelled 'Ridell'.]]

[20] This statement would of course be of interest in any event, but we are able to report that the *graffiti* [Professor Page urges, however, the use of the form *sgraffiti*, which he insists is more correct] in question have been recovered, a discovery of the most intense interest and significance, and which will be detailed in due course, as soon as the authorities at Oxford publish the materials. We are reliant, as ever, on the good offices of Professor Page, who has communicated advance notice of this momentous discovery.

[21] The Old Schools, of course, not the *ersatz* building in The High.

about the ravaging of the Oxford architecture by 'that Jericho builder Hawksmoor'.[22] Babbage observed that The Queen's College was in the process of being ruined, and that there were dreadful plans drawn up for Worcester, Magdalen and many other colleges and university buildings that would be laid waste [as was St Alfred's in 1740] by the vandal Hawksmoor.

"Well, Magdalen will probably dither, and the appalling thing will never get built." [Which indeed was so, for only an experimental part, now crumbling and rather comically known as 'New Buildings', was built, so the rest of the college was spared.]

"That is as may be, but the Radcliffe monies that have accrued are so substantial that they are going to pull down all these houses in Catte Street, some of which used to be occupied by scriveners, and put up a library in their stead. Have you seen the designs?"

"I have, and they are quite dreadful. The Radcliffe Library will have the appearance of a mausoleum in the shape of some malformed mammary. There will be absolutely no room for books in the interior of this great tit, and they will get lost. The only good characteristic will be its endomastic echo."

Murphy's worst fears were realised, and the designs which he had seen (presumably those of 1715) were not dissimilar from those from which the Radcliffe Library was finally built, starting in 1737. It is probably a convenient point to mention the comparable rebuilding of the Library at Trinity, Dublin, that was undertaken in recent years. The plan was to enlarge it on its original site and to reinforce the foundations by the simple expedient of pouring concrete into the lower basement rooms which had been cleared for the purpose. This was done by the firm of Ayres' the builders (calling themselves by the appalling name of 'Ayres' the Civil Enginayres') whose enthusiasm was more commendable than their expertise: for having filled the space in question, the operative, Mr Derry Ayre himself, noticed that there was still a gap above it, whereupon he ordered more concrete to be poured in. Satisfied with a job well done, and beyond the call of the letter strict, he went away, sure that he would be commended by his distinguished client.

Deplorably, his fawlty zeal resulted in a considerable part of the rare book collection in the new building being permanently enshrined in concrete. The visitor to the Berkeley Library at Trinity, where appearances are realistically deceptive, will see in the catalogue sundry references to 'concreted books', these being that part of the collection that is now ossified for posterity. If this were not tragedy enough, the MSS detailed at the beginning of chapter 3 of the present work, and on which considerable reliance has been placed, are among those to have suffered this fate. There is a silver halide lining to this chapter of accidents, however, in that photostatic

---

[22] A characteristic Murphian phrase whence, of course, the modern corruption 'Gerry builder' derives, Jericho being one of the parts of Oxford ruined by his depredations.

copies of the MSS in question are in our possession, and although somewhat turned up at the edges, are serviceable and clear, though not, of course a true substitute for the original. Nevertheless, they will be reproduced in their entirety in the companion volume, thereby, we hope, stifling the repeated cavilling of Professor Heinz Zeit.

No such good fortune has accompanied the Genizah fragments so earnestly sought by Professor Page, however. As the reader will doubtless recall, these fell into the hands[23] of Professor Ker at Cambridge, due to an unfortunate chain of events. The fragments are no more, and the end of the sorry tale is this. Professor Ker had entrusted the Genizah MSS to Sir Fred Kermit, one of the Syndics of the Cambridge University Press, who were to publish them prior to their being deposited in the University Library. Before such a deposition could take place, and indeed before the photographic work had been carried out, Sir Fred moved house, and carefully packed the Murphy sources, with the rest of his priceless collection of first editions and MSS, into suitable receptacles – tea chests and the like. Came the Monday morning, and the workmen turned up on his doorstep, to whom he indicated the boxes and other containers which they duly took away. It was only later that Sir Fred realised that these were not representatives of the removal firm, but the dustcart men, who had duly 'trashed' his Shakespeare First Folios and Quartos, his MS collection, and more important, the Murphy fragments. Although he is now in a madhouse, still attempting to sue Cambridge City Council for dereliction of duty, he is at least alive. Professor Ker, however, is dead. Hearing of the incident, he was beside himself with rage, and attacked Sir Fred, whom he attempted to garotte with a metal-covered violin string.[24] Absent-minded Sir Fred might be, but he turns out to have been a black belt practitioner in the Japanese art of Karate, and Ker was fatally floored in his argument.

Some say that God moves in a mysterious way; but it is self-evident that there is no mystery about the manner in which events such as these should unfold according to

---

[23] "A particularly apt phrase," says Professor Page, "for Ker more or less destroyed them as soon as he touched them. The man's exactly what his Cambridge undergraduates say he is – I fear it is an indelicate word spelt out by his initials. Again, the science of onanastics, or rather its sister science (or should I say daughter science) acronymics, is not without relevance here." Professor Ker appears somehow to have seen this comment and, apart from offering physical violence, had communicated with us in the following manner:

> That's rich, that is. Jack the Ripper is the most notorious shredder of incunabula and manuscripts that you are likely to find. The Murphy MSS fell to bits in his hands at that monstrous British Academy lecture. No wonder the Countess took them back. As to his stupid play upon my name, he is clearly ignorant of the English language. Any reputable dictionary will disabuse you [irrelevant comment suppressed] of the notion that he is anything but an abject cretan. The word in question is spelt with an aitch, as in *when, why* and *what,* so I am perfectly happy to sign myself,

> W.A.N.Ker

[24] What he was doing with a G string in his pocket is unexplained.

a clearly defined Law. It is that Law, and the life of its progenitor, that this book has sought to document, we hope not unsuccessfully.

Murphy stayed in Oxford for a considerable period after he had gained his degree. Due, at least in part, to the influence of the Master of Pembroke, he became a Jacobite. When Johnson was at Pembroke, Dr Panting had been Master; in the Lodgings there had been discussions between him and Murphy's set on the question of the validity of the Jacobite claim which was supported by the Master, yet vociferously opposed by Murphy at that time. Later in his life, however, Murphy became convinced of the rectitude of the Jacobite cause. He was also eventually to espouse the cause of Pictish nationalism, mistakenly thinking the Picts to be oppressed Celts, his sympathy for whom led him to pursue a renewed interest in the Celtic languages.

From time to time he visited Stanton Harcourt,[25] where Pope often stayed with His Lordship. [It is to be regretted that investigations at Pope's Tower in the Manor grounds have failed to reveal the rumoured records of these visits. All that is known of them at present is perforce from secondary sources.] One reason for seeking Pope was to enquire if he had any memory of the colour of Swift's hair which, regrettably, he had not, protesting:

Why has not man a microscopic eye?
For this plain reason, man is not a fly!

On another occasion they discussed the problem of the toast, and other manifestations of the malevolence of chance, upon which the poet pronounced:

Not chaos-like, together crushed and bruised,
But, as the world harmoniously confused:
Where order in variety we see,
And where, though all things differ, all agree.

It was also during these years that Murphy made a considerable reputation for himself as a scientist, and so was a regular visitor to the establishment at Great Tew, not very far from Oxford. There, a group of eminent thinkers of the day, earlier granted the title of The Royal Society, met from time to time as an alternative to London. This illustrious assemblage devoted itself to the discussion of many important discoveries and theories of the day. Murphy's contribution seems to have

---

[25] This was no mean journey from Oxford, even on horseback. The journey became longer and longer, for the first time Murphy came by the conventional route by way of Eynsham, but vehemently objected to paying a toll at the Swinford Bridge. The next time he rode further West to Cumnor, but then found he had to pay the ferryman to cross the river near Eaton. Thereupon he rode still further West to Kingston Bagpuize, and crossed the Isis by bridge, where he was set upon by highwaymen. It remains to be explained why he did not venture on the Witney turnpike, in any case a shorter route to Eynsham.

involved at least two disparate topics, namely his strong advocacy for a duodecimal system of numeration (in this he had apparently been vigorously supported by Newton, President of the Society until his death in 1732, and with whom, it transpires, Murphy had struck up a most cordial friendship many years earlier) and an important discovery: what he called the operation of 'particulate factors' in the mechanism of inheritance.

The only known, or rather extant, evidence for these discussions involving Murphy comes from a document found in the so-called Falkland Desk, when the piece recently came up for auction, though it eluded the attentions of Professor Page. [The theory that these papers were taken to the Falkland Isles can be discounted, as will be seen shortly]. This document mentions both the topic of inheritance and the duodecimal system of measurement. Virtually nothing of Murphy's *De numeris duodecimis* survives, though a portion of it was found by Faraday (a later member of the Royal Society, who happened to be a bookbinder) as a pastedown in a book of an erotic character which he chanced to be rebinding. Otherwise, all we have is a short eye-witness account[26] of a meeting at which Murphy expounded his system, reported in a later chapter.

As to the question of 'particulate factors', there is some evidence from the Falkland Desk document itself, since it records a part of a discussion in the Falkland Arms, Great Tew, on the night of […] when the question was aired at length. It transpires that the children sired by Murphy at various stages of his career had been […] in number [due to this and the previous figure being in Murphy's as yet undeciphered notation, precision in this matter has yet to be established] and their father had been entirely fascinated by the fact that although many had black hair, some were blond, and a distinct proportion were red-heads. His consuming interest in the subject was occasioned, as we know, by his frustrated efforts to discover his true paternity. If in this he failed, he nevertheless succeeded (through his observations of the progeny of cattle, and of the products of his own fecundity) in founding the modern science of genetics.

He postulated that there were two types of 'particulate factors', namely those that were *latent* and those which were *semblant*. Furthermore, these factors could be *potent* or *weak*. Little exegesis [I am grateful to Dr Jean Poole of the Uneversity of Hampshire for much help in this passage] is required to see that these are the phenotypes and genotypes of modern genetics, in their dominant and recessive forms. It is evident that Murphy was homozygous, having inherited a recessive allele from his biological father (who was similarly homozygous, as we know from his red hair) and his mother must have been heterozygous, having a dominant dark-haired allele. This being so, Murphy's children out of a red-headed partner would all have been red-headed, and out of a heterozygous recessive like his mother the

---

[26] Professor Page would prefer the phrase 'ear-witness account': he also says that the book was not of an erotic character, a point on which he has promised to enlarge in due course.

103

probability would have been ·5 (though this does not mean the 1:1 ratio between red-haireds and other colours would necessarily have been realised). Having regard to the consanguinity with many of the females by which he had issue, and the frequency with which these relationships took place, Murphy must have come to the appropriate conclusions. These, together with his observations concerning his multitudinous connexions with females outside this gene pool (which he called the Law of Random Miscegenation), must have supplied him with sufficient information to discover the ratio involved in patterns of dominant and recessive genes, especially in view of his apparent intention to vie with the Elector of Saxony in the matter of progeny, which would have ensured a sample capable of statistical significance.

Whether or not he was able to determine what is erroneously known as the 'Mendelian' ratio must wait for the final decipherment of the numbers found in the source, which are in Murphy's duodecimal notation. It does not seem unlikely, however, that $\sqsubset$ - $\sqsupset$ - $\sqsupset$ - $\int$ should represent the ratios 9:3:3:1, though we should approach such an obvious decipherment with proper scholarly caution. Whatever this formula turns out to be, nevertheless, we know that it was hailed by the enthusiastic Sir Francis Dashwood (himself a member of the Royal Society from 1746) as 'Murphy's Law'.[27]

As with so many of his other major discoveries, the science of Geneticks, as he styled it, had to be recovered much later, due to the operation of a Murphy's Law very different from that hailed by Dashwood. The evidence which Murphy had collected was sent, apparently at the suggestion of Genno,[28] his former Professor of Philosophy at Bologna, to a monastery in Brno, Moravia. It must be assumed that the papers were put on one side and virtually lost until 1866, when Mendel, supposedly working with peas, brought out the theory of inheritance as his own. The annexation of the theory by this means ironically parallelled the annexation of

---

[27] The facts have been carefully stated here since the conclusion that Murphy had hit upon the 'Law of Segregation' (1:2:1, expressed as $\int$- > -$\int$ in Murphy's notation), and the more complex 9:3:3:1 ratio (when 2 characters are being inherited at the same time) is disputed. It is hotly contested by Dick Hawkins, the Oxford Professor for the Publick Understanding of Astrology, who also objects to the truth, exposed in a following paragraph of ours, concerning Darwin. What his qualifications in genetics might be, we do not know (the populist books such as *The Deaf Bellringer* show that he has very little grasp of the subject) but his main thesis is that "a doubly recessive characteristic such as red-hairedness could not possibly be quantified accurately in a human context: we are not dealing with *Drosophila* [*D. melanogaster,* the fruit-fly often used in genetic experiments] or similar orgasms that can be relied upon to reproduce many filial generations rapidly, but with the human male, which is not capable of multiple organisms of a similar nature, and is therefore a very different kettle of fish [[jar of flies? hatful of rabbits?]]."

[28] "It strikes one that it is entirely appropriate that Genno is the Italian for Janus," writes Professor Page. "I hope to be able to furnish you with a substantial contribution on the science of onomastics as it pertains to Murphy, but for the present it is obvious that Genno was indeed Janus faced." Murphy was still pursuing the problem of the toast with his former teacher who still, it seems, declined to give an answer.

its supposed place of origin as Brünn, so Abbot Mendel is forever condemned to being an Austrian as well as a charlatan.

As to the contribution of Darwin, it is clear that he had also been 'anticipated' (to put the most charitable construction on the matter) by Murphy. He (Murphy) had observed that the intellectual vigour of many of his countrymen seemed to decline with each generation, noting that the most gifted of Ireland's sons were whisked away to seminaries in Italy, France and the Low Countries. Apart from a few indiscretions in these places, the fecundity of these men was denied to them, and more particularly to their native land, by their vows of chastity. This process Murphy termed 'Unnatural Selection', arguing that it was the opposite of the proper order of things, inducing what he called 'the Survival of the Unfittest', which likewise was against the principles which operated in the natural realm, as he pointed out.[29]

All that is known about this important, some would say seminal, series of observations is recoverable only from secondary sources, since the original papers were lost when Murphy lodged with Betsy Bowker in London, as related in chapter 6. One such secondary source is a letter from Bernoulli to Murphy, in which he recalled some of the incidents relating to Murphy's stay in Italy. This letter is obviously a reply to one from Murphy, enlisting his old friend's help in tracing Professor Genno. Bernouilli was unable to help in this matter, but quoted the Italian proverb *Butta una fardola per pigliar un luccio* (referring, roughly speaking, to the use of a sprat to catch a mackerel).[30] This is probably intended as a pun on the word 'butter', of relevance in connexion with the matter of the gravity-defying buttered toast, the reason for Murphy's pursuance of Genno. Bernoulli also referred to the 'twice sod' *crambe repetita* (i.e. 'twice seethed' – in this sense, SOD being of course the past participle of SEETHE – the *crambe* being a reference to the cabbage and hairy bacon beloved of Murphy, as detailed in chapter 2).

Unfortunately, this letter was among the documents that were lost in the disaster which overtook Sir Fred Kermit, as recounted earlier in this chapter, and which brought about the felling of Professor Ker in one fall swipe. Even without the

---

[29] Professor Richard Hawkins, being a Catholic of a somewhat fundamentalist persuasion, will have nothing do with Darwin's theories nor with "slurs concerning the Irish priesthood, which then and now is on record as being entirely and blamelessly celibate". Since his reading of newspapers seems to be confined to *The Tablet,* we must admire his faith and dismiss his science. Indeed, his knowledge of the latter is apparently the result of a semester of study at the University of the Deep South, Alabama, where he majored in O.T.* Religion. His comments that "Wilberforce, although not a Catholic, made a monkey out of Darwin", and that "Abbot Mendel's discoveries showed that the wrinkles of the Natural Law are smoothly reconciled by the Divine Law" must be viewed in this light.

*[is this Old Testament or Old-Time?]

[30] "*Very* roughly", insists Professor Page.

necessary documentation, however, Ker's theory that this phrase is the origin of 'Sod's Law' – which he glossed as 'The Law of the Twice Cooked' – is half-baked.

To end this chapter on a more positive note, however, we can report the recovery of an important Murphy document, a record of his stay at Oxford. The *Schola Linguarum Hebraicae et Graecae* in the Schools quadrangle was, as we know, much frequented by Murphy. It has now been converted into a gentlemen's lavatory.[31] Naturally, such a place attracts what are often referred to as *graffiti,* so not much attention was taken of the scrawls on the walls beyond the cursory. As chance would have it, however, Professor Page (prior to his being incapacitated at the Bore's Head dinner as recounted above), needed to relieve himself. Needless to say, he had done so many times before at this most convenient place. His optician, however, had newly prescribed trifocal lenses for Page's spectacles, so he was now able to read the *graffiti* at all levels, high and low, without dissolution or having to climb. Here, to his amazement, he confronted a handwriting with which he was gratifyingly familiar, that of Murphy himself! He was scarcely able to contain himself [[actually, he didn't, for his sodden trousers were undone all the way to the office of the astounded Bodley's Librarian]], shouting *Eureka, eureka!* as he went to report his discovery.

The authorities acted with uncommendable dispatch, for the surface of the wall was at once declared a Bodleian Additional MS, and preparations were made for its removal, preservation and publication. The lamentable consequences of its rather over-prompt removal was that every scrap of writing, apart from the Bodleian MS number, was destroyed. All is not lost, however, for it has since been discovered that someone studying at the Ruskin School of Drawing made a sketch of the wall before its inscriptions had been accidentally erased. Although Professor Page's injuries still preclude his following up this line of enquiry, we have high hopes that there will be a satisfactory outcome to this chapter of accidents.

On the question of Geneticks [Printer – this is not a footnote, merely an addendum] the workings of Murphy's Law of Random Miscegenation has been upheld in recent work. A blood-group survey of a Somerset village was undertaken in order to ascertain how many of the families could be traced back to early times. The results had to be left unpublished as they proved that families that should not have been related had closer ties of a recent nature than it would have been politic to reveal. A similar survey in Israel, this time based on mitochondrial DNA, unfortunately showed that the forbears of most of the extreme Zionist faction were Arab, and that the purest Jewish blood-line was to be found amongst the *falashas,* the black Ethiopic Jews, but whose claims to be descended from Moses were always resisted. Wrongly, it seems.

---

[31] Recently, however, we hear that it has been converted back, or rather assigned to some new purpose which is deemed more suitable by Dr Loon, the Secretary, who had pronounced that it had become 'a tramp's loo'.

V. OXFORD, WYCOMBE, LONDON & The Celtic Realms

Chance is the known result of unknown causes [1]

O N the following page we are privileged to print the *editio princeps* of the missing Bodleian MS Add. 69. Through the kind offices of Dr Rose Madder, director of the Ruskin School of Fine Art in Oxford, we are able to reproduce a sketch of the wall of the former *Schola Linguarum Hebraicae et Graecae* in the Schools quadrangle of the Bodleian Library. Hitherto it was thought to have been drawn by someone studying at the Ruskin School, but Dr Madder has discovered that it was executed by none other than Professor Bo Zart, on his then recent visit to Oxford. This explains the rather poor quality of the draughtmanship, says Dr Madder, drawing on her extensive knowledge of the matter. Unfortunately, Professor Zart cannot at present be contacted, since he is somewhere in France, studying a newly discovered site of immense significance from the standpoints of prehistoric art and anthropology, and which must remain unidentified. (As this narrative is being revised for the press, however, Mme Crowe-Magnon – née Anne de Thal – has told us that the site involved is the hitherto highly secret complex of caves at Le Faux, whose art treasures are being systematically recorded by researchers at the Collage d'Europe under the direction of Professor Zart.)

It will immediately be seen from the reproduction that the wall in front of the artist is adequately drawn and most of the important inscriptions show up reasonably well on the printed page. We shall not pre-empt Professor Page's detailed study of the texts, but this opportunity cannot pass without pointing to the Murphy signature (or rather, his surname) occurring in the maxim *Hic Morphi adfuerit*. This is clearly visible between the two sanitary vessels which are depicted. (Professor Page has promised to elaborate on the frequentative nature of the verb-form *adfuerit*, as opposed to *aderat*, clearly a point of much significance to Murpheans.) The inscription is partly obscured by *and Kilroy was here, too*, in a later hand.

The other glosses, which in the print can barely be made out are: *I shall return*, the signatory of which appears to be MacArthur, and *Je Reviens* to which the name Christian Dior is appended.

The motto 'If you can read this you are not a member of Freddies' is not worth mentioning, being a somewhat gratuitous reference to the supposed lack of

---

[1] This quotation, attributed to Voltaire, is undoubtedly a Murphy aphorism dating from the years when Voltaire was in England (1726–9) under various guises such as Lord Bolingbroke, the Rabbi Akib, and many others.

The former Bodleian MS Add. 69
(wrongly numbered)
Facing Wall

ditto, foot of Right-hand Wall   *detail*

detail of Facing Wall

academic prowess of the college of which Murphy was an *alumnus*. It is in any event rather obscured by the familiar Latin lines *veni vidi vici*, to which the signature Christine Keeler has been subscribed. Professor Page is of the opinion that this must be one of the Marmalade Keilers, but we have our doubts concerning this identification. These lines, in turn, have been mutilated *posteriori manu* by someone with little knowledge of Latin, to read *vidi, vanci, veni*, which of course is nonsense.

Although the facing wall is tolerably well rendered in the sketch, the contents of the wall subtending at 90° are virtually illegible. Notes by the artist, however, enable some sort of reconstruction to be made. The inscriptions DEANZ MEANZ FINEZ, and 'Matriculation makes you deaf' may be passed over, together with aphorisms wrongly attributed to various philosophers such as Jean-Paul Sinatre.

'Procrastinate now' may be left for another occasion, but 'Repatriate the Picts' is a curious coincidence, bearing in mind Murphy's enthusiasm for the Pictish cause. Equally curious, therefore, is the palimpsest 'A wise Pict knows his father' and 'Pictish nationalism is a ticklish issue' (to which is added variously and *not to be sneezed at* and *a tissue of lies*). Another significant coincidence is the signature (only barely visible in our plate) 'Oscar Fingal O'Fflahertie Wills Wilde', with its *addendum* 'Who [are] they?'. This, or these, occurs, or occur, just above a motto originally reading 'People before cars' (a reference to the abandoned proposition that Christ Church Meadow be despoiled by a by-pass), which a glossator has emended to 'leg before wicket'. At the other end of the wall there is an important inscription in a far older hand. Without wishing to anticipate such conclusions as may finally be reached by Professor Page, this hand seems very similar to Murphy's own, but if not, is very closely contemporary. It reads: *estne ⊏⊔ positio Hibernica ⊔⊏?* As noted in the previous chapter, the symbol ⊏ seems overwhelmingly likely to stand for the number 9 in Murphy's system of numeration, otherwise virtually undeciphered at present; the symbol ⊏ could hardly be 100, for this would be inconsistent with the duodecimal system (the equivalent of 100 x 100 would be 144 x 144 = 20736, equally inexplicable, if not grossly wrong). So the significance of this part of the source remains elusive for the present.

Returning to the astonishing epigraphic coincidence that unites Wilde with Murphy, a substantial amount of research is required in order to establish how Wilde came to quote so many of Murphy's aphorisms. One that comes to mind immediately is Murphy's 'the Gods bestowed on him the gift of perpetual old age' *à propos* Cadwallader, which was re-used by Wilde in describing Max Beerbohm. All that can be said at present is that there is a likelihood of a missing Murphy source, perhaps known to Sheridan or Goldsmith, that existed in Ireland at least until the time of Wilde and Shaw (all of these authors having drawn freely on Murphy's *mots justes*).

As to the main part of the wall, the legend above the light fitment, *Lumen ad revelationem genitalium*, is of course misspelt, again showing a woefully rudimentary knowledge of Latin. The last word should read *gentium*, the quotation being of course from St Luke, 'a light to lighten the gentiles', an attempt at jocularity. In worse taste are the inscriptions which run up the leftmost part of the wall. At the bottom, inscribed in what may loosely be termed bas-relief, there is 'If you can read this you are […]ing on your boot', above which is, in a different, somewhat stiff, hand, 'and the angle of the dangle must be 45°'; above this are the words (also *posteriori manu*, this time somewhat florid) 'What an acute observation', to which is superadded (another hand, somewhat formal) 'On the contrary, I find it obtuse; surely the angle of dangle…'[this is interrupted, in yet another hand, by:] 'Having read thus far, what you read first is no longer true.' Finally, uppermost of this group may be seen (in a fresh hand of a copper-plate character): 'I find this to be true throughout life'.

We must needs curtail our discussion of the Bodleian source and await the careful analysis that Professor Page has promised us. He is presently in America, tracking down some additional Murphy materials. His somewhat hasty departure was occasioned by some sort of difficulty at St Alfred's, concerning the revision of the College Statutes, which he referred to as "a blunder ranking with the publication of the Breeches, Vinegar and Wicked Bibles combined". [[Difficulty it was. The details have been furnished to the present editor by his friend Dunstan, until recently the Classics don at St Mary-the-Less who has unfortunately been suspended for "unwonted intimacy" with his pupils at St Mildred's. Although he protests that he was only checking that their clothing was entirely in conformity with the requirements for attending Schools in sub-fusc uniform, his meticulous examination of their underwear, making certain that it was entirely in black, except for the statutory white tie, was thought to be excessive. That he also gave each of them a garter embroidered with what he called "tricky hidden quantities" and the legend *fututio perfectum* was viewed particularly seriously by the unlettered Proctors who thought it to be a reference to the Latin Future Perfect tense, and therefore an illegal 'crib'. But one, as Professor Page would doubtless put it, divagates somewhat.

The St Alfred's Statutes were somewhat out of date in that scholars of the College were prevented from entering into marriage during their undergraduate years. All that was needed was a simple clause allowing scholars to be treated in the same way as commoners and graduates. But Professor Page, ever alert to the niceties of such things, pressed for the use of a more antique formula, beginning, "A Scholar on the Foundation of the College may, provided that three terms have elapsed since his first election …" Only when the new Statutes of the College had been printed and distributed was it apparent that the Press seemed to have employed a Japanese type-setter and that Professor Page had not read the proof-sheets with his usual care (before her untimely death, Queenie used to read proofs to him at the fireside, so that he could check them against the typescript, after which she would listen to him reading the typescript in order to check it against the proofs, so domestic bliss and scholarly accuracy were at one). The unfortunate error meant that such copies of the document as could be retrieved were pulped, and a revised reprint was hurriedly circulated.

This incident very nearly bankrupted the College (High Table dinner was immediately reduced to three courses, and other stringent economies had to be endured); Dunstan, on the other hand, became quite rich, for he had 'cornered the market' in the rejected First Edition, copies of which he then sold for vast sums of money. These transactions he described as a "cunning stunt" (a phrase erroneously and wholly anachronistically attributed to the late Warden Spooner of New College). As a result of this piece of 'wheeler-dealing', he has ceased to contest his suspension, and has moved to California with Helen Bedworthy, formerly of St Mildred's.]]

Until Professor Page returns from what we hope will emerge as a fruitful research visit to America, we have to rely on the Melissa letters for many of the events in Murphy's life recounted below. No hope of the Pope documents mentioned in the previous chapter can now be entertained, for the poet seems to have regarded the papers as particularly special, to the extent that he left them entailed to the then Lord Harcourt (Simon, who with Pope was at one time a prominent member of the Dashwood fraternity) and his descendants, with instructions that in the event of the line coming to an end, the papers should be incremated. The present (or rather the late) Lord Harcourt's solicitors acted at once and upon his death burned the MSS, there being no male heir. Although representations were made to them, they insisted that "with no title there is no title" to the papers, and it would in any event have been too late to save them.

It was a similar case when the executors of an old estate saw fit to burn a considerable quantity of books and manuscripts which, since they could not read or understand them, the heirs were unwilling to have pass into other hands. A local cobbler rescued some of the vellum from the blaze, seeing that it might be useful for cutting shoe patterns. The vicar of the parish heard of this and bought all that was left, including one of St Austin's treatises, cut out and marked in the shape of some rustic foot. These remnants, together with *incunabula* on Canon and Civil Law that were also rescued, he gave to the Bodleian Library in 1868. [[The vicar was none other than the Revd David Royce, Vicar of Nether Swell, the parish next to Nether Piddle, mentioned in part of the narrative presented in the previous chapter. There is no reason to suppose that any of the Murphy documents perished in this way. It is worthy of note that Carlyle's *History of the French Revolution* met a similar fate at the hands of the maid of Mrs Taylor, a friend of John Stuart Mill to whom Carlyle's MS had been lent. Mill's discomfiture over the consuming of the book was mitigated by his consummation of passion with Mrs Taylor when the pair later married.]]

So the last visit that Murphy is known to have made to Stanton Harcourt is recorded solely in the collection of letters to which we have referred. The visit, by Murphy and Melissa together, was of comparatively little consequence in itself. Pope read to Murphy some extracts from his *Essay on Man*, the only significance of which, for our purposes, was that Murphy parodied them in his *Essay on Woman*, of which more later. Whether or not he recited his parody to Pope on this occasion is not recorded. On leaving the village to go to London, the pair were set upon by ruffians, not twenty-five miles on their new journey. They had originally decided to go by coach, but although the activities of the Society for the Reformation of Manners had been lately curtailed, boats and coaches were still reluctant to ply their trade on a Sunday; so they rode instead. It was ironic, therefore [[hardly; the event conformed exactly to The Law]] that before they reached Tetsworth they heard the unmistakable sound of the bells of wagon horses fast approaching behind them. As convention demanded, they pulled off the London road, following an adjacent track. No sooner had they done so, than two footpads set upon them. Murphy, engaging both of them, bravely urged Melissa to escape; but she demurred. More insistently he said:

"Miss Blunt, I implore you to get away from this."

"Mr Sharpe," she replied, "have you not noticed …"

The rest was drowned out by Murphy's loud cries, as the two thugs started to take his clothing from him, while brandishing a particularly evil-looking knife. When she saw what they were about to do, Melissa took no account of her own safety, but cracked one of the thugs on the head with a stout branch she had found, belabouring the other with a whip she wielded with her other hand. The ruffians retreated, seemingly in the direction of Oxford.

"I'll do to him what he meant to do to you," said Melissa.

"Do what? To which one?"

"You weren't listening," she said, unfairly. "Those supposed robbers were speaking in Welsh. They are two disreputable servants from Jesus College, Dylan Davies and Walford Thomas, under Milkweed the Butler, through whose offices they were commissioned by my uncle. They were about to re-enact a scene from mediæval history, when Heloissa's uncle sent two men after Abaelardus to …"

"Jaysus!"

"Yes, they were from my uncle's college, as was the kitchen-knife."

"O Sweet Mercy! Stap m' vitals!"

"They would asssuredly have been stapped, My Dear, had those fiends done their worst! As for my dear uncle, I shall return the compliment to him. At the very least I shall have a ferret put down his breeches. That will circumscribe his activities. And it will pay him back, by the by, for what he said about you that night at Wycombe when he told me that 'our family is not so poor as to have to send you off to Ireland to seek a husband at a cheaper rate'. For this remark, I propose …[2] O, No! Here is another robber!"

---

[2] Whatever it was, it resulted in Jesus dispensing with Cadwallader's services, as seen on

This one was on horseback, masked and coming from the London direction. He slid down from his mount with a practised movement, the gleaming pistols in either hand never wavering.

"So," he said, "you are half dressed, Sir. Permit me to relieve you of the rest of your splendid vesture." In the end, he took only Murphy's dandified cloak and distinctive feather-topped hat, both of which he immediately put on, discarding his own serviceable, if rather dull, garments. He then robbed them of all their money, together with Melissa's jewels and Murphy's fob watch, and almost before they were aware of it, he had remounted and continued on his way with a sweeping bow to Melissa, saying:

"Dick Turpin bids you Good Day!"

"Dick Turpin!", breathed Melissa, entranced; and they both walked a little way along the track to see round the bend and catch another glimpse of the jaunty highwayman.

What they saw, however, was a sight for sore eyes. The two Welshmen had now set upon Turpin, whose dress led them to believe it was Murphy. The highwayman made short shrift of them, discharging both of his weapons at the same time, and aiming somewhat lower than the liver: they had no money on their now mutilated persons, so Turpin galloped on in the direction of Oxford, leaving them writhing.

"Poetic justice!", said Murphy.

"Yes," replied Melissa,

> "Tall Turpin turned the tables on such turpitude
> Preserving thus the playthings of Miss Plenitude
> And hunting down the hunters of My Dear
> He shot them, ball for ball, from front to rear."

Speaking of poetry, the reader may conclude from an earlier part of this narration that the two lately married lovers were travelling *incognito*. The letters include another poetic fragment that shows that Mr Sharpe and Miss Blunt were merely pet names [Professor Ker's suggestion that there might have been a connexion with Pope's Martha Blount is quite without foundation]. The surviving lines, full of poetic and musical allusion, are entitled *To Mr Sharpe from Miss Blunt*, and run as follows:

> [...] his pencil's sharp;
> His lead he dips along the line of love
> Though usage must unpoint the prick 'ere long
> He ploughs the easy furrow 'till he's blunt.
> At length, entwined in counterpointed song,
> Comes now his final cadence in her [... *deest*]

The incident came to an end when the two scoundrels had crawled to where Melissa and Murphy now stood. The latter were invisible to the felons, however, for Murphy had put on Melissa's brown-green cloak and was leaning against a tree and Melissa was some yards away, looking in her saddlebag for her spare cloak. So it was that the two mistook Murphy for a tree, and painfully relieved themselves before staggering on in the direction of Tetsworth. Far from being mortified by this experience, Murphy dined out on the story. It was doubtless by such means that the curious eccentric and appropriately named Dr Birch should have come upon the idea of disguising himself, while fishing, as a tree. This historian and collector of biographical facts, who died in 1766, collected no fish, however. After several years of autodendrophily and ridicule by his friends he gave up, and devoted himself to literature.

Murphy, on the other hand, devoted himself to Lady Vane, a notorious woman of pleasure (in January 1737, Lord Vane offered a £100 reward for the recovery of his wife, who at that time had newly eloped). Lady Mary Wortley Montagu wrote of her that "she does not pique herself on Fidelity to any one Man (which is but a narrow Way of thinking), but she boasts that she had always been true to her Nation and, notwithstanding foreign Attacks, has always reserved her Charms for the Use of her own Countrymen". Murphy was hardly one of her countrymen (on this point Lady Mary may have been purposefully misleading, for reasons that will emerge in due course); but he was aware of Lady Vane's reputation and so ensured that he was adequately distanced from the pox. On one occasion he engaged her first on a Waterman's barge on the Thames, where he "dipt his Machine in the Canal and performed most manfully, and then on Westminster Bridge, where, in Armour Complete, did he engage her on this noble Edifice, the Whim of the Thames rolling below amusing him very much". [[Dr Thrush would have been proud to know that at last Murphy had taken precautionary measures; but she would have been less thrilled that these were more against the possibility of disease than out of any other consideration, least of all for the woman.]]

Some of Lady Vane's exploits were printed in Smollett's *Peregrine Pickle*: as is common knowledge, she persuaded Smollett to include some *Memoirs of a Lady of Quality* in the later chapters of that already derivative book (though it is not so widely known that Murphy appears but thinly disguised both in the *Memoirs* and in the body of that so-called novel). Melissa, meanwhile, had gone off in search of Dick Turpin, for whom she had taken a great fancy. These events can therefore be dated with some confidence, between 1737 (the date of Lady Vane's elopement) and 1739, when Dick Turpin was caught and executed (the role of the enamoured Melissa in his downfall at York – where that Lady was at that time *incognita*, and eager to find if hanged felons displayed the priapism of which she had heard – has yet to be chronicled satisfactorily by historians).

The seventeen-forties were full of incident for Murphy. In 1740, when there was a serious outbreak of smallpox in Germany, there was renewed interest in inoculation against the disease in England. It had already been initiated in 1717, eventually leading to the curtailment of the incidence of the disease in These Islands. As noted in chapter 3, it was Lady Mary Wortley Montagu – a friend of Lord Dashwood, Lady Vane and more particularly, Murphy – who is credited with the smallpox discovery. It would be entirely within the canons of The Law, whose origins this book is devoted to elucidating, that it should have been Murphy's own discovery, which time has usurped as someone else's; and it is true that Lady Mary and Murphy were very close (both in age – there was but a year between them, and in that Lady Mary made determined efforts to seduce him away from Lady Vane, and indeed Melissa); but scholarship must rely on fact rather than instinct, documentation rather than theory, so, reluctantly, we must say that there is no evidence to support Murphy's cause in this matter [[In any case the chronology is against it, for in 1717, Murphy was at Trinity College.

Nevertheless, Murphy's discovery concerning the complexion of milkmaids, wrongly glossed in a previous chapter, led him to write an important communication to Melissa on the subject, of which only a few sentences survive. On the subject of Lady Vane, he said he knew how to protect "the likes of her from the *whores' pox*, by the natural *vacacillation* such as protects the Wycombe milkmaids from the attentions of Lord …" And there the most informative sentence halts abruptly. It is known that at one time the Royal Society had some Dashwood papers and books (one of which came into the hands of Faraday, as will be seen in the next chapter), so it seems more than likely that the infamous Jenner, who was to promulgate what he chose to call *vaccination* against smallpox some forty years after the Great Man's death, had access to Murphy's notes on the subject. The crude alteration of the terminology does little to disguise his expropriation, for a calligraphic misunderstanding misled the supposed discoverer into assuming that Murphy was referring to *horsepox*, a non-existent disease whose connexion with cowpox Jenner was forced to explain in the most circumstantial and, dare it be said, vacillatory manner in order to gloss over the improbable link between stable and dairy, or, as Murphy would have expressed it, "betwixt horsebox and cowpaps". As he did. But *à propos* another connexion, not this. The law may be flouted by such acts of piracy, but The Law is not blind to them.]]

For the important years of 1740 onwards we still have to rely principally on the letters, for there is scant documentary evidence otherwise. There can be no doubt that Swift's papers in America would shed much light on the question, if and when they become available to scholarship. The Huntington collection is entirely familiar to scholars, but several important and hitherto unnoticed papers are housed in the nearby Library at the State University of Santa Veronica (pop. 5,200, elev. 214). There is some difficulty in obtaining access to these papers, due to the intransigence of the librarian, Ms van Dyke. Professor Page, on sabbatical leave in California, kindly undertook to obtain photostatic copies of the documents, but the venture was frustrated by his unfamiliarity with certain Californian academic conventions. A party was given for incoming Faculty, at which Dunstan was also present. Professor Page had over-indulged somewhat: as a result, as the principle of 'positive discrimination' was being explained to him by Dunstan, Page loudly expostulated that he supposed this policy would result in a one-legged black lesbian illiterate being appointed as a Professor of English, whereupon Ms van Dyke, who holds the rank of Professor and is undeniably of darkish hue, kicked Professor Page illustratively in the groin. We say 'illustratively' to some purpose: the blow was made the more severe in that the limb which delivered it appears to have been a mechanical contrivance, and incapacitated Professor Page for several weeks.

As luck would have it, however, the University's policy of positive discrimination resulted in an unlikely ally in the comely shape of Mrs Gonzalez. A personable woman of considerable quality both academically (she graduated *summa cum laude* from Harvard in Classical Philology) and socially (coming from an old Virginia family), she was unable to secure even the most menial employment until after her marriage to the Conde Nasti y González (known as Paco, though his philoprogenitive father was known as Rápido González – and of course his mother was Doña Ferrentez, a Trojan matriarch of the same line as El Greco). When the Count was away tending his estates in Spain, she applied for, and instantly obtained, a position as library secretary at Auto Concepcion college, Santa Veronica. It seems that her surname was assumed to be of Mexican origin, and this, rather than her other qualifications (which she wisely suppressed) was her *entrée* to the University. She has written to us as follows:

Dear Professor O'Toole,

I think you have heard* from Professor Page in regard to the unfortunate mishap concerning Professor Virago van Dyke. He wrote her from the medical center, but I was not quick enough to intercept his letter to her. Although I had warned him of the necessity, he seems to have been unable to address her as Ms, beginning as follows (I quote): "One cannot bring oneself to address an animate object as a manuscript: if Miss or Mrs will not do, then one could compromise with the fuller form of Mistress, do you not think? The simpler solution would be Professor, since that is generally taken as epicene (though this is philologically doubtful) but I gather you do not use this title in such a context."

* [Professor Page wrote as follows:

Medical Center
(of course, they can't spell properly)
Santa Veronica University
(motto: *Jesus Wept*)
C a l i f o r n i a

Dear Gerald,

I have had another mishap, which I would be obliged should remain unrecorded in your monograph. I am very ill and cannot say anything more, being entirely constant in incontinence. My recovery may be expedited, however, by the charming lady who called upon me today, who says she will write you (by which she means write *to* you). Did you know that *verónica* means 'speedwell'? Strange, the quirks of language.

As ever,

Jack]

I guess it was inevitable that this would call forth the reply which I enclose [the letter is printed more or less as it stands]:

mister page you shit – ive gotten youre slimy limy letter you sent me about inanimut objects and mistresses and other shit about getting off on the rong foot wich I shall send to the race bored, the sex boar and the disabled bawds – your for it you shit and if you think you get anything about those crummy papers from me youve gottanother think coming you limy mother-[...] shit, and shit what you said at the party about me being iliterate shit ive a doctors in marxist feminist perspectives and a masters [[Mistress's?]] in wimins studys besides majoring in soshiologi and world litricher from saffo to german greir so shit yourself limy noall.

Virago van Dyke

and dont you try to set foot in this libery. V.D.

All of this has caused Professor Page to lose interest in the papers, though he strongly denies it: I have a suspicion that he feigns interest in order to have a little company – possibly more than that, since he seems to be very gallant and attentive. Anyway, he has suggested that I help you, which I will be pleased to do. I can transcribe any papers you wish, but xeroxing might prove difficult. Also, to avert suspicion of the Dyke (by name and nature), please address me as Ms Gonzalez. It would never do to be 'Mrs', let alone Countess. Oh, and although my name is Constance, (Professor Page calls me the Hon Con for some reason and quotes from Dean Swift about my being Constance in his inconstancy) I have adopted Concepcion here (my husband calls me *conejo* – which means little rabbit – but it doesn't seem suitable). Where was I? Oh yes, I shan't be here much longer, so it would be wise to write me at the American Embassy in Madrid – the people there will know how to contact me.

C.G.

Here it is my sad duty to record the passing, in California, of Professor Page, who has devoted much time, coupled with great scholarly acumen, to this project. During the course of this narrative, some allusions have been made to a certain propensity of his in regard to accidents: it was indeed this propensity that finally ushered in his demise. He had mastered the art of driving "on the wrong side of the road" as he dubbed it, but was still unfamiliar with certain American conventions. In Britain and Ireland, the simple sign 'No Entry' suffices; but in the U.S.A. the sign (invented, so some say, by a descendant of Murphy rebelling against the peremptory nature of its British equivalent) is something like 'Go back, you're going the WRONG WAY'. Professor Page was indeed going the wrong way; and in the opposite direction one heavy truck was overtaking another, at considerable speed; as a tragic result, a scholar, friend and gentleman is dead. Let his memorial be a share in the endeavour which I shall hope soon to complete.

[Additional note. The accident was occasioned, at least in part, as a consequence of discussions between Professor Page and some eminent Oxford scientists at St Catherine's College on the subject of residual vorticity, a subject apparently discussed in one or more of the lost Murphy Falklands papers. As a result of this, Page maintained that, although in the Southern hemisphere it was correct to drive on the right-hand side of the road, in the Northern hemisphere such a practice was injurious to the atmosphere and therefore not only to the weather but also, because of the ensuing negative ionisation, to the psychological well-being of those living north of the equator. We have been fortunate in obtaining the opinion of that indefatigable environmental campaigner Sir Percy Vere, who has explained that "the residual vorticity in question is set up, not by driving on the right *per se*, but by the circulation in an anticlockwise direction around traffic islands and the like". Thus, in common with the subject of this biography, Professor Page may well be said to have died for his beliefs.]

[[Additional additional note. The view expressed above, apparently sanctioned by Professor O'Toole, is wholly erroneous, according to Professor Rick O'Shea, now of the Ballsbridge Institute of Ballistics, Dublin. "It fails to take account of the Rossby waves, themselves an effect of the Coriolis forces acting on the planetary vorticity of the earth. In the Northern hemisphere the resultant high altitude westerly winds first follow a cyclonic path towards the pole, but as latitude increases, are deflected towards the equator, in turn to be deflected northwards again. Page's supposition that bathwater drains clockwise in the Northern hemisphere, anti-clockwise in the Southern and straight down at the Equator, is pure fantasy."]]

It transpires that Professor Page's *obiter dicta* were to have been the promised contribution on the subject of onomastics. He appears to have revived his interest in the subject, this having waned when his daughter became pregnant. [[It seems that Prudence Virginia Concepta Page was badly let down by her erstwhile lover, Justin Pediment, who left her as soon as he found her to be with child.]] Professor Page's notes, which are disarranged and fragmentary, allude to the fact that his late wife Regina's middle name was Iphegenia which "allowed one to save a considerable sum on the lettering of her gravestone". When, unhappily, Professor Page came to rest in

the same grave, the executors, both for the sake of symmetry and expense, kept to the same succinct style of lettering and employed the Latin form of his middle name for the middle initial. This can be seen in the sketch of the monument (by his son, Christopher Robin Aloysius Page – the reader will be amused that the Murphyesque Aloysius crops up again on these pages) reproduced here. Unfortunately, the depredations of vandals had not been removed at the time the drawing was made (though some of its shortcomings appear to be due to its being a kind of palimpsest).

Apart from the sentence alluded to above, the major part of Page's disquisition on the subject of onomastics ("or rather", as he says in the note, "its subdiscipline, acronymics") is concerned with incidents recorded in one of the Melissa letters, events which we have attempted to reconstruct in the following paragraphs.

Despite being married, Melissa and Murphy seemed to go their separate ways. Indeed, Melissa appears to have been the only female of his intimates who avoided becoming pregnant. Whether or not the wheel had turned nearly full circle and that she (in common with Murphy's 'father') was infertile, will never be known. What is known, however, is that Murphy had several dalliances with other women – such as the infamous Lady Vane, Lady Mary Wortley Montagu and several other eminent ladies of the time.

For her part, Melissa had a brief association with Dick Turpin, as we know, but dropped him [[it was the hangman that finally dropped him, though]] in favour of other pursuits, one of which was referred to as The Peacock. This was a Negro servant of Lord Montagu's, who had a reputation as a dandy and, for a consideration, as a ladies' man. Juno, as she styles herself in the letters (the reader will doubtless recall that she had a commanding physique) was not averse to tendering the necessary fee for his attentions, so the liaison became known as 'Juno and the Peacock'. [[Professor O'Toole did not trouble to explain the phonetic problems entailed in this and other passages, for the Irish pronunciation of some words as 'tea' still retains the phonological value heard in eighteenth-century English. 'Tea' was pronounced 'Tay', as in many parts of Ireland today; 'Peacock', likewise, must be rendered 'Paycock'. The present editor is uncertain as to whether Professor Page's lost notes on the subject had picked up this point, and its implications.]]

'Juno' had been told of the qualities of the servant at one of the many Wycombe gatherings which she and Murphy had attended. On this occasion they overheard a

Levantine, Dr Fulān el-Fulānī, telling a fascinated group of the company about life in a Harem. According to the learned doctor, there were two distinct categories of eunuchs, white and black, only the latter being admitted into the Harem itself.

"But I thought …", interrupted Murphy

"You thought correctly," rejoined el-Fulānī, "and it was for this very reason that although the whites were merely castrated, the blacks lose the entire organs of generation, and yet are still not on any account admitted to the inner sanctum of the Harem. Only the white eunuchs are the guardians of the Sultan's wives, attend upon their persons and are answerable for their conduct."

"That would seem dashed illogical," said one of the party, "for surely the white should be exchanged for the black."

"And the other way about," added Murphy.

"Formerly, they say," answered the Levantine, "the Harem was served by white eunuchs or by castrated Negroes, but, upon an unlucky day a certain Sultan (I think it was Amrat III), walking in a park belonging to one of his country Seraglios, happened to observe a gelding which vigorously mounted a mare and seemed in some sort to perform the function of a stallion. The Sultan was struck at this novelty and, immediately reflecting how far analogy might probably extend, ('The pathetic phallacy,' muttered Murphy) he thought himself how very unsafe his ladies were with their present guards, which latter might partake of the forbidden fruit of the Sultana, in particular. In haste to ensure the chastity of his wives, he instantly returned home and amputation ensued through the whole Seraglio."

"Oo!" said Juno [Melissa].

"A detestable practice!" said another.

"Not so detestable as other Turkish practices which a Christian could neither contemplate nor mention," said yet another, "the which, as the inscription on the goddess' rump over there warns us, leads to perdition".

"Indeed. It is an odious circumstance which, though a stain to my narrative, candour will not suffer me to conceal. As has been confirmed to me by Mahmood Mamaki, Interpreter of Oriental Lays to the King of England, there is too much reason to believe that the Turks are greatly addicted to that detestable vice which nature starts at and which, if there were not too certain proof that such crimes have been perpetrated, no innocent man could suppose possible …"

"What crimes?" said Juno, in an undertone.

"Sodomy," whispered Murphy.

"Oo!" she repeated.

Murphy's Law

"I found," said Lady Mary, "that the Turkish ladies I saw in the steambaths were generally fatter than English men would generally find attractive."

She looked pointedly at 'Juno' and then at Murphy, who rapidly changed the subject saying:

"And what of your Negro servant, Lady Mary, is he an eunuch?"

"By no means," she answered, looking upward at the statue of Priapus in a decidedly excited state, "His evidence of manhood, when I have on occasion glimpsed him bathing, is considerable."

Juno was immediately captivated by this description, as Lady Mary had intended her to be (for Lady Mary's stall was still set out for Murphy). So the two women retired for deeper conversation, leaning against the statue of Priapus [of which more in due course, when Professor Page's notes pertaining to the inscriptions on these monuments will be set forth, when they are released by his son, Christopher Robyn (as he now irritatingly respells it, likewise with Alois, for some unaccountable reason) Page. "It is not a question of *releasing*," says the latter in what looks like a typical Page footnote, "I need to be assured that my father's idiosyncrasies are not ridiculed in your book. You shall not sully the Page name in your pages in any way whatever. C.R.A.P."].

Murphy, meanwhile, found himself talking to el-Fulānī and a fascinatingly ugly young man [Melissa's words – the man in question was Wilkes]. For some unaccountable reason, the subject had changed from black and white men to black and white birds, and there was a discussion as to the true identity of the penguin (at that time the term was erroneously applied to the Great Auk [as still the French persist with their *pinguoin*]) and the etymology of the word, which none of the company could guess [[and neither can the Oxford English Dictionary]], apart from Lloyd, who facetiously said that it probably came from the Welsh for his fellow poet, Paul ('The Aged') Whitehead, for 'white head' would be *pen gwyn* in that language [[and may well be the true etymology, though the Welsh bow may have been drawn at a venture]]. The learned Doctor el-Fulānī said that the penguin was a rather ludicrous bird and that is why its Arabic name was *Butrīq*. He had to explain himself further, which was unfortunate, for he was unaware of Murphy's race.

"*Butrīq*," he said, "is merely the Arabic form of Patrick, serving for any Irishman, the Penguin and the Irish sharing the same endearingly comic characteristics."

The blow, delivered almost instantly by Murphy, missed the Levantine, who had chanced to turn aside. Instead, its full force was felt by Wilkes, who staggered backwards in the direction of Lady Mary and Melissa. He came to a jolting stop at the Statue of the god of Lust at which, in order to regain his balance, he took hold of a convenient protuberance on the statue. This immediately broke off, however,

121

causing much merriment from those who had heard the previous tale of amputation in the Harem.

Wilkes, with high good humour despite the unwarranted blow, said:

"Past tense, or rather imperfect tense, I think."

[This was a reference to the inscription on the statue which read, *Peni tento, non penitenti*, which must be translated as '*une bite tendue, sans pénitence*' that is, a 'p*n*s tense, not penitence'.] As a result of this incident, the statue, restored to its former glory (the flaming reed held by the Priapic figure was hardly damaged) was later moved to Medmenham Abbey, where it was placed in an outside setting, indeed, one appropriate to the garden-god. The statue of Venus was also removed to the Abbey garden at the same time, for similar reasons of safety.

This female statue was a handsome representation of the goddess of Love, bending over to pull a thorn from her foot. In doing so, she exposed the full beauty of her cheeks to the viewer, on which callipygian expanse was written, beginning in the centre, then running to the right of her generous flanks (what Wilkes described as "two nether hills of snow") the words of Virgil,

> hic locus est, partis ubi se via findit in ambas

referring to that place where Aeneas was shown the parting of the ways. On the one hand, under the walls of Dis, Elysium beckoned

> … Ditis magni sub moenia tendit
> hac iter Elysium nobis

But, as the forward path (rightward in regard to the inscription) was bliss, the other, *a posteriori*[3] the rearward, was perdition, sending the offender to merciless Tartarus

> … at laeva malorum
> exercet poenas, et ad impia Tartara mittit.

In its new location at the Abbey, the Virgilian warning was countered by a French motto on the door nearby, for Rabelais' words 'Fay ce que voudras', by enjoining the hedonist to do as he will, are in flat contradiction to the Latin injunction.] [[Professor Page, silent on this matter, neverthless pointed out that Rabelais was none other than Swift's Alcofribas Nasier, and rightly observed that 'Mahmood Mamaki, Interpreter of Oriental Lays to the King of England' was one of Voltaire's pseudonymns. Page's notes on the inscriptions on the statuary and walls were voluminous but somewhat coy in their avoidance of their true subjects. The diatribe on the onomastics of the *Buṭrīq* incident, though possibly more incisive, is regrettably illegible. Rabelais' motto is still to be seen on the lintel of the door at the Abbey, though the stonework is

---

[3] Or perhaps *a tergo.*

crumbling and the letters will not long survive. The statues vanished many years ago.]]

Wilkes' overwhelming ugliness seemed to be no hindrance to his conquests which, though not approaching in number those of Murphy himself, were more numerous than Giacomo Casanova's. When in England, the Chevalier Casanova paid £100 (a generous consideration in those days) for the pleasure of relieving the remarkably pretty Marianne Charpion of her virginity. Having pocketed the money, the eighteen-year-old reneged on the deal. Not long afterward, she surrendered her maidenhead to Murphy. There is a full record of this event in our source: it will suffice to document that when he asked her if she were a virgin, she replied "Not yet". When Miss Charpion was twenty-eight, she took up with Wilkes, who kept her for three years until the arrangement ended in a quarrel.

Wilkes is supposed to have written much scurrilous verse, including the parody of Dryden's 'Creator Spirit, by whose aid' which was chanted by the 'Nuns' to the tune of *Veni creator*[4] at various mock-monkish rites enacted at Wycombe and later at Medmenham Abbey. The first stanza of this, 'The Maid's Prayer', runs:

Creator Pego, by whose aid,
Thy humble suppliant was made;
O Source of Bliss and God of Love,
Shed thy influence from above;
Come, and thy sacred Unction bring
To sanctify me while I sing.

The 'Monks' sang their own 'Universal Prayer', beginning:

Mother of all, in every age
In ev'ry Clime adored

---

[4] This information, given to Professor O'Toole by Fr Innocent Bliss, is quite wrong. The metre and that of its supposed tune are very different. The hymn was in fact sung to an air from *The Beggar's Opera,* "O Polly you might have toy'd and kist, By keeping them off, you keep them on". Though of a slightly different form, this is substantially the same tune as that now known as 'Golden Slumbers'. There can be little doubt that Murphy wrote all, or most, of 'Creator Pego', for the stanzas beginning

From loathed Hymen set me free
Enter a Temple worthy thee

are found in one of the early Melissa letters, dating from long before Wilkes became a member of the Society of St Francis. These lines won the approbation of Pitt when he first heard them from Wilkes, who later published them. It is likely that the reason for Pitt's turning against Wilkes was that he had learned that the latter was a plagiarist rather than a mere padorist. Whatever the truth of this, in the printed version the last three stanzas have fewer lines, so these were clearly by Murphy, even if the first two had been composed, or adapted, by Wilkes.

By Saint, by Savage, and by Sage
If modest, or if whor'd…[5]

Another rite celebrated at the Hell Fire Club was based on the amusing antics of Sir Francis in Rome, where the 'Chevalier Ashewd' (as Charles de Brosse rendered the name in his memoir of Dashwood) had dressed up as Cardinal Ottoboni in a mock conclave of Cardinals, intoning prayers that were not to be found in the service-books. These prayers were rewritten as part of the flagellation liturgy that commemorated Dashwood's adventure in the Sistine Chapel. On Good Friday, each member of the congregation took a small scourge on entry, and as the candles were extinguished, severally took off their clothing, garment by garment, as the light dimmed; finally, in the dark, they scourged themselves, accompanied with theatrical groans and wailings. This Dashwood viewed as pure stage effect and, fortified by a good quantity of wine, entered the Chapel in a large watchman's coat and "demurely took his scourge from the priest and advanced to the end of the Chapel", in the words of Horace Walpole, who witnessed the affair. When the lights had been extinguished "he drew from beneath his coat an English horsewhip and flogged right and left quite down the chapel and made his escape, the congregation exclaiming *Il diavolo! Il diavolo!* and thinking the evil one was upon them with a vengeance. The consequences of this frolic might have been serious to him, had he not immediately fled the Papal dominions."

The flagellation was re-enacted in a slightly different form by the Friars of St Francis at Wycombe: it is better to gloss over the details. The 'monks' were clothed in watermen's outfits: these, rather than the watchman's costume worn by Dashwood at the Sistine Chapel, were chosen on account of the aquatic activities that usually followed the liturgical doings of the Friars. The ladies were clothed only in Nuns' smocks (a reference to *The Nun in her Smock*, a licentious work translated from the French, published in 1724 by Edmond Curll, one of the authors vilified by Pope in *The Dunciad*). Of the liturgy itself, it is sufficient to say that it was the fleshiest parts of the ladies' unsmocked anatomy that were scourged. This part of the ceremony was followed by the injunction 'sursum pego' intoned by the celebrant, to which the response (by the 'monks' only) was 'habemus ad cunnum'; in turn, the celebrant's 'gratias agamus domino pego nostro' was answered (this time by the 'nuns' alone) 'dignum et justum est'.

Any participant that forgot his lines through having taken too much pre-communion wine could study the inscriptions on the walls of the chapel which acted as prompts, and were, as one observer of these "old monkish rhymes" described them, "as

---

[5] Also by Murphy, though the evidence for this cannot be printed here, nor can 'The Dying Lover to his Pr*ck', both of which were later also circulated under Wilkes' name. The melody used at Wycombe is unknown, but the verses were doubtless sung to a 'Poulter's measure' hymn tune. The present editor regrets that The Printer has again requested that the footnotes be curtailed.

obscene and indelicate as can well be conceived even by an impure imagination, so it is as well for chaste eyes and ears that they are in the Latin tongue". In truth, however, it was more likely a lady who should forget her lines, for the men tended to drink with caution until the *Postcommunio*, on account of the possibility of what was termed *languidulus monachi*. It is said that "the particular flower that adorned the gardens at Wycombe, Monksdroop (not to be confused with *Aconitum*, Monks*hood*, which was called Monks*helmet* at Wycombe), was named after this condition on account of its languidly pensile [sic] fronds". For this information we are indebted to Mr Basil Leefe, horticulturalist, gourmand and member of the Dilettante Society, a sister body to the Friars, also originating in the eighteenth century, of which Dashwood and his cronies were members in common. Mr Leefe's wife Lettice, also a distinguished botanist and herbalist, points out that "another favoured plant at Wycombe was *Clitoria Master Batesia*, [surely this should be *Doctor Batesia*, for Bates was Dashwood's physician, but no matter] though only *C. ternatea* is listed by the RHS. As with the genus in general, it is rather tender, and not much seen". We are indebted to this lady for her full exposition.

Returning to the matter in hand, it is hard to credit that Dashwood, author of much of this impious liturgy, should have been the compiler of an abridged Book of Common Prayer. It is indeed a supreme irony that another member of the Hell Fire fraternity should have collaborated with Dashwood in this project, the results of their labour later becoming accepted as the American prayerbook. (Although Franklin became a Monk of Medmenham only after Murphy's death, through intermediaries he was nevertheless able to steal the currency of many ideas from the subject of our biography and palm these off as his own.)

On one notorious occasion, the celebration had barely reached its climax (and Murphy was *in limine*) when spies were discovered. Chaos ensued ("a beresk state of chassis", to use Murphy's own words, as reported by Melissa), and the pair were obliged to avoid discovery by the rather cowardly method of running away (or, as expressed by Melissa, "we won't wait to see which side our bread is buttered"). To which Murphy replied:

> How right you are, my dear gazelle
> To fetch us up to hide
> For those who come to know us well
> Cannot alway confide
> For never was there piece of toast
> However long or wide
> But fell upon the sandy floor
> And on the buttered side

The way the final quatrain was adapted and put about as original by the nineteenth-century James Payn (though this was at least called 'Parody' when published in *Chambers' Journal*) will not strike the reader as remarkable by now; nor yet that the lines, especially the first few, were lifted and worked upon by Tom Hood the Younger in the same century, in his *Muddled Metaphors*. Muddled indeed.

It was on the same occasion that the young Wilkes failed to escape from the spies, partly because he had been too entranced by Melissa's conversation and partly because he failed to heed Dashwood's warning that the Fraternity had been discovered, and the celebrants must flee. Somewhat unfairly, he blamed Dashwood for his disgrace as a result of this incident (though his ultimate downfall was brought about by the publication of a poem entirely composed by Murphy, as related in a subsequent chapter) and nursed a grudge against His Lordship for the rest of his life. He also nursed an admiration for Melissa, this being the chief reason for his continued attendance at Wycombe despite subsequent antipathy towards Dashwood. Melissa's letters record that he tried to seduce her after the occasion when the statue of Priapus met its unfortunate accident. "He winked at me, most horribly – you know what his eyes are like – but it wasn't so much the wink, than the look in his other eye." Unwisely, Wilkes compared himself with the statue, to which Melissa replied "then you are but a broken Man, possess'd merely of Stones like enormous Stertian Berries, which are not Charm enough".

The slight obscurity of this passage has been clarified by Dr Leefe, who has pointed out that "*stertian berries* are what we would call nasturtium seeds, whose wrinkled shape might well be held, by someone vulgar, to resemble the organs of procreation in question. I prefer, by the way, to be called Dr Leefe because I dislike the full form of my name, Laetitia, also its hypocoristic form Lettice, and even more do I dislike Titty, that my schoolfriends unfairly called me, to which I flatly refused to answer." We are obliged for this intelligence [Professor Page would doubtless have kept us abreast of the etymology of 'Lettuce', issuing, as it does, from the Latin *lactuce*].

Despite these setbacks in the quest for source material alluded to earlier, we are able to trace Murphy's movements in 1742, for he was in Dublin, his past misdemeanours apparently having been forgiven, to take part in the celebrations when the 'College of the Holy and Undivided Trinity near Dublin' became the University of Dublin. In April he also witnessed the first performance of Handel's *Messiah*, which he condemned roundly, as follows:

> I fail to see why I was persuaded to pay half a Guinea, and even a British Sixpence on the Book, to witness this Joy to great Chaos. The wretched Work was postponed many Times, for good Reason. Though it gained Applause from the Irish Publick, it will not catch on with a more discerning Audience. The German Tongue is so far removed from the English, and it's *Genius* so contrary, that Herr Hændel (or *Mister Handel* as he now styles himself) is quite unable to understand that the Word 'surely' has but two real Sillables which he risibly sets as three. The Phrase 'He shall feed his Flock' is set with the Accent on *Shall*, making the Pastoral Theme sound more akin to a Prussian Battle Order, and the Word *Chastisement* is set as though accented on

the second, rather than the first Sillable, which is a gross Distortion of the English Tongue. I allow the Subject of *Messiah* to drop by it's own portentous Weight.

On the above passage (recovered from fragments in our own collection, to be documented more fully below) we are fortunate to have no fewer than two commentators. Dr Root (a colleague of the late Professor Page) reminds us that the phrase "allow the subject … to drop by its own portentous weight" was quoted by G. B. Shaw in an unfavourable review of Dvořák's *Requiem* when performed in Birmingham. He further points out that the trisyllabic "surely" in "Surely he hath borne our griefs" was later modified by Handel together with other corrections, and that the setting of "He *shall* feed" was changed in various ways by later editors, and performers would often take matters into their own hands by prolonging the note to 'he' over the bar-line, with even more disastrous results. "I recall," he says, "the rendition by the famous Contralto Frau Büsten-Halter which made this passage tolerably realistic in that it vaguely characterised the bleating of stray sheep, but in truth it must be said that the noise of her hee-haw delivery more nearly resembled the braying of a deranged donkey. Murphy was right on most of these matters of accentuation, at least, but not about 'chastisement', of course. Is this a reference to some Hibernian pronunciation?"

Dr Footling (of whom more in a moment) disabuses Dr Root of the latter, and farcical, notion. "Murphy, if it was he, would be correct in pointing to a gross misaccentuation. 'Chastisement' is correctly a proparoxytone. It seems likely (Miss Stake, a pupil of mine, is undertaking a study of this and allied questions for an advanced degree) that the popularity of Handel's *Messiah* and its uncorrected blunder actually influenced the language: due to the rarity of the word, heard virtually in this context alone, the wrong pronunciation prevailed, like 'formidable', once heard coming only from the lips of ignorant newsreaders. Other examples adduced by my pupil are 'Dayity' for 'Deity', a mispronunciation popularised by a late organist of King's of my former University [Dr Boris Woodcock] as Dr Root informs us."

The rest of this note must needs be curtailed, although Dr Footling insists that "the spelling *it's* in this and the following extract cannot possibly be a correct transcription, or if so, rules the document as unauthentic".

We need point only to Gilbert White in *The Natural History of Selbourne*, where this use of the apostrophe is found copiously. Take letter XXV of August 30, 1769:

> I knew a gentleman who kept a tame snake, which was in it's person as sweet as any animal while in good humour and unalarmed; but as soon as a stranger, or a dog or cat, came in, it fell to hissing and filled the room with such nauseous *effluvia* as rendered it hardly supportable.

Dr Footling is the successor at St Alfred's to the late and lamented Professor Page. Due to the financial difficulties of the university and in that college, now known as the Home of Lost Courses, Page's post has been 'frozen'. Dr Quibble was to have succeeded him (as Quibble put it, "to the Professorship held, albeit with a feeble and accident-prone grasp, by the mutilated Page", a comment entirely worthy of the odious Quibble) but Nemesis was to overtake him at the annual festivities at his Cambridge College, St Vitus's. Hitherto, St Vitus's Ball had been held without mishap, but some malfunctioning of the reproducing apparatus used by the 'disc-jockey' caused this functionary to ride his recordings at a faster pace than intended, and the canter developed into a headlong galop. Quibble, dancing like a demented Dervish with Miss Happ, eventually fell to the ground in a state of exhaustion which she colourfully described as "knackered". Quibble quivered quaggily, after which his querimonious condition qualmishly deteriorated quite quickly, to the extent that the quadrumane quat and quondam textual critic found his quietus, called at last to the Higher Criticism.

The appalling possibility of Quibble tripping in Professor Page's footsteps was thus averted by Fate [[or rather, The Law]], and a junior colleague from the same Cambridge College was appointed in his stead. Until the Professorship is 'unfrozen', Dr Marc Antony Everest Footling will rejoice in the title Professor Elect [[the misprint in the *University Gazette* was corrected before it raised its ugly head publicly, by an assiduras poof-reader: the supposed Japanese typesetter turned out to be a disgruntled would-be author who had also been discovered sabotaging the examination papers of the Final Honours School of Theology, where a reference to the publication *Künstliche Hymnen* should have appeared.]] We are grateful for Dr Footling's interest, sometimes misguided, in the subject of this monograph, to whom we turn again.

By August, 1742, Swift was very ill, and Murphy visited him frequently, partly out of natural solicitude, and partly because he still hoped for progress in the matter of hair colour. On one occasion, he was present when Handel came to see the Dean. Despite Swift's part in the promotion of *The Beggars' Opera*, Handel seems not to have borne any grudge, and for his part Swift seems to have taken back his ill-formed judgement that Handel was "a fiddler and consequently a rogue". [[As Dr Footling correctly states, however, this remark was nothing to do with Handel. Furthermore, he adds, the idea bandied about that Murphy was the model for Gay's MacHeath (with Melissa and Lady Mary as the rivals for his hand) is hopelessly out of tune with the known facts, let alone the chronology.]] The meeting between Swift and Handel has been recorded as follows:

> Swift fell into a deep Melancholy, and knew no Body; I was told that the last sensible Words he uttered were on this Occasion: Mr *Handel*, when about to quit *Ireland* went to take his leave of him: The Servant was a considerable Time, e'er he could make the Dean understand him; which, when he did he cry'd, "Oh! a *German*, and a Genius! A Prodigy! Admit him." The Servant did do, just to let Mr *Handel* behold the Ruins of the greatest Wit that ever lived along the Tide of Time, where All at length are lost.

In the following year [1743], Murphy attended a performance of *Messiah* in London, out of curiosity. "I was amaz'd," he wrote, "that the Londoners were as impressionable and uncritical of the Work as the Irish. If you will only take the Precaution to go in long after it commences and to come out long before it is over, you will not find it wearisome. The King, having heard Three Parts of it, had too late formed the same Opinion, and determined to leave during one of the more clangorous and repetitive Choruses. Unfortunately, as he rose to leave, that Band of his loyal Subjects which formed the Audience took this for Approbation and also came to it's Feet, effectively barring his Route of Departure, much to His Majestie's Annoyance."

Again, Dr Root draws attention to the surprising resemblance between part of this passage and a criticism by George Bernard Shaw (this time of Gounod's *Redemption*). This, he feels, is evidence that Shaw must have had access to Murphy papers, possibly those earlier seen by Wilde. Dr Root also confirms that this tradition of standing for the 'Halleluia Chorus' does indeed date from this incident, though he informs us that Murphy's explanation was not quite correct. The King's attempt to leave was occasioned by bodily needs: "this much," says Dr Root, "is evinced by a note of a personal nature to the King's dressmaker, now lost, but which was transcribed, along with other important source materials, in a pamphlet published in 1948. The same pamphlet also records *inter alia* the documentary evidence bearing on Murphy's part in the *Fireworks Music* fiasco."

Dr Footling (in addition to a reiterated obloquy on the spelling *it's*) gives *Halleluia* as another instance of a mispronunciation perpetuated by composers, and quotes a story about a rehearsal where the choirboys at St Alfred's, Oxford, were mangling the word *Alleluia* even further by adding extraneous notes to the penultimate syllable. "Boys", enjoined Dr Thorne, Master of the Quiresters, "do not sit on the *loo*."

We shall take the incident of the *Fireworks Music* out of chronological order, so that the references to Handel and his noisome art might be finished with. It is well known that the peace of Aix-la-Chapelle was celebrated in 1749 and that Handel, seeking to repair relations with the King (whom he had slighted earlier when the latter was Elector of Hanover) provided a score for wind band to accompany the fireworks display. Despite the fireworks being set off by mistake, and the whole event having to be abandoned, Handel seems to have been restored to favour. The hand of Murphy may be discerned clearly in this event, though his exact role has not been established with certaintly. Documents show that he met Handel in Oxford at the opening of the Holywell Music Room in the previous year. Despite his lack of regard for Handel, he seems to have made some overtures (if this is the right word) in regard to the forthcoming peace celebrations.

Dr Root tells us that the same documents (preserved in the pamphlet of 1948 alluded to earlier) indicate that Murphy may well have been part of a Jacobite sabotage unit called the Scottish Highland Instruments of Terror, and that the *fracas* was deliberate, having the added benefit for Murphy of discrediting Handel and blowing up Henry Fielding (who that year published *Tom Jones*, many of whose escapades were lifted bodily from Murphy's life, as was noted in a previous chapter) and Tobias Smollett (who the year before had published *Roderick Random*, also, as we know, bearing heavily on Murphy and his adventures). The plot failed, as we have seen. Handel was restored to Royal favour, and there is no evidence that Fielding or Smollett received the slightest injury.

Indeed, there is no evidence of anything. As Thomas Fuller, in *The Holy State and the Profane State* (1642) rightly said, "Learning hath gained most by those books which the printers have lost". The pamphlet published in 1948 to which Dr Root alludes, and which clearly contained valuable Murphiana, is now untraceable. The only known copy was last seen in the British Museum [[now Library]], but repeated requests for it have called forth the statement that it perished, along with other documents and books, during enemy action during the war. Miss Slay, Senior Curator at the Department of Displaced Books at the Museum [[Library]], has categorically stated that the long-term effects of bomb blast were responsible for the destruction of much of this part of the holdings.

The involvement of Murphy in the Jacobite cause is authoritatively substantiated in documents which we shall present in the Appendix (we fear that the projected companion volume of documents has been precluded by various circumstances). In the seventeen-forties, Murphy had become obsessed with Celtic matters. In 1744 he went to Brittany to observe the stone circles there (this incident is chronicled by Tommy Lipps, the MacHinery Professor of Engineering at Aberdour Uinversity, in his book entitled *The Temple of Tarmac*). He then visited Wales, going about under the name Iolo Morganwg in a white sheet (the same in which he had been paraded through the streets of Oxford, upon the orders of the Bawdy Court), in a vain attempt to revive the Druidic order.

In October 1745 he returned briefly to Ireland for Swift's funeral, but as soon as was decent, he left for Cornwall to record the Cornish language, having heard that this ancient tongue was still extant in one locality. He arrived in Cornwall on the day of another funeral, being that of the last known speaker of Cornish. [[Not so; Dolly Pentreath, who died in 1777, was the last native speaker of Cornish. The Manks tongue, the present editor is happy to remind the reader, survived in oral transmission until the nineteenth century.]]

During the earlier part of that year he appears to have been involved in fifth-column work for the Jacobite cause. In January he was in Scotland, advising the Scots that any battle would easily be won against the Hanoverian upstarts, for the whole nation was disaffected by them and their taxes (Smollett's remark about the Prince being "cajoled by the sanguine misrepresentations of a few adventurers, who hoped to profit by the expedition" is pure malice toward Murphy, whose motives were entirely honorable and without guile. Moreover, the Duke of Cumberland's troop was already proven to be wholly ineffectual, for it could not even read a map, being unable to tell the difference between Scotland and Wales). [The army marched towards Wales in error, before turning back towards Lichfield, but the mistake was unfortunately rectified; after this fracas the Duke's army became unaccountably more soldierly; but this was hardly Murphy's fault – if fault it can be called, being merely the working of The Law that bears his name.]

By mid-March of the year 1745 the Scots were preparing for the forthcoming skirmish, armed with Murphy's ideas for tactics: on March 23rd he was dispatched south to gain further information about English dispositions, arriving in Carlisle on March 24th, 1744. In April, he followed Cumberland's army to Culloden, and in the ensuing *melée* was lucky to escape both from the English and the Scots. It is said that he tried to disguise himself as a Scotswoman but was pursued by the English (whether they imagined him to be a kilted Scotsman or a nubile Scotswoman is not recorded); he evaded them and changed to trousers only to be pursued by the unfortunate kinswomen of the Scots soldiers (here, the garments saved him from mutilation). He fled South, and never returned to Scotland.

Our reader may ponder one or two apparent chronological discrepancies, in that Murphy's first journey South was unusually rapid, starting in 1745 and ending in 1744. The explanation… [[which would have been forthcoming from Professor O'Toole – whose death intervened before he was able to complete this note – is a simple one. The Scots had adopted January 1st as the beginning of the legal year in 1600: in England, however, the year began on March 25th. Hence the apparent discrepancy which was not rectified until the passing of the Calendar (New Style) Act in 1750. The consequent adjustments enacted in 1752 are also significant, as will be evident in the following chapter. The ability to travel between one time dimension and another led Murphy to his theory of Relativity, to which reference is made below.]] The present editor must now relinquish the [[double]] and indeed most of his single [square] brackets and record the untimely death of Professor O'Toole.

Gerald O'Toole met his tragic death accidentally during celebrations in connexion with the re-opening of the Irish canal system. As the reader will be aware, the first English canal was opened in 1757, but soon after, Isambard Kingdom Murphy was at work on a system in Ireland. It is true that the 'navigators' (as the excavators were then called) moving in an easterly direction bypassed those proceeding towards them from the west, but despite the scoffing of commentators who have recorded these events, this was a mischance repeated by the French engineers at the construction of the Panama canal.[6] One result of this incident was that the word 'navigators'

---

[6] De Lesseps and Eiffel began work in 1881, but this and other disasters bankrupted the Panama Canal Company by 1889, the year of the completion of the Parisian folly that bears Eiffel's name (though he cribbed the design from an underling). The distraction of this calamitous essay into ironmongery must have cost him the necessary concentration which

was henceforward replaced by 'navvies', in order that possible confusion as to their abilities might be lessened. No such problems overtook the canal of 1840 in West Ireland, between the loughs of Corrib and Mask. All went well with this venture, and the stroke of genius was that the waterway was to be supplied by one of the loughs. When the sluice gates were opened for the first time, although the lake drained into the canal as planned, the bed of the latter was unfortunately found to be porous limestone. This minor defect was corrected by the tenacious engineer, and a second supply lake was selected. Only when the workmen cutting the channel towards the canal from this second lake found themselves digging uphill, was the project eventually considered to be unworkable and abandoned.

Finally, another attempt was successful, and it was this whose centenary was to be marked by the celebrations: several period features were to re-enacted; for example, progress down the canal was to be effected in the unsinkable boat invented in 1765, to which some modifications had been made since the original version unfortunately sank on its maiden voyage (not unlike the new bus service from Shannon Airport in 1982, inaugurated by the Mayor of Limerick, which took three replacement buses to get him out of the Car Park). The modifications were not sufficient, however, and the replica, like its parent, sank without trace. The rising of the water might have been noticed had it not been for Professor O'Toole's somewhat lengthy and soporific speech. The result of his eloquence was that all hands perished, from the neck down.

It remains a matter of conjecture as to whether important documents were on his person at the time. If so, they were never found. To compound the uncertainty, the documentation to which O'Toole constantly referred has almost all vanished. In his house there remained a large quantity of finely shredded paper, the result of the depredations of Diamond, a pet hamster belonging to O'Toole's daughter. (The reader will not need to be reminded that Diamond was also the name of Newton's dog, which anticipated the hamster's doings in that it – the dog – ate the whole script of Newton's *Principia* before it had been delivered to the press. On discovering that he would have to write the book anew, the scientist is said to have uttered the wondrously – if not doubtfully – restrained "Diamond, O Diamond!"). Forensic scientists from Trinity College, Dublin, have established that some of the shreds were from old-fashioned photostatic paper: it is overwhelmingly likely, in the opinion of the present editor, that they were copies of the 'concreted' books in Trinity Library. Of these and the other fragments, some of which have been dated by C_{14} and other methods to the early eighteenth century, we shall never know for certain what they contained.

---

the more important project required. In accordance with The Law, this act of *hubris* gave the Americans the opportunity to change the course of history, for in 1901 they had engineered (to use the term loosely) a licence to construct the canal, whose building they recommenced in 1904, the consequences of which are obvious to any historian (and might even have been dimly perceptible to Dr Quibble).

Some of the Melissa letters survived, however, and these show that she and Murphy, despite the attractions of the Peacock and the entreaties of Lady Mary, kept up their affection for each other. One of the letters contains the record of a conversation that is a sequel to one of the Hell Fire Club incidents recorded earlier.

"By the way," said Melissa, "you never told me why you took such a dislike to el-Fulānī. Was it because of his Turkish Practices?"

"No, my Lemon Balm;[7] not at all, at all."

"I am glad of that, in view of our own ... [deesʃ]"

"Exactly. Nor was it entirely because he made that remark about the Penguin being as ludicrous as the Irish."

"What, then, was the reason?"

"That he insulted a Welch friend of mine, implying that he and his compatriots were wont to have congress with sheep."

"What's wrong with that? I mean, it's well enough known that such disgraceful things do happen."

"It was the hypocrisy of it all. Not only did he refer to my friend Owen as Wälsch, which is a German insult meaning 'peasant' [Professor Page would doubtless have protested on this point], but he knew enough of the practice to betray himself."

"How?"

"Because when I pointed out to him the uncouth way he pronounced Owen's name as oen (this being the Welch for 'sheep') he said that 'you think I know bloody nothing about how to speak your language, but I tell you I know about sod oil in this matter'."

"Was not this merely another Levantine mispronunciation, this time of *sod all*?"

"Assuredly not. Sod Oil [the present editor trusts that the reader will recall that in the previous chapter the morphology of the verb 'seethe' and its past participle 'sod' was rehearsed] is grease extracted from sheepskins and used in the pursuance of the very thing that el-Fulānī affected to revile, knowledge that condemned him as a hypocrite, and of practices even worse than those of a sodomite."

"Or SOD, for short."

[A note found in the papers of the late Professor Page discusses the Welsh word *oes* and relates it to the Latin *oesypum* – Greek οἴσυπος, meaning the greasy element

---

[7] No doubt Dr Leefe would have explained the significance of this endearment.

of unwashed wool. This supposed connexion, though highly dubious, might be of considerable interest were it not that *oes* is a word denoting futurity in Welsh (rather than fatuity), so although it might have something to do with sheep oil, it has nothing do with the word in question, *oen*, a sheep.]

VI. OBITER DICTA

The Chapter of accidents is the longest chapter in the book [1]

A S the reader will be aware, this monograph has not been easy in the writing. Professor O'Tõõle had laboured hard, despite many setbacks, to get it into the proof stage; indeed, by 1979, the year of Professor Page's death, the previous chapters were mostly in this state. The passing of Page turned out to be a severe blow to O'Tööle: he found it difficult to regain his energy and enthusiasm for the work. Consequently, the University Press (actually the second, for the Syndics to the original Press decided to renege on their undertakings half-way through the venture) that had been responsible for the volume abandoned the project, and subsequently denied all knowledge of it. Professor O'Tõõle's own death occurred in 1990, the tercentenary year of Murphy's birth, and some one and a half centuries after the opening of the Irish Canal system, the celebration of which was the occasion of his untimely end. Earlier, it was thought that his collection of Murphiana had perished with him. It seems, however, that a few of these priceless documents, especially the Melissa Letters, were housed elsewhere: these have now been rediscovered. Furthermore, it has recently come to light that one of the Delegates of the University Press mentioned above (bUt which for variouS reasons cannot be named) had in his possession a complete set of proofs and other materials relating to the volume, which by a felicitous chance eventually found their way into the hands of the present editor. Representations to O'Tõõle's own University Press elicited the generous offer to publish the recovered monograph, under the present editorship. A consequence of this further shiftting between publishers has been one or two typographical difficulties which, it is hoped, will be ameliorated as soon as possible.

The vicissitudes of bringing together this volume have meant several unconscionable delays, but the present editor is determined that it shall now be printed without further postponement. As a result, many of the recovered materials have not been accorded the full treatment that they deserve. To hold back any longer would not well serve the cause. In any event, some of these materials may be found elsewhere, as will be noted in the next few paragraphs.

---

[1] "This aphorism" (wrote Professor O'Tòòle) "was attributed to Wilkes by Southey. Wilkes ..." (O'Tøøle's note recorded details of the Hell Fire Club, but for the most part these have already appeared in the previous chapter). He went on to observe that the reader would by now be in no doubt as to the true author of this dictum, indeed of a host of others. As a matter of accuracy, the present editor must point out that this chapter is far from being the longest in the book, as perhaps had been originally intended by Professor O'Tœle, for events were to overtake him in this ambition.

Some account of the many Murphy relatives who found fame and fortune was to have been given by Professor O'Tóóle. The daughters of Daniel Murphy, shoemaker, whose relationship to Murphy himself is unclear, have already been mentioned in chapter 3. The simian Edward Murphy, the Roman Catholic Archbishop of Dublin who died in 1728, although a primate *inter pares*, can be ruled out as a *pater inter pares*, but it is relatively certain that he was a relative. James Cavanagh Murphy, born "of obscure parents" in Cork, and who became an architect of some note, seems to have been a grandson, as were both John and Michael Murphy, both rebels, and Patrick who became a weather prophet, not entirely successfully (he seems to have been passably correct on 168 occasions, but utterly wrong 197 times: as our own Murphy said, "some are weather-wise, some are otherwise"). All of these seem to have careers that reflected some aspect of their more famous forbear. This is particularly true of Robert Murphy, born in 1806, who showed many of his grandfather's talents: he was run over by a cart at the age of 11, but as a result of this confinement to his bed, he studied to such effect that he became a brilliant mathematician by the time he was 13. Later, he was elected to a Fellowship at Caius College, Cambridge, but this came to an end when his life of dissipation exceeded that of his colleagues. Noticeably, it seems. The *Dictionary of National Biography* and similar reference books may be consulted for these and other famous Murphy scions (Arthur Murphy, coincidentally a friend of Samuel Johnson after the lexicographer had left Oxford, was not a relative).

Another of Professor O'T°°le's *desiderata* was a thorough documentation of the 'Catastrophe theory', 'Chaos theory' and so forth, and of the works by Parkinson, Peter, and those many other researchers and writers who have collected evidence of the workings of The Law, whether by name or by denial of that name. To give merely one odious example of the latter: *The Principle of the Graduated Hostility of Things*, whose supposed author the present editor will not deign to mention, simply echoes Murphy's findings on the question on the behaviour of buttered toast in a pseudo-mathematical treatment (though it fails to concern itself with the remarkable exception which Murphy had as yet to elucidate). These effusions have not been noticed here; nor have the many research projects in hand at various universities been mentioned, for time and space precludes even the most cursory of surveys. Again, however, the voluminous literature pertaining to the subject may be studied by the reader.

As to the Appendix first proposed by Professor O'Tююle, but which later was to have formed a companion volume, it is feared that this part of the project has had to be abandoned. What he had hoped to bring to fruition would have been (to use Murphy's apt and vivid phrase) "a beautiful quarto page, where a neat rivulet of text shall meander though a meadow of margin"; alas, it cannot be. Although this lays the monograph open to the criticisms of the late Dr Quibble and others concerning the question of references, it would be pointless to delay publication in order to add even more of these to the text, especially in view of the [then] Printer's wishes in regard to extra footnotes. In any case, it should have become obvious to the reader that many of the incidents referred to are common historical knowledge, which can easily be confirmed in any reliable book of reference. Dr Quibble's surprise at the sinking of the unsinkable boat, the activities of the Hell Fire Club, events surrounding the battle of Culloden and a host of other episodes that he had expressed as being "too bizarre to have any foundation of truth" simply betrayed his lack of a proper historical training. Far more 'bizarre' happenings are written on the pages of eighteenth-century history than he could have known, but the more educated reader may easily ascertain the facts for himself, especially concerning the important events mentioned in the course of this monograph.

As to those materials that have perished, it is enough to know that they were transcribed and authenticated by reliable scholars before they disappeared from view. For the elucidation of certain scientific matters in these sources (notably those connected with the Darwinian problem) the present editor is indebted to Dr Kay Mann, whose *The Lachrymal ducts of the Crocodile* tears to shreds the scoffers who imagined themselves to be experts in that subject, it turns out falsely, in the teeth of incisive contrary evidence. Her testimony is particularly important in regard to the Bognorite papers which had been erroneously thought to have perished entirely. Although principally concerning the religious controversy familiar to students of the eighteenth century, the Bongorian papers also alluded to another Law, and another personage, of more interest to us today than some long-forgotten doctrinal quarrel. It is true that some of the papers had vanished, alongside many of those of John Warburton himself, before they found their way into the Landsdowne Collection in the British Library (formerly Museum), as mentioned below. Nevertheless, some fragments of the Bongar Controversy materials have recently come to light that add somewhat to the precious store of extant Murphy documents, especially as they complement those Melissa letters that have survived the ravages of fate.

What follows, then, consists merely of a presentation of those priceless documents, lately uncovered, that follow Murphy's final years. If only in some measure, their interpretation completes the biographical endeavour undertaken by Professor O'Tóòle and his aides. A comment of the Contessa's (Lily's, that is, not her modern counterpart's) serves as an epitaph both for Murphy, as it was intended, but also for his biographer: *natura il fece e poi ruppe la stampa* – nature, having made them, broke the mould.

Some of the doings of the notorious Hell Fire Club have already been chronicled. Although its first meetings were in Wycombe, there was a period of two years when many of the meetings were in London, in the cellar of the *George and Vulture*, Cornhill. The inn burnt down in 1748 [the notion that Murphy had anything to do with this accident is without foundation], so the meetings were thereafter transferred back to Wycombe; by 1755, the splendid premises at Medmenham Abbey had been finished, so the Society of St Francis moved there; but by then, Murphy was of course dead. Nor did he witness the final move to the caves at Wycombe. It is not the purpose of this monograph to write the history of Club, Brotherhood, Society, or whatever it might have been called at one time or another, and indeed it is difficult not to shrink from recording anything of its distasteful doings; but for a considerable period these activities greatly involved Murphy, who as an Apostle held a senior position in the Society, along with many eminent persons of the day, the names of the other eleven members of this inner circle being well documented. Melissa, moreover, had almost as important a status in the complementary Sisterhood, as one of the three Horae. This epithet arose from the stated aim of the Brethren to banish time, as expressed in *The Temple of Venus* by Thompson:

> The winds took pity on the little whore
> And kindly puff'd her to the Cyprian shore
> The circling *Horae* saw the floating car
> And kindly sav'd her, for the God of War.
> Eunomia, Dica and Irene Fair …

It is well established that Melissa was the Dica of the three, though the identities of the others are less easy to ascertain. One of the problems of documentation lies, naturally enough, in the secrecy to which all were sworn, though as Murphy had once observed, "A Secret cannot be kept by three People unless two of them be dead". 'Brother John of Aylesbury', that is, Wilkes (who later was given preferment as 'The Archbishop of Aylesbury'), had his own reasons for breaking that code of secrecy. Yet, in his desire to bring scandal on everyone apart from himself, he succeeded only in engineering his own downfall, and his 'revelations' concerning the Society were not universally believed then, nor can they now be accounted as entirely factual. The more reliable source material was unfortunately disposed of. Some of it, including the Minute Books of the High Steward (Paul 'The Aged' Whitehead) were destroyed at about 1774, the year of Whitehead's death, either by him, or by the Earl of Sandwich who certainly had motive enough to destroy the evidence of his disreputable doings. In addition, according to present members of the Dashwood family, many other papers were burned in a bonfire at Wycombe about a century ago, though this was some time after some ghoul had stolen Whitehead's shrivelled heart from the urn in which it had been preserved in the mausoleum.

The Earl of Sandwich famously told someone: "I have often wondered what catastrophe would bring you to your end; but I think it will be either the pox or the rope." The immediate rejoinder was: "That depends, My Lord, as to whether I embrace your Lordship's mistress or your Lordship's principles." That someone, as the reader will recognise, was Murphy, though history has been rewritten so that the remark is variously attributed, sometimes to Foote, at others to Wilkes. The assumption that Fanny Murray was the mistress in question is also false, for she particularly observed to Murphy that she "wouldn't wish to partake of the Earl's sandwich, either way, preferring quite another filling".

In view of the state of the records, it is difficult to be certain of the exact times and places when Murphy was joining with 'El Faqir Dashwood Pasha' in the toast 'The

Harem', or being Prior for the day, with all the privileges of primofutuiture, under Abbot Francis. But one of the recovered documents records an important incident which has a considerable bearing upon the question of Murphy's last years. He had been in the Isle of Man, attempting to learn the language (his efforts to record the dying moments of Cornish having lately been frustrated): from there he wrote many times to Boyle on the subject of Melissa, for whom he apparently pined, saying "O! dy begins er ve maree!". Boyle spoke no Irish, let alone Manks, so these sentiments were lost on him. Similarly, there were parts of *The Rosy Sequence*, whose significance Boyle seems to have misunderstood, not being a Roman Catholic. Referring to her as his *dulcis memoria*, Murphy went on to quote the lines about 'giving joy to the heart' (less accurately translated by the Revd E. Caswall as 'with sweetness fills the breast') and

> sed super mel et omnia
> dulcis eia presentia

sentiments which could be construed perfectly innocently, were it not for the obvious pun on Melissa's name, the alteration from *ejus*, the plays elsewhere on *paenitentibus* and *petentibus*, and the last lines of the piece. The latter, as our virtuous Professor of Latin at this University (Parfitt G. Knight) correctly points out, should more properly run

> sit nostra te in gloria
> per cuncta semper saecula

but in his unsullied view (he is, after all, from the American South) he insists that they were merely misquoted and misspelt by Murphy, "who also miswrote *eia*, which would be either an interjection of joy, or means 'heyday', rather than *ea* – 'she' – which is anyways wrong, for the reading should be *ejus*". Our clean-living colleague seems to be unaware that Murphy was rather cleverly echoing, though in rather more lurid detail, the sentiments of the Manks, "O, that I would have been with her" (and is doubtless unaware of the Revd E. Caswall's considerably less dignified poetic effusions that circulated round Oxford in his days as an undergraduate at Brasenose).

For her part, Melissa seems also to have been desirous of meeting her husband again, and although the documentation of their next meeting is poor in some respects, there is a very full account of another visit (and possibly Murphy's last) to the Society of St Francis at Wycombe, when there was more than a week of celebrations of the monkish kind. On this occasion, the 'solemn music' which accompanied the liturgy was to be performed on a new invention by Murphy. He had heard of the success of the French composer Gluck's Musical Glasses, or *Harmonica*, in the same year as his own, less successful, participation in the battle of Culloden. The instrument (or rather instruments, for the procedure was after the fashion of turn and turn about, as with handbells) was tried out variously at the *George and Vulture* and at Wycombe, at first by using wine bottles, which produced variable results when played upon by certain ladies. A slightly more successful alternative was later attempted, using wine glasses. The pitch was varied by different levels of liquid filled from a communal pot, and each vessel was set in motion either by a moistened finger circling around the brim, or by other means. Even with the improvements, the haphazard results had not been in keeping with the solemnity of the occasion, nor was decorum improved by the glass eye of Betty Weyms (a noted courtesan and faithful Nun at Wycombe) which was wont to fall into the vessel apportioned to her for playing. Thus, Murphy determined to invent a more reliable instrument than what had become known as the Glass-Eye HarMonica (this last being a reference to another of the regular Nuns, known as Sœur Monique).

His first task was to secure a method of moistening the glasses more efficaciously than the way hitherto employed at Wycombe. Wilkes' description of Lady […] as having a "slimy aquatick […] in which the seed of heaven will congeal into frogspawn" is unfortunately celebrated, for it was quoted later in connexion with Pitt's bride-to-be Hester Temple, by Potter. (The latter was another of the Apostles amongst whom, incidentally, Wilkes was not numbered, which may account for some of his peevishness.) Undeniably, however, the viscosity of the 'blessed unction' applied to the glasses was crucial. How this problem was finally overcome we do not know, but the solution came from Fanny Murray and from his own Melissa, whose mellifluity he had celebrated in the Latin lines already discussed.[2] Fanny Murray was, of course, the dedicatee of *Essay on Woman* supposedly written by Pego Borewell, and put about by Wilkes as though it was his own.

---

[2] The lines "Sicut apis melli semel heret dura revelli" which Wilkes translated as "As the bee goes for honey, the whore goes for money", were hardly by Murphy, as some would have it. Nor would he have written "Spe levis argenti stabulo caput abdet olenti" which might apply to the unsavoury Sister Agnes, but not to Melissa, whom he described as having "the savour of a game pie". These, and other lines of this nature, are too scabrous to translate.

All the copies of an *Essay on Woman* seen by the present editor appear to have had their medallions (a copper engraving of a phallus) removed from the title page. Before his untimely death Professor Page intimated that such a phallus was to be found in at least one Cambridge library, but little has come of this intelligence up to now.

NO MORE FOOTNOTES!
The Printer.

It matters very little now that there are or there are not any more footnotes. The note from The Printer printed above is now doubly redundant. The Oxford so-called Unverity so-called Priss has now decided to expunge the ancient title of The Printer, and to have the whole thing run by a Chief Bottle Washer or something. I ask you. This nameless Press has also stopped publishing anything worthwhile (poetry, many scholarly works and so on) and sent the rest to be published in America, for heaven's sake. At the last minute (or rather, during the first minutes of a new century, though hardly anyone seems to know when it begins – but I – you know the rest) that lot have decided not to publish this monograph, but luckily, O'Toole's own Univversity Press has kindly stepped into the breach by way of honouring the memory of one of its own distinguished scholars. *Si monumentum* … .

Originally, the parody had been addressed by Murphy to Sandwich, beginning

> Awake, my Sandwich, leave all meaner joys
> To Charles and Bob and those poetic boys.
> Let us, since life can little more supply
> Than just to kiss, to procreate and die

Amongst the Brethren, Charles Churchill and Robert Lloyd were perhaps the most distinguished poets, apart, of course, from Murphy himself (though it was Paul 'The Aged' Whitehead who eventually became Poet Laureate).

His later version was closer to Pope's *Essay* and began:

> Awake, Melissa, leave all meaner things
> Our sole ambition, joys that Pego brings
> Let us (since Life can little more supply
> Than just to swive again before we die)

and continued, in later lines

> And let us now our *Pyrenees* explore
> The latest Tracts, the pleasing Depths of yore

(the reference, as Murphy explained in a footnote, being to the Perinæum or Pyrenæum). These lines were later published by Wilkes as

> Awake, my Fanny, leave all meaner things
> This morn shall prove what rapture swiving brings
> Let us (since life can little more supply
> Than just a few good ****s and then we die)

As we know, the true authorship was almost entirely unacknowledged, even to the extent that Potter has also been credited with the poem. The only hint given by Wilkes in his publication was a glancing reference to Rogerus Cunnæus, as contributor of notes to the volume, amongst which the reference to the Pyrenees is indeed to be found. But this malfeasance rebounded on Wilkes, for the publication of the *Essay* brought disgrace, and eventually imprisonment, upon him, The Law being thereby obeyed.

The Law operated in a different manner in respect of the HarMonica, or Mellifluicum as Murphy had at first named his new invention. He had special glasses blown in a particular shape, the *areolae* of each being pieced by a spindle fastened by

---

(footnote from previous page, continued):Thank goodness that this volume will at last see the light. Third time lucky. I am beginning to be fed up to the back teeth with the whole project, worthy though it is. It's just as well that this comment won't get printed, but just in case some moron forgets to expunge it, I will not express myself in the manner that I would otherwise. I shall say no more. J.R.

mastic, the latter being connected to a treadle arrangement. The treadle caused the bulbous vessels to rotate; a finger, moistened with the special unction was applied to each vessel in turn whose note was required, and thus one player, not several, now controlled the arrangement. [The nature of this unction is obscure: Melissa elsewhere described it variously as Apricot or Plum Juice, also referring to Oysters: these confused passages are in French, German, and various other languages – *jus d'abricot*, *Pflaumensaft* and so forth – so there is a distinctly unfruitful polyglot confusion concerning this whole matter]. Now it is dubious that Benjamin Franklin would have known Murphy directly; but it is a fact that Franklin heard an early version of the Glass Harmonica in London, and brought forth his own version in 1761. It is also a fact that he was a frequent visitor to the Hell Fire establishment, even if such visits were after Murphy's death. Crucially, it must also be stated that his description of his so-called invention, as given by him in his writings, is virtually identical with the last part of Murphy's, as preserved by Melissa in a letter from her husband:

> The tinkling Note of the Friary Chamber Pots becomes higher, as you remember, My Sweet, the more they are filled. This Chamber Musick, or something like to it, is employed in the Instrument dedicated to you: the Pitch thereof increases as between the C Cup and the D Cup, and increases yet more through the E Cup, and so on, not forgetting the lesser Cups such as the A Flat, nor the F Sharp and the like, nor yet the magnificent Cups such as the DD. [In a lacunose passage Murphy apparently described the method of obtaining the unction and its application, and the manner of operating the treadle. These details, alas, are lost to us. Significantly, however, he continued:] When these Particulars are all attended to and the Directions observed, the Tone comes forth finely and with the slightest Pressure of the Finger imaginable, and you swell it at Pleasure by adding a little more Pressure, no Instrument affords more Shades, if one may so speak, of the *Forte* and *Piano*. One Anointing with the Unction will serve for a Piece of Musick twice as long as Handel's Water Piece.

Franklin's calumny, by whatsoever intermediary it might have been encouraged, is condemned by the last two sentences, which are more or less quoted *verbatim* in one of his letters. Indeed, in common with many other imitators, Franklin seems to have had no qualms in taking several of Murphy's discoveries, inventions and *mots justes*, indeed *notes justes*, as his own.

The HarMonica featured in a disgraceful incident that did the Society of St Francis no credit. The liturgy had proceeded much as it was wont, with the usual injunction 'Sursum Pego'; this was not obeyed by all the Brotherhood, there being some initiants who were not entirely versed in its ways. So the Latin had to be glossed by the Prior of the day, which happened to be Murphy, who therefore intoned in what should have been a supererogatory fashion, "The members will rise".

It was a poor showing, as Melissa then and later observed. As a result, in the festivities afterwards, many of the Nuns had to have recourse to The Game at Flatts, rightly condemned by Thomson:

Muse drop the curtain, nor behold this act,
Two sisters glorying in a carnal fact;
Shrink at these times, like darker days of yore,
Two sisters playing with one man the whore.

In view of the lack of suitable manhood, Murphy, for his part, was much in demand. Sister Agnes was insistent, but Murphy complimented her on her musicianship, so she was persuaded to play upon the HarMonica while Melissa and he played in an adjoining bedroom, or 'cell', as these facilities were known at Wycombe. Sister Agnes was importunate, but Murphy congratulated her on her command of the instrument, and bade her entertain the company with more of it, which was an air from Mr Handel's *Judas Maccabæus*, lately composed for an establishment of young ladies that had taken the fancy of the Prince of Wales (also one of the Brethren).

During this performance, Murphy entertained another of the Nuns, who was possessed of a raucous voice like a *corno di bassetto* and who, instead of 'sound the trumpet, beat the drums' was heard, on reaching the peak of her own performance, loudly to sing, "beat the strumpet as she strums". After this, Murphy was, in his own words, "tired, but not sorry". The emergent Prior was again set upon by Sister Agnes, but even though exhausted, Murphy was glad to be claimed by yet another Nun, who whisked him off again. She, too, tested the acoustical properties of the cell by a shrill singing, more or less in accord with the music of the HarMonica: this was to the chorus at which Sister Agnes and she had simultaneously arrived. "See," she bawled, "the conquering hero comes!" adding "and that was truly heroic, my dear Prior, for that third tune must be reckoned very handsome in a lover past forty." Lady Mary (for it was she, though, in truth, Murphy was considerably older than fifty, let alone forty) later told the story somewhat differently, *à propos* the yet to be ennobled Edgcumbe. She seems to have been piqued that Murphy would not devote himself more single-handedly to her (though this was by no means the exact phrase she employed).

Sister Agnes ('Extra Virgin') was something of a mystery in the Wycombe establishment. On many occasions she was called to nurse one or other of the Nuns in a secret confinement (incidentally, the horrid slander that this had to be done for one of Dashwood's sisters is wholly untrue, as are the lines:

Like a Hotspur young cock, he began with his mother,
Cheered three sisters one after the other;
And oft tried little Jen, but gained so little ground
Little Jen lost her patience and made him compound.)

Murphy had tried to improve Agnes' low speech, calling himself "Dashwood's Pygmalion". But her advances towards himself he repulsed, not least on account of a lack of attention to her toilet. She emitted a particular odour that he described to the Revd Laurence Sterne as 'ghoti', a spelling, apparently, with which Murphy was demonstrating to him the absurdities of English orthography, and proposing a system which would supplant it. Although this word cannot presently be construed, we may be sure that its significance will be recovered. At least it is known that it inspired Sterne to call his new friend 'The learned Smelfungus', a compliment that Murphy returned by reading him some passages from his *A Sentimental Journey to Melissa.* (Of course, the paths of the two men had already crossed on the occasion of Murphy's marriage.)

To return to the matter of the evening in question, the subject of the *Sentimental Journey* was disappointed that Murphy's exertions had left him with little energy to devote to her. They attempted a little excursion on the rather suggestively shaped lake. Though the design of this and other parts of the Wycombe landscape were not to be discerned by what might be called 'the naked eye', such details were apparent when viewed from Dashwood's ball, the gilded curiosity which he had placed on the top of St Lawrence's Church, and which would accommodate two or three who might view the landscape. The boats that were often taken on the lake were shaped after the fashion of Venetian gondolas, but on this occasion Melissa's gondolier failed to make much progress with his oar. Little indeed came of the ride, for her husband's ardour was dampened and shrivelled by the wet and the cold. This was the occasion, however, on which Murphy composed his Lake Poem, beginning:

> Happy Spark of heavenly Flame!
> Pride and Wonder of Man's Frame!
> Why is Pleasure so soon flying ?
> Why so short this Bliss of dying?
> Cease, fond Pego, cease the strife,
> And yet indulge a moment's life.

As the reader will not fail to recognise, *The Dying Christian to his Soul* was the model of this parody; nor will he be unaware that this, too, was counterfeited by Wilkes, and published as *The Dying Lover to his [***]ck.*

After their time on the lake, the two went back to the house and repaired to the Inner Sanctum of the Chapel. It was here that Murphy became embroiled in what were nothing but perfectly harmless pastimes, despite posterity having mistakenly recorded these events as the following of evil practices, the so-called Black Magic of Wycombe.

The assembled company was clustered round the Pentacle, or Pentangle as they variously called it (later known as the Pentagram). There were, besides a few lesser lights, Sterne, Potter, Wilkes, Lloyd and Churchill (the Lords Sandwich, March and Despenser were detained by other activities in other parts of the house), the painter

Hogarth (whose representation of Murphy, reproduced on p.148, is the only one known to have been preserved) and Stanhope, the son of Lord Chesterfield (to whom Murphy had written some memorable letters: the many troubles that Murphy had overcome made him uniquely able to offer sound advice on the ways of the world, though, as he observed, advice is seldom welcome; and those who need it the most always want it the least). Among the Nuns, there were Melissa, Fanny Murray (the Ladies Vane and Montagu Wortley being engaged elsewhere, as was Lucy Cooper), Sister Agnes and Betty Weyms (who had again mislaid her glass eye) and the Chevalier D'Eon de Beaumont (no one seems certain as to whether he or she was a Brother or a Nun, but the Chevalier is known to have "played the part of a Mollie").

According to an entirely unreliable, not to say vicious, account of these proceedings, the darkened *Thalamus* or Inner Sanctum witnessed "execrable occult arts and unimaginable cavortings between and within the sexes". It is true that Melissa's beautiful auburn hair was revealed to Hogarth at this gathering, but her state of undress was merely the result of an accident with a candle as Murphy was demonstrating various properties of ropes with her assistance. Far from being an orgy of whips and lashes, halters and bindings to stakes as described elsewhere with signal misinformation and malice, Murphy was merely recounting some shipboard adventures connected with his Italian travels (the very same that had been drawn upon by the plagiarist Smollett) and explaining about the sailors' ropes. He had observed on many occasions that however carefully their ropes were wound and stowed after use, when they came to be required again, they emerged mysteriously knotted. Murphy's mathematical bent led him to seek an explanation for this, which he called his Knot Theory. As many readers will be aware, this has lately been considered anew by science, and paraded, without acknowledgement, as though it were a new discovery. The truth, of course, is quite otherwise.

So it was that, a new candle having been lit, and Melissa having discarded her charred clothes, Murphy demonstrated the properties of the Pentacle on the floor, whose five lines formed an endless knot: this phenomenon, as he displayed, was at the heart of his theory of the inevitable knotting of ropes, fishing lines, and the like. There was no kinkiness as he wound the ropes around Melissa, but he showed that as soon as they were laid on the ground (the ropes) the kinks, unbidden and ineluctable, were there for all to see. At this point in his peroration, however, a minatory noise was heard outside, to the dismay of many of the distinguished members of the Society who were wary of discovery in such circumstances. The ladies stayed their ground, but the men, now unaccountably without attire, prevailed on Murphy to effect some form of escape.

By the time Lord Bute (for it was he) and his cronies had entered the place, the Nuns were looking demure and, apart from the Pentacle and the ropes, all evidence of "Black magic" was absent. The Brotherhood, to a man (though the escapers included the Chevalier) had retreated to the dentilled ledges above, where they clung to the curious gargoyles that were a feature of the Inner Sanctum. In the flickering light of the candle the fugitives were virtually invisible, but their hold was somewhat tenous, due to each man by turn having to grip the same gargoyle as his neighbour, his feet having to tread a common dentil. So the appearance of the assembly, as they could be glimpsed but dimly below, was of a frieze made up of so many naked Saint Andrews, crucified saltire-fashion, each bearing a look of agony to match.

Melissa, *sotto voce*, warned them to be careful, saying "Rory, although you were formed for the ruin of our sex, this is not the time to fall into my arms". Any futher advice from her was interrupted, however, by Bute and his henchmen, who were still determinedly searching the *penetralia* of the Sanctum and, when His Lordship was not engaged in showing off his ankles to the ladies, joined him in threatening exemplary punishment to the yet undiscovered malefactors. This the Brothers took seriously, for assemblies such as the Hell Fire Club had been outlawed many years earlier, and Witchcraft was still a heinous offence. So when the noise below was sufficient to cover his voice, Murphy enjoined his companions with the immortal words, "We must hang together, or assuredly we shall hang separately".

As the searchers below wandered into one corner, Murphy had moved along and had managed to reach the end of the Sanctum and its Oriel window (though its shape was not precisely that). Having gone through the window, he turned and poked his head within, silently encouraging his fellows carefully to move, in stages, towards it. So the company now eerily resembled a progress of naked crabs, one by one dropping though the window. Although the descent outside was cushioned to some extent, the pillow consisted of bramble bushes and blackthorn; so, contrary to Scripture, the crucified were scourged after their main ordeal. Murphy, managing to stifle what would have been a scream (he was, after all, experienced in this kind of manoeuvre), called up to Sterne to seal his lips, no matter how exquisite the discomforts of the fall, and likewise in the same vein to the emerging Hogarth, who was much taken with the adventure. On the ground, Sterne was gibbering:

"I am a stoic, my dear Murphy, a stoic as much as the great and learned Lipsius who composed a work the day he was born."

"They should have wiped it up," said Murphy shortly, "and said no more about it."

Meanwhile, most of the Brethren had descended, but one of the last, probably Stanhope, overcome by the cold and the pain of his fall, cried out volubly. Murphy tried to soothe him, saying that an injury is much sooner forgotten than an insult, but the noise had been heard within. This was as well for Melissa, for she was by now in much in fear of the search including the *thalamus* where she had hidden certain "engines of pleasure" as she called them, which would have "given the Game at Flatts away". Bute was still parading his calves and threatening to seek out her "line of booty" (a puerile pun on his own name and a reference to Hogarth's 'Line of Beauty' on the lower part of the female figure, discussed in his *Analysis of Beauty*): he was thus fortunately distracted by the shout, towards which he now moved, saying, in his abominable Welsh accent: "Curved is the line of booty, but straight the line of dooty."

This boded ill for those outside, who must surely be discovered. But "the chapter of accidents" as Murphy expressed it to Stanhope, was not yet at an end. No sooner had Bute and his coadjutors purposed to seek the cause of the noise, than Wilkes, the last of the frozen frieze, lost his grip and tumbled from his shaky foothold, arriving spreadeagled on the Pentacle, to the astonishment of all. The immobile body was turned over by Bute's elegant foot, and at once recognised. The prognathous jaw, the prurigo of his complexion, together with the proptosis and convergent strabismus of the eyes that contributed to Wilkes' legendary ugliness were immediately apparent to the men (though it was Melissa who had descibed this peculiarity "as if one eye Upon the other were a spy"), as was the distressing phimosis to the women ("so much worse," said Melissa on another occasion, "than an ingrowing toenail"). Bute was well pleased with his booty, and bore his trophy away. This incident marked the entirely literal beginning of Wilkes' downfall and sealed the enmity between the two men.

Here, the sources become more than usually elusive, for Melissa's epistolary narrative is interrupted here. Thus, the depredations of Fate have not allowed us to follow much of Murphy's subsequent career in any great detail. Purely by chance, however, the last chapter of Murphy's life can be sketched in, however meagrely, by another source, close to Murphy himself. The Richards family still maintain that they are descended from Murphy himself, and that he entered into a common-law marriage with a Bronwen Richards on one of his Welsh visits. She bore a child to him whom she called Rhydderch, for reasons at which we can only guess. All that is known is that the child had the Murphy red hair, and was a boy of ten or so at the time of Murphy's death. The family, acquiring later respectability, assumed the name Morphy-Richards, but the first element had to be dropped as the result of a hotly contested lawsuit brought by a manufacturer of household goods against the descendants and which became known as the 'Burnt Toast Case', in which the Judge appears to have been more than usually befuddled by the conflicting evidence. It is true that the witnesses were less than coherent, for apart from speaking largely in Welsh, they seemed to talk more about the gravitational properties of toast than of their claims to the Murphy name; but the Judge, calling for scientific testimony on the subject, seems to have lost the drift of the case entirely.

Tragically, the Judge was electrocuted when attempting to prise out a recalcitrant piece of toast during the course of a demonstration of what the forensic expert, Dr Croustade, called the 'Murphy effect'. It is remarkable that the flash of enlightenment that came to His Lordship, albeit too late, was an unwitting echo of Murphy's own end, as will be seen.

The retrial that followed the death of Mr Justice Chard-Wigge was less spectacular, but the new judge was even more eccentric, and the prosecution of Messrs William

Posters and William Stickers, on an entirely trumped-up charge, succeeded, to the astonishment of the court. In the Morphy case that followed, judgement was unaccountably given for the plaintiffs. During the course of the hearing, there were revelations that should have showed, beyond all doubt, that the defendants had genuine Murphy documents in their possession. According to Professor Richard Head, who was present at both trials, there was a reference to a letter from Professor Genno of Antwerp that had been preserved by the family. This was in the form of a triumphant reply to Murphy, touching upon the subject of the mysterious contravention of The Law, which had been the cause of much perturbation.

According to Head, then Head of the Department of Cultural Studies (whatever that might be) in the University of East Glamorgan (wherever that might be), the letter was unaccountably in an obscure dialect of Welsh, which his colleagues had so far been unable to decipher. Recently, however, he has moved to the University of Tredegar, where there is more of an emphasis on the Welsh language, for which reason he is more confident of success. He writes:

Oddi Wrth: **Yr Athro ap Richard Head**
Pennaeth Sefydliad Astudiaethau Pen Pidyr
Prifysgol Llygoden Mihangel
Y Drededgar
Sir Morgannwg

Dear James Ridell,

My collegues here are in the process of decyphering the letter about which we corresponded breifly. It seems that it is not the original after all, but an

Opposite Page:
Unpublished later version of Hogarth's *Strolling actresses dressing in a Barn,* which was revised to record the Wycombe incident. Barely to be made out in the top right hand corner is Murphy (encircled) peering in. Sister Agnes is on the right, Betty Weyms, on the left of Melissa, is misrepresented as being enroped.
There are two Hogarth paintings (oil on canvas) in the Fitzwilliam Museum, Cambridge, entitled *Before* and *After,* the first showing a female resisting the advances of her swain, the second (in which both parties are shown exhausted and dishevelled) indicating that such resistance was not long-lived. Although the date of these works (1730–1) could be made to fit the chronology of Murphy's known history, the present editor is unconvinced that they represent an encounter between him and Melissa (who is not known to have succumbed to such behaviour. Resistance, that is. Nor do their somewhat solemn countenances illustrate Murphy's well-known phrase "tired, but not sorry"). From Knock, in Ireland (where he is on sabbatical leave from Germany) Professor Dr Dr Terri Fick has kindly sent me a lengthy analysis of the scenes: although I cannot match his deep penetration, he concurs with my own superficial handling of the subject.

anotated copy, which is why there is Welsh in it. It also contains Dutch or Flemish, which we are endevouring to translate, apart from the bits of Latin which we shall have to go elsewhere for, since this University does not deal with dead languages. My collegues at the Advanced Institute for the Advanced Study of Welsh Letters (which is a misnomer, since it handles Breton, Cornish, Cumbro-Pictish as well as Welsh) have every confidents that they will be able to solve the hole thing in a very quick trice, if not sooner.

Yours very sincerly,

Dick

Proffessor Pritchard Head

PS. Some of the Welsh anotations have already been translated. I enclose versions of some two of them. Another, rendered into English verse by my collegue Ffred Ffansis Ffani, reads:

The mountain girls are sweeter
The valley girls are fatter
The former might be meeter
But the RAM prefers the latter

It is a discusting slander to say that Murphy was refering to unnaturural practises [indeed, previous chapters have shown that he was reluctant to embrace such couplings] and which is implied in an English travisty of this holesome Welsh ryme circulating in a book purporting to be about life in North Wales (I think it was a Paycock and Bull story by some one called Thomas Headlong Hall). It is well known that Wales is divided into two desparate parts, the North being reffered to as The Mountains and the South as The Valleys. So the diffrence between the girls of *mynydd* and *cwm* is the diffrence between North and South. Of coarse, he prefers those of The Valleys for their mountainous features.

Although the above letter was written a year ago, there is every likelihood of what Richard (now Pritchard) Head describes as a 'brakethrew' in this important matter. He has, at least, forwarded the document to an expert in Theosophistry at a distinguished university in Germany. For the present, however, the narrative must take a different, but equally important direction, that of Murphy's search for his true lineage. Naturally, the death of Swift in October 1745 was a heavy blow to Murphy: apart from the close bonds of affection between the two men, the severing of this link cut off the last realistic possibility of determining his parentage. It was in this vein that he talked to his old friend Dick Boyle, with whom he had met up again some years later, probably after 1750, for one of the subjects that they discussed was the approaching changing of the calendar, in conformity with the Act of that year.

As has been noted, the inconsistencies as between the Gregorian and Julian calendars were to bedevil the chronology of many of Murphy's activities, not least those surrounding the Scottish episodes. The proposed standardisation of the English calendar rightly exercised him greatly; unknown to him, however, this event was to prove particularly catastrophic in regard to the manner in which he was to enter the laurel-strewn glades of immortality. In its wisdom, the British Parliament failed to foresee the unforeseen ramifications (these were Murphy's words) contingent upon such changes. Events in the twentieth century have underlined his concerns. The German Government (then the West-German), on deciding to standardise the clock to conform with a Central European Time, made meticulous preparations for the event. Unlike the changing of the English calendar, when eleven days were to be lost, the Germans were to lose only one hour, but days or hours, the anticipation of possible problems is the key to a smooth transition to a new era.

Accordingly, the Germans had made painstaking provision for the adding on of the lost hour for pension and insurance purposes; furthermore, the registration of births and deaths (and possibly marriages following unexpectedly upon either or both) that might occur between what would have been the hours of One and Two in the morning were to be deemed to have taken place between Two and Three; and a truly astonishing number of other measures were passed by the Bundestag in anticipation of the time-change. In short, the Teutonic genius for detail was demonstrated in the most gratifyingly comprehensive manner. This genius had reckoned, however, without the action of The Law. Accordingly, the train that left Munich station, carrying dignitaries who were to have celebrated the confluence of time with their Swiss counterparts, missed the connexion at the Swiss border, this train having left an hour earlier, apparently in ignorance of the Time-table changes on the German side. As Swift had earlier said, "In Konstanz there is no constancy"; and the train of thought expressed in Milton's exquisite ode *On Time* is also a pertinent comment on the regularity of the Swiss railway system.

Had the Bundestag been more literate, or had it been party to the discussion of Boyle and Murphy on the subject of time, its deliberations might have taken into account the unaccountable. But this is a matter of conjecture, though in the sense enunciated by Bernoulli, of course. (A descendant of Bernoulli became a senior officer in the Swiss Navy and became an eminent authority on maritime chronometrics; his ground-breaking book, *Latitude*, is too well known to mention.) The discussions with Boyle included reminiscences of the days when he and Murphy were undergraduates together, including a recounting of the various attempts to dislodge Swift's wig, and the moment when the unbewigged pate had at last been revealed.

"Well, now," said Boyle, "This is the first I have heard of all this. I knew nothing of the eagle carrying off the wig."

"Yes, and after all that trouble I had trying to get a glimpse of his hair to ascertain its colour, the eagle revealed that what there was of it was grey: so I shall never know whether or not it was originally red. I should have tried to spy on him in the bath, though that sort of thing got me almost as much into trouble at Oxford as Acteon."

"Acteon? I didn't know he was up at Oxford. What sort of trouble?"

Murphy explained that he had been accused simultaneously of being a 'Peeping Tom' and of exposing himself, to which Boyle reasonably replied that the arrangements at the Hell Fire Club included chamber-pots on the sideboards and elsewhere so that the participants could relieve themselves without leaving the room.

"And, as I recall, there was no false modesty displayed by either sex," continued Boyle.

"That is so. And since the hair thus revealed, what Lily calls the *quei capille*, rarely goes grey until an advanced age, unlike the hair of the head …"

"My dear fellow," said Boyle, "you seem to have forgotten that even in respect of its manifestation on the head, there is grey hair and grey hair."

"What are you talking about? Spare me the riddle-me-ree. It sounds like that old-fashioned song 'White sand and grey sand'."

"Precisely."

"Boyle, 'tis an eejit y'are. I will throttle you upon the instant if you don't explain at once."

"Since you appear to know nothing of it, there are several sorts of grey hair, especially in middle age, before it has achieved its final colour. One kind, *videlicet* iron-grey, often pertains to persons who in their youth had dark hair; then there is white hair, which frequently succeeds blond hair, and …"

"I cannot believe this. And …"

"Salt-and-pepper grey, as they call it, which …"

"Follows from red hair."

"Precisely. And because, as we both remember well, the Dean had piercing blue eyes, he is unlikely to have had dark hair in his prime. So all you have to do is remember whether it was white hair or grey hair that the great bird revealed when it bore away the Dean's wig."

Of the rest of this conversation there is no record that can be discovered. We must needs pass on to some of the scientific observations alluded to in a previous chapter, known only from the paste-downs in a book that came into the possession of Michael Faraday, and which was thought to be of an erotic nature. As Professor Page pointed out in one of his surviving notes, the book in question was salacious only to the prudish, and was a Spanish translation of some of the lives of the Desert

Fathers. The Inquisition had seen to it that the uplifting lives of St Mary the Harlot and of St Pelagia the Harlot were omitted, but that of Abbot Caspian escaped their censorship.

The Abbot was wont to walk in the desert naked, except for a hat with which to ward off the relentless sun. Many times the Devil appeared to him in various forms, as was often the fate of the saintly. One such appearance to a hermit was in the form of a snake, whose blandishments he fought off with a copy of the Gospels: it vanished, leaving only, as the chronicle relates, a vile smell (though the ascetic regimen of the hermit, his cramped cave offering little room for hygiene, may well have contributed largely to this assault on the senses). To the hermit, in common with Abbot Caspian, the Devil also appeared in one of his most favoured guises, as a beautiful woman.

So it was that the Abbot was confronted by the woman, whose charms took him aback. She had no hat, which, he being a priest, may have disturbed him more than the fact that she, too, was naked. Abbot Caspian modestly covered himself with the only garment to hand, as it were. The beautiful woman told him to raise his right hand, which instruction the Abbot obeyed without demur, holding the hat somewhat earnestly to his nether parts with the other hand. The she-Devil then made him raise his left hand, which he did, now shielding himself with even greater care, the hat in his right hand. "Now raise both of your hands," she said, which also he did. "*Y, veridade milagro!*" according to the narrative, "the hat stayed in its place, unaided". The devout Spaniards took this miracle to heart and many copies of the book circulated before the Inquisition had it withdrawn.

For this reason, the book is now scarce, but a choice copy formerly in the possession of the then Lord Dashwood of Wycombe, was being rebound by Faraday. He found that its previous binding contained fragments of Murphy's notes, some of which relate to the duodecimal system, and which are drawn upon below. By themselves, the notes are virtually unintelligible; added to other documentation, however, some kind of interpretation can be advanced. Nevertheless, the recovery of this latter source-material has not been a simple matter, since it was part of a collection of papers left behind at Murphy's lodgings, the history of which is as follows.

His landlady was Betsy Bawker, who, before she retired and took in lodgers such as Murphy, was the cook to John Warburton, Somerset Herald and collector of MSS, amongst which were plays of Shakespeare and his contemporaries. Of these, only a slim folio volume survives, in what is now the Lansdowne collection at the British Library [formerly Museum], to which the following note is appended:

> After I had been many years Collecting these MSS Playes, through my own carelessness and the Ignora[n]ce of my Ser[vant]. in whose hands I had lodgd them they was unluckley burnd or put under Pye bottoms, excepting ye three which followes. J.W.

It can only be assumed that she dealt with Murphy's papers in a similar fashion, though a portion of one of these MSS, badly burnt, was seen and described by Dick Hawkins, Professor for the Publick Understanding of Astrology and Fellow of Old College, Oxford. He, a devout Catholic, found them in a crypt in a London Oratory, in a charred box bearing the name Burns, Oates and Washboard. Hawkins immediately recognised the papers for what they were and, as luck would have it, he communicated their contents to Professor O'Tôôle before they again disappeared, burnt, according to the Burns staff, as rubbish. The cyphers in this recovered source allow some sense to be made of the Faraday paste-downs, together with a passage in the Melissa papers where she records a speech made by Murphy when he was canvassing support for his duodecimal method of calculation. In one of her letters to a friend, she quotes the speech more or less *verbatim*, as follows:

"My idea, of a duodecimal system of numbers, merely conforms with nature. How can ten of anything be apportioned into three? Nor can ten be quartered, save by having recourse to an irrational fraction. Twelve is the natural quantity of nature. It is common knowledge that hens lay their eggs in dozens."

"What about scores of cabbages?" said a heckler.

"My score would be corrected to four-and-twenty, which would have a beneficial effect on man's longevity. This unit would also conform with my New Guinea, for the New – and cheaper – Pound (here I would rectify the error of the King Carolus Magnus) would comprise twelve present Shillings, each of twelve present Pence. Thus the New Guineas would be something of an equivalent to the old Pounds. In weights there would be twelve Ounces to the Pound, twelve Pounds to the Stone, which would make the porter's burthen lighter. The sum of twelve Stones would be a Grossweight.

"The defects of the Chaldean system will be made good by having a circle of 144 degrees, called duodecans: so a right angle would measure 36 duodecans. This would coincide with the clock, which would save much troublous noise from the clangorous striking that so besets our towns and cities. For there would be twelve hours in the day, each of 144 duodecans.

"The Week would consist of six Days. The Lord laboured on these six Days and rested on the seventh. Therefore it is blasphemous for us to usurpate His Day to our terrestrial Week. Due to the quiddities of nature, there would needs be five Weeks in a Month, making 30 Days in each and every Month. This number is unfortunate, but must be borne for the sake of the Moon. Christmas Eve, falling on the day after the 23rd of Duodecember (the Months would be rationally named) would begin the five Holidays named after the appropriate Feasts, there following Christmas Day, St Stephen's, St John's and Innocents', but all unnumbered. Every fourth Year, the Feast of St Thomas of Canterbury would be intercalated, giving in such a year six days of Christmas. This would mean that Uniumber the First would always fall on a Monday (if these names were to be retained, docked of the otiose Sunday), as with all the other months. There would also be adjustments at other dates, notably in the duodecennials, in order to keep course with the sun.

"In this way, Parliament would have a rational calendar to hand, and far from robbing the populace of eleven days of its several lives by its meddlings, it would gain five, even six, Holidays in the year.

"As to the cyphers themselves …" [Note by the late Professor O'Tôôle: Although the Melissa papers are unclear as to the precise form of these cyphers, the MS that Hawkins recorded contained a series of number forms, some of them not unlike those of modern Arabic, with the lower dot signifying a multiplication of the foregoing number by twelve, a supralineal dot division by twelve, and so forth. This is now known to be the explanation of the curious figures on the lost Bodleian MS removed from the *Schola Linguarum Hebraicae et Graecae*, in the phrase *estne* ⊏⊔ *positio Hibernica* ⊔⊏*?* The MS appears to have been in the nature of a demonstration of the rational qualities of this numeration, including divisibility by three. We must remind ourselves that the *Schola Linguarum Hebraicae et Graecae* shared the same part of the building in the Schools quadrangle at Oxford with the *Schola Arithmeticae et Geometricae*, so it is a perfectly logical place for there to be some record of Murphy's mathematical thoughts. The hitherto cryptic inscription can now be read as: 'is 96 the Irish *positio* 69?' The precise significance of this conundrum, and of the word *positio*, eludes us for the present. …].

The prophetic words of Murphy concerning the mutilation of the calendar by Parliament could not have been more cogent, as will shortly be evident. As, from time to time, he returned to Melissa, so he returned, at last, to his own, his native land. It was on the windswept hills around Killarney that the light of his genius was extinguished. It is noteworthy, not to say suspicious, that there again seems to be a parallel with an event in the life of Benjamin Franklin, the supposed discoverer of the lightning conductor. Murphy was flying his kite on the McGillycuddy's Reeks (not the Boggeragh Mountains as was once rumoured, though it is almost certain he had previously taken Melissa there to Boggerah) when a severe thunderstorm broke out. Lightning struck the kite and communicated itself to Murphy, who thereby discovered for the world the principle of the lightning conductor. It is curious to record that although The Church has resisted science in many of its forms and repressed many practitioners of science, it was not slow to equip its towers and steeples with the lightning conductor, almost superstitiously. Franklin, to whose name this discovery is generally credited, was thus anticipated by Murphy: the remarkably feeble reason for this misattribution is that Franklin survived and Murphy's enlightenment left him dead as a Bombay duck. It has been said that a postmortem might have saved his life, but this is unlikely: as Professor Milton Keynes once put it in a posthumous lecture, "In the long run, we are all dead". What is beyond doubt, however, are the circumstances of his death, for they were set down, soon after the event, by an eye witness. It is thus that we know the exact time and date of his death, which occurred at midday on Sunday, September 13, 1752.

Or would have done, had not Parliament, in its wisdom, decreed that the day following the second of September, 1752, should be accounted as the fourteenth, in pursuance of the Calendar (New Style) Act of 1750. Riots ensued, as people protested against the loss of eleven days from their lives. Rightly so, but the greater tragedy, that Murphy was robbed of the due commemoration of his death-date, seemed to pass unnoticed.

His last words have been variously chronicled. This is another manifestation of The Law: the recorded versions of Last Words are rarely the last word in accuracy. On his deathbed, Willam Pitt the younger is widely supposed to have said "O my country! How I leave my country!" Or was it "*love* my country"? Or was it, as seems entirely more probable, "I think I could eat one of Bellamy's veal pies". There is an even more poignant analogy with the *obiter dicta* of the beloved monarch of Britain, George V, whose last words are usually recorded as being "Look after the Empire". His real last words were, however, a riposte to an interfering nurse who (not knowing that the Royal Physician had already taken steps to hasten the King's demise so that it would be announced with due solemnity in the quality morning papers) recommended that His Majesty pay a recuperative visit to Bongor: the King replied "Bugger Bangor!". Murphy, whose death was hastened merely by the working of his own Law, was heard to utter a sibilant cry on his sideration as he sizzled into oblivion. The eyewitness recorded this as "Shit!"; an alternative interpretation, however, now preferred by posterity, is that his Last Words were a characteristic invocation of the Deity, "*Semper Opus Dei*".

"In short," as the Contessa di Ritornella had once said, before what were to become the Murphy fragments were presented to her, "SOD".

The evidence now

Tragic death of Noted Murphy Scholar

Dr James Ridell, of the University of Man (and whose mother keeps the tobacconist shop on the Esplanade at Douglas) was tragically killed in London on Tuesday, at a ceremony that was to have commemorated the residence of the famous R A Murphy at a house in Hanover Square. Unfortunately, the plaque which Dr Ridell was to have unveiled came detached from the wall as he pulled the cord in order to reveal it, and he was hit fatally upon the temple by the memorial. This accident leaves the eagerly anticipated book on Murphy, which has claimed the life of more than one scholar, unfinished, though the papers lying on his desk have been preserved.

At the well-attended funeral, the Bishop of Sodor and Man spoke of his many qualities, quoting the verse from the Psalms to the effect that 'The words of his mouth were softer than butter'. "Melancholy occasions such as this", he continued for some twenty minutes, "leave us bereft of meaningful words."

James Ridell was an active participant in the Peel Archaeological Society and a Churchwarden at St Lukewarm's at Laxey, an office which fell

Lex Morphi

Inst. für Theologisches Spitzfindigheit

Universität Gottesheit

Esteemed Colleague:

On the matter of the translation of the document about which you recently enquired.

It appears that the Janus-faced Genno was writing, unaccountably, in Flemish. My colleague Bertholin Van der Graaf, Leydig Professor of Intersitial studies at the University of Grottinghem has translated the relevant parts of the letter for me, which I now forward to you. I hope it makes sense. It merely says « About the toast. The solution is simple. There is nothing remarkable about the way it fell. That it landed buttered-side up was not against God or His natural Order. You see, it is obvious, indeed transparently so, that you buttered the wrong side. »

Murphy's Law

Professor Emeritus P.D.Quirk, D.M., F.R.C.O.G   Talipes Surae
                                              Caigher Point
                                              Calf of Man
                                              Isle of Man

In festo Valerii, episc., 2005

Dear Mr Melrose,

In confirmation of yesterday's telephone call, Yes, under poor Jimmy's will I am both his executor & the copyright holder of the near-complete book which I sent you. His widow Blodwen has made the stipulation that it is to be printed without alteration, exactly as it stands, except for such necessary preliminaries and whatever explanation might be needed to be added at the end. With this proviso I can authorise publication, the Munster Press having relinquished any rights they may have had in the book (copy of letter enclosed).

You ask me if there are any further materials that might be rescued from his University rooms at Port Soderick or from his house (apart from the translation of the Genno letter – erroneously known as the Holland Fragment – & the press cutting, both of which you have already received). The short answer is No, the longer answer being that there are serried ranks of tightly-filled box-files and an assortment of papers scattered over the vasty field of available surfaces of his study. Although these testify that there was much to have been done, most of the documentation was clearly rejected, either by O'Toole or by Jimmy. An instance is the file of so-called formulations of 'Murphy's Law' such as 'Celibacy is not hereditary' & 'A short cut is the longest distance between two points'; these (both supposedly Albanian proverbs) and thousands of similar derivatives of authentic Murphyana, Jimmy rightly scorned to include in the book. Especially unoriginal is the Sock Theory: M had already made the observation that unattached hosiery collects itself into anything but pairs; this was on the occasion of one of his Italian escapades (which, for some reason, does not seem to have been included in the book).

Another file contains a large assortment of notes by Professor Page, hardly any of which seem to have much bearing on matters in hand. A further voluminous file houses an ill-tempered correspondence between J and his late colleague Candida Thrush. One of these is a letter from her that begins 'By the way,' and concerns the somewhat irrelevant life-habits of the swift (not The Dean, of course) which, she tells us, copulates on the wing, that is to say, in mid-air. It was she, I might add, who prevented me from giving the Tiresias

Lecture to the Medical School at Jimmy's University,
on the grounds that I was a male Obstetrician. This,
and the fact that it was to be on the subject 'Hormonal
disorders influencing sex-reversal in the foetal brain-
architecture' led to her beating up each and every
board member of the University Department of Medicine
single-handed. My second suggestion, though it had
orginally met with approval, eventually suffered a like
fate; the poster announcing 'Some unusual perinatal
conditions' caused some ribaldry when it was defaced
with the typical undergraduate comment 'Mary had a
little lamb'. Moreover, by this time CT had enlisted
an ally in the form of some lout of preternatural
ugliness, an antipodean with pince-nez from the Spa
University of Leamington. The upshot was that the Vice-
Chancellor, with all his insolence of office, cancelled
the whole proceedings on the grounds of bad blood
which he feared might cause (not his phrase) academic
gangrene.

Poignantly, Jimmy's last printed words were "I shall
say no more." So I suppose there is no more to be said.
There was to have been an Appendix to the book, but
all that was contained in the box-file so marked was
a scrap or two of illegible remarks;* so the appendix
seems to have succumbed to peritonitis.

You have requested details about my biography.
I scarcely think that this would be relevant, as I
have no connection with the Murphy project – apart
from being, as it were, its midwife. There is a
certain irony in my having been an Obstetrican until
my retirement. I was a consultant at the University
Hospital in Cardiff for some time, where my efficacy
of delivery was, if I may say so, legendary (in which
regard I make no doubt that Professor Page would
have commented on the relevance of his studies of
acronymics, on which, with "its step-daughter science,
hypocoristics" he dwelt at length in one of the papers
kept by Jimmy, already mentioned). Nevertheless, I
had to leave there due to an allergy. Increasingly,
the gravid women with whom I dealt belonged to what
are erroneously called 'ethnic minorities'. Eventually
these were so much in the majority that the odour of
curry from their waters, which pervaded the delivery
room, overcame me on more than one occasion: so my
personal physician, Dr Paneer, advised me to seek
employ where I would not be exposed to Sudan III (not
an Eastern Potentate, but a potent enough allergic
agent) when ministering to neonates. That is why I
moved to the West Country, for midwifery is good in
Bath, at which I was appointed Professor of Perinatal
Problematics, a post which I held until my retirement.

As to my education, I was at DNC, Oxford, (not Brasenose College, with which it is often confused),
the medical school there, & the Regional Hospital at
Munster, Ireland. My military service in the Welsh
Guards (part of the 5th Infantry Brigade which made
up the Falklands Task Force) was somewhat curtailed
when it was thought that my expertise was not quite
appropriate to the task (though I did deliver a
prolapsed sheep on a remote hill, but had to wait a
very long time to be rescued as I had lost my bearings,
& the sheep with its newborn lamb did not act as
sufficient identification for the helicopters which
were trying to find me).

The family connection to which you refer is a little
convoluted, & best kept under the carpet. *Sub rosa* is
a better phrase, but I am not quite sure how it applies
in this instance, though the matter is certainly a
rather thorny one. My wife Bethan was a Richards, the
family referred to in the book as once having been
known as the Morphi-Richards (this is the correct
spelling). Bedwyr Richards (though he should better
have been called Lawnslot) married Buddug Brangwyn:
they had four daughters, Bronwen, Bethan (my wife)
Betsan & Blodwen (Jimmy's widow). You would be correct
therefore in supposing that Jimmy was my brother-in-
law. Or might be.

After Blod's birth, Bedwyr disappeared, as did Bron.
Rumour has it that Blod was the result of an unnatural
union between Bed & Bron, but Buddug always brought her
(Blod) up as though she were her daughter. Beth thinks
that Bron went on to marry a taciturn chap called Tegid
& that he & Bronwen now live at Gaufron, but I have not
managed to keep abreast of all of this family history.
I hope this clarifies things.

I have recently heard from a former colleague who
now works for a laboratory in London which does DNA
analysis for a large number of cases of disputed
parentage. He says that a staggering 1 in 10 supposed
progeny are not related to their presumed fathers,
providing a striking confirmation of what was said
on p.106 of *Lex Morphi*, and nicely illustrating the
familial problems of Murphy and his own subsequent
divarications (as Professor Page would probably
describe them).

As you see, I have now retired to my homeland,
which quite coincidentally was Jimmy's too. There have
been Quirks here for generations (it is an old Manx
family). Oddly enough, Professor Page seems to have met
Randulf, my grandfather, at Cambridge many years ago:
one of his notes refers to him, unaccountably, as 'that
philogynist'. On the contrary, grandfather Randy made a

name for himself as a *philologist* (he did the whole of
De Bella Gallicana into Manx).

Much of the land (the unentailed part) on which this
house stands had been offered to the National Trust:
they had accepted the gift in principle (this being the
reason why the Calf of Man was actually marked NT on
some earlier maps), but a new broom in the shape of a
chimaera (or not!) decided that restoring the tenements
of rightly-forgotten Liverpuddlian crooners, meddling
with villages and hunts, stopping people from bathing
as they wish & restoring ghastly eyesores for the sole
purpose of providing temples for Lesbian marriages
has resulted in me & many others giving up on the
thing. Her watchword is 'popular culture' (two words
actually, but a contradiction in terms): she seems
not to understand that she is a victim of the Cult
of Commerce. Indeed, she would be rather more popular
if she didn't turn villagers out of their homes in
favour of Public Relations & she would also better let
people swim in the altogether rather than the replusive
garments seen in the Sunday supplements read by her &
her fellow cultists. Enough of that.

As to my publications, these too are best left
unmentioned. My article in the *Dictionary of Notional
Biography*, for example, was entirely rewritten by the
so-called editors, despite repeated representations to
the O.U.P. So I have disowned it, for no one reading it
could possibly conceive that it was about Marie Stopes,
due to the appalling misconceptions in which the
editors were instrumental. (You will find references
to my various contributions to *Archaelogia Manxiana* in
my *Who's Who* entry, but it can hardly be thought that
these would have much bearing.)

I trust that the foregoing is of some use to you. I
hope that you will reach the consummation devoutly to
be wished in this important venture, which will be a
fitting memorial to Jimmy, not to speak of O'Toole &
Murphy himself.

With best wishes,

Yours sincerely,

[signature]

Desmond Quirk
* Actually, some of the illegible remarks have been
elucidated by a friend currently staying here. One
seems to be a note recorded by Professor O'Toole to
the effect that a misunderstanding (well, a *fracas*

162

actually) apparently occurred when the word *moron* was
uttered to Murphy at some point during his druidic
quest: it was intended as a reference to the colour
of his hair (my friend tells me that the word is Welsh
for 'carrots'), but was misinterpreted. A similar,
but opposite, misunderstanding occurred when M was in
Ireland & a girl addressed him as *maroon*, to which he
objected on the grounds that he was looking for a redhaired father, not someone stranded on a desert island.
O'T points out in his note (which seems to be somewhat
confused) that *maroon* is a term of endearment, not
particularly colourful, in Irish.

My friend Peredur (i.e. Perceval) also points out
that Bedwyr is the Welsh for Bedivere, hence his little
joke about Lawnslot (Lancelot) which I incorporated
earlier in this letter. He also told me that Buddug
is the equivalent of Boadicea (which I knew) & that
Cynfelin was Shakespeare's Cymbeline (which I did
not, & since when I have not slept One Wink). And on
the same subject (Is there no Way for Men to be, but
Women ...?), I lately discovered that Thrush's crony
from Leamington whom I thought to be a man is in fact
a crone (hardly a Golden Lad or Girl, more a Chimney
Sweeper). Far from being the embodiment of civilization
like the urbane Sir Les (the Australian Minister of
Culture who has appeared from time to time on British
Television), she has no culture at all. I can't
remember the name of this harridan spinster – it is
something like Sneer – but at all events the matter is
not particularly germane to the contents of the book.

PS. In dating my letter according to the observance
of Bishop Valerius' day, I note that the same Kalendar
was used in Ireland in Murphy's time. It is not that
of the Sarum use: that pertaining to old Manx usage and
that of Murphy was also current in Spain at one time,
but now variously changed by those who meddle in such
things, and who now presumably celebrate themselves *in
die omnium stultorum*.

PPS. I mentioned my allergy to Sudan III in the
parturient bodily fluids, but even more evil-smelling
were the perinatal pongs of the yuppies of Bath
amongst whom, a few years ago in the antenatal ward
of the maternity unit, there seemed to be a fashion
in pregnancy cravings for asparagus. When these ladies
gave birth, it was like being imprisoned in a silage
clamp. This reminds me of Botch-Suture, who makes a
discreditable appearance on the pages of the book in
hand. When I was last in Cambridge he was, believe
it or not, appointed as the Queen's Physician. When
a notice to this effect was posted on the Faculty of

Medicine Notice Board, a wag annotated the announcement
with 'God Save the Queen'. Out of the mouths ...

On the subject of cravings, one of my ladies in
Bath (one of the Olivers, a well-known local family)
presented with an unusual *post partum* urge to eat
pickled beetroot, which she satisfied by getting her
husband to smuggle a jar of this comestible into the
ward set aside for nursing mothers. Unfortunately,
she seems to have been unaware of its properties,
& when her bed-pan was filled with what she thought
to be blood, the fright caused her milk instantly to
be turned to cheese.** Luckily, the acute Dr B.D.I.
Askew, who had got wind of the earlier asparagus craze,
quickly deduced that it was another manifestation of
not-so-golden showers & so the problem was bottled up
before it became another *cause célèbre*.

I wonder whether some of the readers of the volume
will realise that the *Mitre* & the *Golden Cross* are no
more. In my time as an Oxford undergraduate and at the
(Old) Radcliffe, these revered establishments must have
been much as Murphy knew them, but they have now become
gaming parlours or the like. Ironically, however, the
Old Bank has become an hotel & the old Post Office,
also in The High, now deals in antique currency – *plus
ça bureau de change.*

** As Dr Paneer will tell you, such an event more
usually causes what is known in the trade as nest-
layette evaporated milk.

PPPS. I have recently become aware of the astounding
possibility that more Murphy fragments are lying in a
bank vault somewhere. The only thing I know about these
documents is that one of them refers to a portrait
(on panel) of King Alfred that used to take pride of
place in the Hall of the College that bears his name.
In Murphy's time there, however, it fell from its
place during some raucous Sunday festivities of which
the Founder would hardly have approved. Having become
dislodged, the panel hit a candelabrum on High Table,
ignited, & almost at once burnt to a cinder (apart from
the College motto, which survived from the foot of the
picture). Lamentably (according to a note by Professor
Page in the relevant file, which now makes more sense
than I had realised), the document recording the
canonisation of St Alfred by Pope Benedict IV in 900
was hidden behind the portrait, & it, together with a
quantity of otherwise unknown Proverbs of Alfred, & the
proof that the College was the only one to be founded
by the King (of Blessed and Glorious Memory), were all
consumed in the fire.

If & when we can recover these documents, more light

will doubtless be shed on these & other important
questions. Until then, all I can say is that Page noted
that the portrait of the King (flanked by his personal
armorial bearings & those of the College) was inscribed
ÆLFR[EDUS] : FUND[ATOR] : HIC COLL[EGII] : SOLI (I am not
very good at this sort of thing, so I hope that I have
stitched up the Latin correctly: I am much more used
to dealing with Caesarean sections; & my expertise
in suturing ruptured cracks is of a wholly different
kind).

The portrait, according to one of Page's diatribes,
vaguely resembled that which was once said to hang
in a rival Oxford College that spuriously traced its
origins to Alfred. Suspiciously, this disappeared
at about the same time as the St Alfred's one was
immolated, so the only evidence for this supposed
portrait is merely an engraving published by Spelman in
1678, which shows the King looking somewhat perplexed,
as well he might. (Intelligence has just reached
me that, even more suspiciously, University College
claim to have *rediscovered* the painting upon which the
1678 engraving was based: manifestly, the thing is a
forgery, made up from Spelman, in a further attempt to
justify the College's unfounded claims upon Alfred.)
His true likeness, that had once graced the Hall of
his genuine foundation, however, showed a more serene
expression: he was pictured studiously contemplating
the composition of one of his Proverbs, an endeavour
that caused him to overlook the culinary task that had
mistakenly been delegated to him.

The proverb in question seems to have been in a
North Saxon dialect of Old English (I summarise page
after page of Page's notes). P rendered this into a
slightly more modern diction as follows.

Thus quoth Alfred:
It be well said, a timely stitch preventeth IX;
but be there XII, the Ist unrav'lleth them
like unto Hot Cakes.
P. commented upon there being 9 words in the first line
of the distich & 12 in the second, carefully imitated
in his translation, which numbers have something
to do with the Golden Mean. He also expatiated at
length on the Murphean aspects of this proverb. He
further noted that the original panel, as described by
Murphy, had a representation of the College (as it was
before Hawksmoor's depredations) below the King. The
superscription read COLL: NOST: OLIM S: FREDDESWEDDES.
This, said Page, is why St Alfred's was popularly known
as 'Freddies', a theory which seems (even to me, who
knows next to nothing of these things) utter rubbish.

Talking of rubbish, the lower quadrangle of the

college, on being much dilated by Hawksmoor, had
to be aborted & scraped up before a more successful
termination of his efforts came to fruition: the
malformed new building subsided into a heap of rubble
due to inadequate foundations having been laid. Thus
quoth Murphy.

   This much seems to have been what Page had
discovered, but there are probably many more materials
that we may hope will come to light in what must be
described in the cache of documents that he saw, but
were subsequently mixed up in some shady deal over here
in which the parotitic Thrush was involved. Luckily,
Jimmy managed to get them shifted, under an obscure
I.O.M. statute that prevents aliens from holding
unidentified securities in Manx Banks. So, armed with
the relevant clause, he got them out of the clutches
of the Thrush & removed them to a Zurich safe-deposit.
Alas, J seems to have hidden the number of the box all
too well, so it is at present unknown. Bit of a facer,
that; well, in short, a SOD.

The Spielman Portrait of St Alfred, referred to on p.165.

Copy kindly furnished by Dr Tyas, Fellow of St Alfred's College, Oxford.

Additional Note. It appears that Dr Dr Terri Fick (whose views are quoted on p.149) has changed his opinion about Hogarth's *Before* and *After*. Accordingly, Professor Quirk has kindly acquiesced to its use on the dust cover of this book.